What She Wants

What She Wants

LUCINDA BETTS

APHRODISIA

KENSINGTON PUBLISHING CORP.

http://www.kensingtonbooks.com

APHRODISIA BOOKS are published by

Kensington Publishing Corp.
119 West 40th Street
New York, NY 10018

ISBN-13: 978-0-7582-3459-9
ISBN-10: 0-7582-3459-7

First Trade Paperback Printing: July 2009

10 9 8 7 6 5 4 3 2 1

Printed in the United States of America

To WTT always.
To SKK for her wicked red pen, her wicked wit,
and her kind heart.
To NH, who always roots for me, and to the critiquers at
RWC and Romance Critters.

1

Laughter and chatter filled the night, but Dr. Ann Fallon stood silently, the muscles in her neck as taut as a bowstring. She needed this job.

Speckled in silvery lights, geneticists from across the country drank champagne and ate canapés in the moonlit courtyard. The spring breeze caught the banner welcoming the conference to San Diego's Hotel del Coronado, making the gold letters ripple.

If she landed the professorship, her life would improve a lot—but most importantly, her family would be safe. They could savor the sweet taste of freedom again.

She scanned the crowd, looking for gray hair and stooped shoulders. If she could find Dr. Stoller, charm him like she'd never charmed anyone, convince him she'd be the best biologist Harvard ever hired . . .

She walked toward the white-linened table covered in Camembert cheese and succulent blackberries. Lush strawberries and thin slices of Edam gleamed in the lantern light. Snippets of dialogue floated over her like flower petals at a wedding.

She allowed the conversations to register. Did anyone mention Dr. Carl Stoller? Two men argued about statistics at the far end of the patio. With hearing no human could match, she listened to an announcement of tenure from behind the open bar, and one woman told another something about panda SNPs by the waterfall. But was anyone talking about search committees? Was anyone gossiping about whom Harvard would hire?

And as she picked up a heavy china hotel plate, she watched her fingers tremble—because her dearest wishes might come true this weekend. Trying not to rely on hope, she ignored the melons and kiwi. She put several succulent blackberries on her plate instead. Turning away from the table, she picked a berry from her plate, anticipating its sweetness.

Before she could eat it, though, a half-forgotten scent assaulted her; if someone had come up and slapped her, the effect would have been the same. She froze, shock and horror icing her veins.

How could that scent be here? How could the predator have found her now, after fifteen years?

Despite her denial, the brooding fragrance inexorably swirled over her palate. Italian bergamot and jacaranda twined around cedar and a twist of vetiver root. It held something else, too, something unnatural. Its magic could ruin her, destroy her. With the slightest crook in his finger, the predator could command her body—and she would love every second of it. Then she would die.

The fragrance cast its thrall even now, even as she inhaled her second breath of it—but refusal made her choke. This couldn't be happening. Not here. Not now! She'd worked too hard.

The black scent relentlessly permeated her blood. Its magic crept across her skin like a spider's feet. The brooding feeling slithered over her nipples and made them hard as sure as her lover's tongue would have. It snaked between her thighs, over her wrists, behind her ears.

She couldn't deny the fact. A predator watched her. It watched her as its dark fragrance assaulted her, took her hostage for its own needs. The predator expected her to drop her plate and find his arms, his bed, his hands.

She exhaled and straightened her shoulders. She didn't have to lay down and accept this. She was no longer the weak girl child she'd been all those years ago.

Slowly, she put the berry back on the plate. Her eyes scanned the crowd as she choked back rage. How had he found her?

Again that preternatural lust heated her blood, and she turned, her ears focused. Was he there by the waterfall? She should run away, but she started toward it, inhaling the sophisticated perfume and the magic it masked. She had to see his face. She needed to see his hands. She wouldn't imagine them on her stomach, on her breasts. She wouldn't imagine his fingers around her neck, his cock between her thighs. If she could just get behind the person in front of her—

The sharp squeal of microphone feedback filled the courtyard, and the excited crowd thickened. The waterfall—and the predator behind it—might be on another planet for as much as she could reach it now. A news camera with a CBS emblem on the side panned toward the speaker, and Ann shrank back. Her kind always shrank from cameras.

"Welcome, everyone!" A woman's cheerful voice echoed through the mike. "Welcome to the twenty-third annual meeting of the American Genetics Society."

A smattering of applause filled the courtyard, but Ann stood silently holding her plate as she searched the faces behind the speaker. The AGS president droned, but Ann heard none of her speech. Where was the predator?

That dark sensation danced over her skin again, teasing her wrists and breasts—and someone moved near the waterfall, shifting most of his body behind the rushing water. Her nose caught the faintest whiff of bergamot. Where had he gone?

Catching a glimpse of dark hair, Ann stepped to her left, trying to see him better. He—

Cold fingers touched the back of her shoulder.

She jumped and barely managed to swallow a yelp as she stepped back. She couldn't let a predator take her here, not in front of her peers—not in front of the people from Harvard.

"Hello, Ann." The soft tone didn't intrude on the woman behind the microphone, but Ann's heart leaped.

And then she exhaled with relief. He was *not* a predator.

"Hello, Dr. Stoller." Harvard. She hoped her smile didn't look as weak as it felt. How long would the crush of bodies between her and the waterfall protect her from the predator's perfume?

"I trust you had an uneventful trip." He held out his hand, speckled with gray hairs. His lightweight tweed jacket did little to hide his stooped shoulders, but his smile was warm. "I startled you. My apologies."

"No." Embarrassment made her nervous. She needed to impress this man. More than anything she needed to impress him. "I just—" She waved her hands, wondering how to finish the sentence, but he saved her the indignity.

"Don't worry." His genteel laugh eased her tension. "A lot of people are jumpy when they make Harvard's short list."

She gave a self-deprecating laugh, pushing her fear to the back of her mind. "I'm in good company, then." She smiled, feeling like a fraud. At the height of his career, this man had discovered that only the exon portion of a gene coded for proteins, and she'd just shaken hands with him. "Was your trip comfortable?" she asked.

"It was pouring in Cambridge when I left. The Old Yard was terribly flooded."

Ann swallowed, wondering what it must be like to be so familiar with Harvard and its surroundings. What would it be like to offer her family the protection of Harvard's name—and money?

"And you may call me Carl, if you please," he said. "No need for this *doctor* business, not anymore."

"Thank you, Carl." What did he mean, *not anymore*? Had they decided on her? She cleared her throat, trying not to count unhatched chickens. "So, are you giving a presentation this trip?" she asked. "Or do you have a poster in one of the sessions?"

"Neither." He shook his graying head and gave her a small smile. His blue eyes were bright and young in defiance of his posture. "I've stepped back from research these days, left it for you younger scientists." He tapped his forehead. "Keeping all the proteins straight isn't as easy as it once was."

"I doubt that very much," Ann said. "I'm sure you've forgotten more than what these experts know."

"You're being kind." He shook his head with a rueful expression, his hairy eyebrows high. "I'm here to watch presentations this year. Two people in particular have my attention."

Ann smiled with what she hoped looked like confidence. She understood him perfectly. He was going to watch her and her competition, then decide who to hire. Perhaps the safety of her family remained within her reach—if she could avoid the predator. "Well, I hope you see something you like."

"I'm certain I will." He plucked a tiny pastry from a passing waiter and ate it with a satisfied expression. "Exquisite," he said. Then he wiped his fingers on the napkin and met her eyes. "I'll be at your talk with my colleague from the West Coast, and my money's on you to outshine the competition."

She had picked a berry off her plate, and she put it down now. "That is the nicest compliment I've received in a long time."

"You deserve it. Your work is remarkable." Carl smiled. "At my age, I've learned it's nice to have admirers."

"Yes," she agreed. "It is."

"And do you have any with you? Admirers, that is."

He wasn't hitting on her; he was trying to determine if she had an attachment. All else being equal, universities preferred to hire someone single, someone who'd never take time off for marriage or child care.

"No," she lied. For once she felt glad her lover insisted on secrecy. She'd always suspected he'd exaggerated the need to appear single, but now . . . "I'm here alone." She handed her plate to a passing waiter, the blackberries untasted.

Stoller nodded, his expression too closed to read. "That's a shame," he said. "I understand the party at the end of the meeting is quite grand. Almost like a wedding reception. It's much more entertaining to attend with a friend."

"Perhaps you'll save me a dance then."

"I was hoping for more than a dance." His blue eyes met hers. "Would you accompany me?"

"I'd find that very enjoyable. I look forward—" But fear choked her words to a stop. That perfume. The predator had found her—and stared even as she nodded good night to Stoller. "I look forward to it," she managed to say as she savored the fragrance against her will.

Across the spanning patio space, she saw dark pupils gleaming, bringing to mind hot, hot mouths and hungry caresses. The tall man, his hair black as a Percheron's coat, radiated power . . . and danger. He made her think of a stallion scenting a mare, his nostrils dilated.

"Are you well?" Dr. Stoller asked, looking in the direction of her gaze.

Ann couldn't answer.

A tiny woman with a pixie haircut stood next to the dark-haired man, a calm look in her eye. With a slow nod, the man curled his broad fingers around the woman's neck, her hip resting familiarly against his thigh.

"I'm fine." She dragged her eyes back to Dr. Stoller, trying to make her words true.

"Then I hope to see you at Dr. Reinhart's talk," Stoller said, with a careful wink. "We'll certainly be there, listening carefully."

Ann nodded. Even through her distraction she realized Carl was naming her competition. The dark-haired man turned more fully toward her, wrapping his long fingers around the neck of the tiny woman, and Ann knew she needed to leave. Now. The longer she bathed in this brooding scent, the harder it would be to disentangle herself.

She wanted to push the tiny woman with the auburn hair into the waterfall and take her place, placing the predator's fingers around her neck and begging him to squeeze. As it was, she barely resisted the temptation to throw herself into his arms.

"Thank you," she said, her voice weak. Maybe she could ask Dr. Stoller to escort her to the lobby? "Dr. Stoller—"

"Please." He held up his hand. "Call me Carl. Now if you'll excuse me, I see someone with whom I must speak."

"Thank you, Carl," she said, knowing she couldn't ask him to take her to the lobby now. "Good night."

He walked away, leaving her alone in the crowd.

She exhaled, trying to find some core of strength. She needed to run, get to her hotel room, away from the being who would ruin her life—but she couldn't move.

In a swirl of subtle fragrances, lust pulled her eyes toward her enemy. It woke a craving in her, a craving too dark to bear. Her sisters had gone so willingly to their deaths, strangled by predators' hands. And now the predator's hand reached across the auburn-haired woman's throat, and desire coiled in Ann's belly.

He could close his powerful fingers around her tiny neck and snuff the life from her. He could claim her last breath, that final whispered gasp, for his own. He could free her soul into the balmy night.

The beauty of his power spun its spell, leaving Ann's wrists longing for his lips, leaving her tongue hungry for his.

Ann could so easily be in the tiny woman's shoes. The unnatural scent floating between them made her crave the attention the other woman received—even if it meant Ann's own death. A predator always killed his prey, eventually.

This predator didn't kill now, though. His fingertips purposefully traced the line of the tiny woman's collarbone, his eyes still locked on Ann's. His sexuality was so blatant—so dangerous—that her heart pounded. She could almost imagine him as the alpha stallion pawing the ground, shaking the earth beneath his hooves with his lust.

And the fragrance made her want to submit to his will, his strength.

She exhaled, anger winning the war against fear and lust—at least temporarily. If he thought she was some filly, some weak thing with whom to trifle, he was wrong. He could no more crush her neck in his palm than he could sprout wings and fly.

She could protect herself. She might not have the strength to fight, but she could run. Ann turned and walked through the door, her eyes on the elevator.

Ann.

What was that? Pain tore through her head, leaving her stunned. Leaning against the wall, she pushed her temples to try to counteract the searing pressure.

Anemone, honey. I need you.

Mom? She must be imagining this. She hadn't heard from any family member in fifteen years. *Mom?*

I'm here. You have to listen to me. The predator has found you. You must stop him. The pressure in her skull lifted as her brain relearned the mindlink of her childhood.

Oh, Mom, I love you. In a haze of pain and shock, she remembered to breathe. After so many years isolated and alone, she wanted to put her head in her mother's lap and savor her company. *Where are you?*

I can't tell you, and I love you, too, but you need to listen to me. Are you listening?

Yes.

Do you know where the predator is? Right this minute?

Yes! He's behind me. How did you—

Hide! her mother said. Ann glanced around the crowded lobby and spied a darkened hall. Not looking behind her, she walked toward it. It led to a series of conference rooms. She tried the first glass-paned door. It was open.

Okay. Using her animal vision, she walked through the darkened room until she found a chair. *I'm alone.*

Keep alert. I don't want you near the predator until you've heard me.

I don't want to be near the predator at all. I barely escaped just now. I wanted to—

That's why I'm reaching out to you, but first you have to promise you won't try to find me.

What are you talking about?

Just promise!

How can I do that?

Promise me.

Ann paused, not wanting to lie, but also not wanting to give up on her mother if she were in trouble.

Promise me, her mother insisted.

Ann pushed her selfish needs aside. What else could she do? *I promise.*

Thank you. Ann heard the softness in her mother's voice, remembered the gentleness in it as she'd read her poems and sung to her. In that moment, she would have done anything to feel her mother's arms wrapped around her, to feel like she belonged someplace.

Now listen to me. Her mom's voice sounded intense now, no hint of lullaby. *I don't have a lot of time. The predators. I know how they seduce us—and you can stop it.*

How?

You're the only one who can do it. With your resistance, we can save all our kind.

How?

You have to go back to him. You have to get near him, search his pockets, his car, his hotel room.

What?

I've discovered their secret.

Their secret?

They're just humans. They created a pheromone, genetically modified it from something. And they've bottled it in two small vials. Silver. They're passing them among themselves. You have to find them.

Pheromones? That's how they . . . seduce us? Shock poured through her. She'd always thought the predators were supernatural. *They don't have magic?*

No magic, her mother said. *They're simply human men with a terrible drug.*

They couldn't be human. Her mind raced over the implications, seeking a flaw in her mother's statement—and she found it. *That doesn't make sense. Whenever they seduced us, it drove them mad. They created something that was just as bad for them as for us.*

That was fifteen years ago, Anemone. It was a trial run.

What are you talking about?

They've refined it. The pheromone they've concocted now—seducin, they call it—it lures us like rats to the Pied Piper. Ap-

parently this new seducin doesn't drive the wearer insane, but it's just as much of an aphrodisiac as it ever was for us.

They're human? She swallowed. *Really?*

Yes. Someone has designed a trap.

What for? What do they want with us?

I don't know yet. She could tell her mother was distracted, could feel her peering over her shoulder. *Listen, Ann.* She envisioned the fear in her mom's eyes. *You need to find the vials and smash them, flush the perfume, destroy it.*

Destroying the vials would break the predators' hold on them, but would it solve the problem? *Shouldn't we destroy the lab first? They'll just make more. We need to—*

Don't worry about the lab. I've got that covered. Can you take care of the vials?

Of course I'll do it, Mom. To save her family.

You're strong enough now—I know it. Now I have to run—

Be careful!

The predators, they're coming as we speak. Don't try to find me. Don't use the mindlink. They can track us. I love you—

Her mother's voice broke off.

Mom?

No one answered.

"Mom?" Her voice sounded so lonely in the empty conference room. "Mom?" she asked again, but Ann was alone.

She sat back in the chair. The residual thrum the mindlink left in her head almost felt like her mother's arms. Ann could save them! She could free them from the predators, and when she landed that job at Harvard, she could run together with her mother and her siblings.

Then the daydream gave way to reality.

She realized what her mother asked. Finding those vials would take all her strength. She'd have to walk right up to the predator and touch his pockets. . . . Easier if she were kissing him.

Easier still if she asked someone else to help her. Daniel! Her lover would be immune to the pheromone, and he was strong. Maybe he could help her search for the vials.

Of course, that would mean she'd have to tell him the truth.

Ann stood and tried to tell herself she didn't mind telling him her true nature. She tried to imagine Daniel at her side rummaging through the predator's room. He'd help her. Especially once he knew what was at stake for her.

She opened the conference-room door and headed to the elevators, hoping the predator was gone.

He wasn't. He stood by the far doorway, his eyes on her as she exited the dim hall.

With her chin high, she headed for the elevator. Students walked past him through the door to his right, but he ignored them. He leaned down and nipped his companion's ear. With her lobe between his teeth, his deliberate fingers traced the woman's shoulder and spiraled down her arm in slow circles. He caressed the woman's breast, cupping it in his palm and brushing his thumb over the areola.

As she watched the scene, a jagged bolt of desire raced through Ann. The woman's wide eyes were locked on something Ann couldn't see—but beneath her pixie cut, her face flushed.

Ann pressed the up button for the elevator.

Across the lobby, the predator released his companion and walked toward the elevator, toward Ann. He moved like a panther. She saw that the predator wore an official name tag.

The urge to run shot through her veins, but the door pinged open and she went inside. She pushed the close-door button and stuck her key card into the slot for the concierge floor.

He gave her a seductive grin and raised one dark eyebrow. *You haven't escaped me yet*, his expression seemed to say.

But she had—or, rather, she would.

2

Chiron crossed the lobby in three long strides, his fists ready. He had to stop Sutherland from getting into the elevator with the woman in the red dress.

The woman stopped Sutherland first, though. She quickly slid a key card through the reader and pressed a button. The elevator closed before Sutherland could get in.

Chiron caught a glimpse of the woman's face as the doors closed. Beneath her austere ballerina bun, she looked scared, her eyes locked on Sutherland's. Her hand clutched the skirt of her formal dress.

Chiron breathed a little easier—her fear was good. If she wasn't ignorant of the danger, she might live a little longer. Sutherland and his girlfriend had killed, at least once, and Chiron would stop them from killing again—or die trying.

He stood in the lobby's throng, not wanting to draw Sutherland's attention to himself. How badly did Sutherland want the austere blonde? Would he take the next elevator to follow her? The stairs? No. Sutherland glanced at his girlfriend, a tiny woman with auburn hair, and pointed toward the bar. She nodded and followed him.

Chiron considered tailing them—as he had in every off-duty moment of the last two years—but he'd gotten nothing for his trouble, except a warning from the squad sergeant. He would have killed Sutherland months ago, but then he would never find Akantha's remains. Would he ever discover what really happened to her? He had been protecting Akantha for so long. Even in her death, he didn't want to let her go.

"Take the next elevator," Chiron told a small crowd of conference-goers. If following Sutherland were a fruitless task, maybe following Sutherland's red-dressed quarry wouldn't be. Maybe she knew what Sutherland was up to, could somehow lead him to Akantha's remains. He pressed the button, and the door slid open.

Stepping inside, he slid in the key card for the concierge level and glowered—the elevator doors were too damned slow. Maybe he could save her. Maybe he could save the blonde where he'd failed Akantha. If the elevator ever moved.

"Damn." Chiron slid the card again, hoping to convince the doors to shut. Akantha's red hair had been a wild mass, hair more fitting for a Plains pony than a woman. She'd been leaning on Sutherland's arm that night, her lips curled as she'd delivered a flirtatious jab. She'd always been good at those. She'd always been good at staying just out of Chiron's reach, too, but that memory wouldn't help him now.

As the elevator whirred up the flights, Akantha's final smile flashed though his mind, stabbing his gut and twisting. What had Sutherland done to her, with her? If she'd been tortured . . . If she'd suffered . . . Almost two years later, the guilt nearly choked him. If he'd been man enough to hold her affection just a little longer . . . If he could have protected her . . .

Stop it. Laments could last centuries, and they never cured a thing.

His brain refused to listen, though. Akantha's face—flushed with desire—flashed through his mind. "Chiron," she'd said, her long fingers possessively hanging on Sutherland's arm. "This night is mine. Leave me be."

Thankfully the elevator doors opened before the memory played itself out. Touching his gun, Chiron relegated the sorrow to a dark pocket of his mind and stepped into the silent hallway. He stayed focused now, turning the corner as quietly as he could.

"Jesus!" She nearly jumped out of her skin. Behind her heavy-rimmed glasses, her eyes were wide with fear. The air felt strange in the hallway—it crackled with ozone. "You scared the crap out of me," she said.

"Relax. I'm a cop." He reached for his badge. Something had seriously freaked her out. Erik Sutherland.

"A cop." She took a deep breath, and he watched her relax. He could tell she was glad to have him here.

He showed her his badge. "Kai Atlanta. San Diego PD."

"PD as in Police Department," she said. It wasn't a question. He had the feeling she was trying to calm herself.

"Yeah." He drew out the word. "What else would it mean?"

The muscles in her shoulders loosened, and although she didn't smile, he could see her thinking about it.

"You have an MD?" she asked. Even pulled back in a severe ballerina bun, her hair was beautiful, like spun gold. Straight fringe crossed her forehead in a clean line, and each strand was impossibly thick and neat.

"I'm not a doctor," he said.

"If you're not a doc, PD doesn't stand for Parkinson's disease, then. Rules out progressive disease, too."

She was teasing him, he realized. "I guess it does." What the hell was progressive disease?

"If you're a chemist, PD might stand for palladium." She inspected his thighs and chest, boldly. "But you don't look like any chemist I've ever met."

"Not a chemist," he agreed. The light down the hall made her bared shoulders gleam. What would the thin red straps of her dress feel like under his fingertip? "But I understand chemistry perfectly well."

She ignored the innuendo. "If you looked more like an electrical engineer, I might suggest partial discharge."

"I don't know anything about partial discharge." He met her eyes, trying to unnerve her, but she unnerved him instead. Blue specked the green of her irises, reminding him of the Aegean in the summer. He could pull off those glasses and—he stopped the thought. "For me, discharge is complete—or nonexistent. I don't do anything halfway."

This got her, and she started to laugh. The line in the middle of her forehead disappeared. He realized the ozone charge he'd first noticed was gone, too. Had he imagined it?

"You done trying to impress me?" he asked.

"I don't know." A smile played in her eyes, and the color was back in her face. "Did it work?"

"I'm impressed." He shook his head. "But not by your encyclopedic knowledge of PD abbreviations."

"What then? My fashion sense?"

He laughed again, although the way her red dress slid over her full breasts made a fashion statement of its own. "I'm impressed you didn't spray me with mace or try some fancy kung fu on me."

"Why?"

"You thought I was someone else coming out of that elevator, didn't you?"

"I—"

He didn't give her a chance to lie. "You're right to be afraid of Erik Sutherland."

She paused a minute as if considering something. Did she know something about him? "Who?" she said, finally. She looked as innocent as a newborn lamb, but he didn't trust it.

He'd learned enough about trust to sum it up in one word: *don't.*

"Erik Sutherland. Dark-haired guy stands about a foot taller than everyone else—"

"Except you."

He ignored the observation, but she was right. "He's with a small auburn-haired woman."

She nodded. "I saw him—them."

"What'd you two talk about?"

"Talk?" Her eyebrows arched in surprise over the top of the dark rim of her glasses. "We didn't . . . talk."

Did they fuck? That didn't seem likely. For one thing, this woman seemed too afraid. For another, Sutherland's girlfriend rarely left his side. "You didn't talk over the phone before the conference?"

"No."

"Not behind the waterfall where no one was watching?" He nodded, trying to encourage her into confessing something, anything. He'd seen Sutherland looking at her, stalking her. He'd seen recognition between the two of them, hadn't he? "You'd be surprised what the hotel staff pretends not to see. All I have to do is ask."

She stepped back, her eyes narrowed. "I don't think I like what you're suggesting. Why would I lie to anyone, much less a cop?"

"People have all sorts of reasons to lie." He should know. He'd been living a lie for nearly four millennia.

"Look." Her voice tightened. "If you're bringing me in for questioning or something, I'll call my lawyer. Otherwise, leave me alone."

"Did Sutherland tell you what his affiliation is? Where he works?"

"Good night, Mr. Atlanta."

"Hold on." He'd pushed her too far, and she'd leave now.

urprised him. "I'm just asking you what you talked
held up his hands, wishing he could prove his good

"And I'm just telling you we didn't talk." She shifted the
chain of her tiny purse higher on her shoulder. Her body language told him this conversation was over. "And if you wanted
to know where he works, you should've looked at his name
tag." She shot him a crooked smile, turned, and walked down
the hall. "Detective."

"Very cute." He hoped his words would stop her, but she
kept right on walking. And he couldn't help it then—he admired her fashion sense a second time. At least, he admired the
way her dress moved over her delicious ass as she walked.

"Wait." He let authority drip into his tone and took a business card from his wallet. He walked toward her as she re-
treated. "Take this."

She stopped and turned, looking at his hand. "Why? You
short on dates tonight?"

"If I were, would you call?"

She made an exasperated sound, but he could tell she was
amused—which was a good sign.

"Take it?"

She did.

"Seriously? Erik Sutherland's trouble." He wished people
still used the word "evil" without sounding dramatic. He
wished he could tell her Sutherland was evil without sounding
like a psycho himself.

"What kind of trouble?" She met his eyes. "Does he kidnap
women from genetics conferences? Rape, murder, and pillage?"
Her light tone quavered, belying something . . . Fear? An im-
probable belief that her sarcastic words were true?

"Nothing we can prove." He couldn't prove Akantha was
dead, for example, not in a court of law.

"So, why's he trouble?"

"He's into drugs."

"Drugs?" Her eyebrows dropped, and she shook her head. She didn't believe him. What *did* she know?

"He might want to buy something from you. Equipment. Technology."

"From me?" She shook her head. "That makes no sense. I don't know much about drugs or equipment . . . unless he wants a GPS and a video recorder to cook up some crack."

"That wouldn't work so well." He stared into her eyes a moment, and she didn't flinch. What was her tie with Sutherland?

She shook her head and stepped back. "You're worrying about the wrong woman," she said. "I don't have anything he wants."

With her lush curves, he doubted that. "What are you doing at a genetics conference, if you don't mind me asking?"

"I study wild horses in Nevada. They've got a surprising breeding system—thus the genetics aspect—and I'm presenting the results tomorrow morning."

"Interesting."

She gave him that crooked smile again and held out her hand. "I'm Dr. Ann Fallon."

Fallon. The name suited her somehow. So did the doctorate. "So you use the technology?" he asked, shaking her warm hand.

"Technology?"

"Genetics technology. Amplifying? Splicing?"

"You know a lot about it for a cop."

"I listen to NPR," he said. "You use that stuff?"

"Not really." She shook her head, her sober bun catching the hallway lighting. What would her hair look like if he took it down? Would it flow down to her ass or stop at her shoulders? "I send out samples to labs—hair, occasionally blood samples. I don't know much about the technology used in a lab."

"I find that hard to believe."

She laughed. "To be more specific, I know more about the labs than any average Joe, but ninety percent of the people at this conference know more than I do. I'd be the last person here someone would stalk for technology."

He exhaled. "Just keep the number." He nodded at the business card in her hand. "If Erik Sutherland harasses you, call me."

"Thank you." She slid the card into her purse, and he turned back toward the elevator.

"Wait," she said.

"What?" When he looked at her, that line was back on her forehead.

"You wondered about his affiliation. His name tag said he's from the Brode Institute."

3

"Damn." Ann swiped her keycard to Daniel's room. "Damn, damn, damn." Why had she flirted with the detective like that?

The lock mechanism whirred, and residual adrenaline from her run-in with the predator churned through her veins. She could blame her blathering on fear—but, with a start, she realized she'd be lying to herself.

She blinked at the thought. Her kind were always outsiders, and no matter how well she got along with particular humans, her hidden identity cramped her relationships with them—which was one reason she had never told Daniel her true nature.

For some reason, she hadn't felt that reticence with the detective. In fact, when he'd told her the predator was dangerous, she'd almost asked him to help her—

As she opened the door, her thoughts evaporated.

Light from the moon bathed Daniel in a bone glow, highlighting the planes of his cheeks. His hair was cut to hang at an exact angle, and the cobalt blue of his eyes sparkled with excitement. Modern jazz played from his laptop computer, and he had two bottles of champagne on ice. She knew they'd be delicious. Just like him.

When she walked in, he wrapped his arms around her and buried his face in her neck. His arms felt right. It didn't matter that he was human, not one bit. She wasn't an outsider in his arms. He'd help her. As soon as she asked, he'd help her.

Daniel lifted her chin and kissed her, hard. "I saw you out the window and wanted to do that out in the crowd."

"You should've." She tortured him a little bit. She knew damned well he wouldn't claim her, not in public.

"It's so good to see you." He nibbled her ear. "It's been too long."

"Daniel, I need to ask you a favor." She leaned into him, savoring his strength and scent. The citrus flavor of his cologne mixed deliciously with the heat of his skin.

"Hmmm." He nibbled her ear, his hand on her hip. "I went shopping for my favorite girl."

She looked. Pink and brown boxes fell over each other on the king-sized bed. Satiny teal ribbons draped over some of the larger bags. Brown bags with expensive-looking embossed stickers provided the icing for the cake. She wouldn't need new clothes or jewelry for a year—but nothing in this pile would help her raid the vials from the predator.

"I don't remember how your mouth tastes," he said, wrapping her in his arms.

"We can fix that." She turned, and he lowered his head. Gently, he touched his lips to hers. Sweet and gentle. So, so sweet. She shuddered and he did, too.

Skin gliding over skin, she relearned his feel, and he relearned hers. Slowly, he opened her mouth, and she tasted his flavor, as heady as the champagne.

"My God, I missed you so damned much." Daniel touched

her gently, almost reverently. Like a man drinking water after weeks in the desert.

It's your own damned fault. She kept the thought to herself, though. She didn't want bitterness to intrude on their isolated islands of bliss. Once Harvard came through with their job offer, they wouldn't need to hide.

"What did you want to ask me?"

This wasn't the time. She drew his head back down so she could press her lips against his, so she could caress his cheeks with her hands and remember the rough angles of his face. "I missed you, too," she said.

He growled softly and slid his hand over the bodice of her dress. Through the silk, he palmed her breasts, brushing his thumb against her nipple. Her eyes grew heavy with need for him.

He slid strong hands down over the curve of her ass. As he pulled her against him, she felt his cock press against her stomach, and she surrendered to him. She let him possess her.

Maybe the night's danger added a dimension to her desire. Maybe it had just been too long since she last saw him, but she'd never felt anything like what her lover was doing to her now. Her body shook with need, trembled with desire.

His hands and mouth and scent shaped her into a honeyed, formless slave to his touch.

She unbuttoned his shirt and traced her fingertips across his broad chest. His nipple hardened with the scrape of her fingernail, and she laughed. She started to unsnap his chinos, but he stopped her, wrapping her in his arms. She moaned her disappointment.

"Let's not rush." He touched her cheek and walked toward the champagne. With natural grace, he popped a cork on one of the bottles. Of course, he had glasses.

Her body didn't want to wait, but she knew if she pushed

him, he'd withdraw—and she was too hungry for him. She took a step back. If he didn't want her right now, she'd change his mind.

"Daniel." She let husky desire fill her voice as she slid the spaghetti straps off her shoulder. Her dress slithered to a puddle around her ankles, and she stepped out of it.

He turned from the champagne, blinked in surprise, and gave a low whistle. "Beautiful."

She turned slowly, giving him time to appreciate the way the tiny silk panties clung to her ass. "You like what you see?"

"Oh, yeah." He took a long sip of champagne and set the glass on the end table. "Come here."

With a laugh, she stepped back. "Come get me."

He shook his head, though. He wouldn't play. No lustful lover chasing a pretend coy maiden for him. He had his own rules.

No matter. She'd get him by hook or by crook. She shoved all the boxes and bags from the bed and lounged across the pillows. Half closing her eyes, she licked her lips. "This bed's cold and lonely without you."

He kept his distance still and stayed by the champagne. "Spread your legs, just a little," he said.

She rolled to her side and propped her cheek into her palm. "Like this?" She put one foot flat on the bed, knowing the view would tantalize him.

"Oh, yeah. Spread them more."

She moved her foot back.

"You can do better."

She laughed. "I could do better if you were here with me."

He didn't smile or move. "Your panties are in the way. I think you should move them."

Slowly, she moved her fingers over her ribs and across her hip. She let her fingertips dance over the edge of her panties. "This could be your tongue."

"Your panties." His voice was thick. "Move them. They're blocking my view."

"I could take them off . . ." She hooked her index finger under the string across her hip and started to tug.

"No."

"Oh?" She touched the thin silk separating her hand from her clit. "You mean here?"

"You know I do."

She pushed the thin silk aside, giving him a full view of her swollen clit. "Come here," she said. "I want to—"

"Shh. How can you complain? I'm not even touching you."

Which was the problem. Still, her sex must have glistened with the slippery wetness, since her belly tightened with desire. She knew he liked this, and that made her like it. She'd get what she wanted soon enough.

"Look me in the eye and stroke yourself." Desire deepened his voice. "Show me how you like it."

"You know how I like it." Keeping her panties to the side, she spread herself with two fingers.

She heard him moan and moaned herself.

"You could touch me." She shifted so he could see exactly how much she wanted him.

"You do it."

Had she ever been this wet? Surely her clit had never been this swollen. Hot. Wet.

She rolled onto her back and reached down. *Glide.* She arched her hips in pleasure. *Slide.* Her fingers trailed her slick heat, and she used two to stroke her clit.

"Inside," Daniel said.

So she sunk a finger deep inside, caressing her clit with her thumb.

"I can't stand it—I can't keep my hands off you." Daniel crossed the room and buried his face between her legs. She gasped and removed her hand, but he took it and mumbled, "You do this, too."

His tongue ran the length of her and accompanied her fingers as they circled around her clit. He sucked on her clit and flicked his tongue. She couldn't tell which sensations were caused by him and which by her.

His hands reached up to find her breasts. Gentle fingers caught her nipples, caressed them into hard, tingling tips.

She flexed her hips toward his mouth, unable to hold back one more second. He sucked again, and she saw stars, fireworks, explosions.

Her muscles throbbed and pulsated as they reached for something that wasn't there. Even as she ached for his cock, she gasped at the intensity of her orgasm.

"Take off your clothes, Daniel." She reached toward him. "I need you. Now."

He didn't get naked, though. He didn't fill the still-aching need in her. The orgasm hadn't fulfilled her—it'd left her hungry.

He chuckled and walked toward the champagne. "You'll get what you want soon enough."

Why did she doubt that?

"Tell me about the party, baby." He handed her a glass, the topaz bubbles bursting across the surface of the drink. His hair wasn't even slightly mussed, but his lips were shiny. "Who'd you talk to?"

Pushing aside her need, she sat and took a glass as she considered. The tail end of the orgasm still fluttered through her stomach, and the predator's face flashed through her mind—his brooding eyes, the scent that wrapped around her and refused to let go. And then that detective, Kai Atlanta. The sorrow in his eyes. The strange comfort she'd felt in his company. None of these topics seemed like pillow-talk material.

She should ask for his help now . . . if only she could.

"Well," she said, wondering if he already knew this. "I think I can save my horses." And her family.

"What do you mean?"

"I officially made Harvard's short, short list. It's down to two people and I'm one of them."

He blinked and then grinned. "What? You're one of the finalists?"

"I am." The thrill of success bubbled through her. She could claim him in public now. "Dr. Stoller told me himself."

"That's fantastic." Daniel sat on the bed and wrapped her in his arms, but not before she saw his expression. He looked worried; the tiny lines around his eyes deepened.

"What's the matter?"

"The matter?" he asked. "Nothing. It's fantastic. It's absolutely fantastic. What'd Stoller tell you?"

"I think he likes me best," she said. Daniel's expression seemed so earnest, she must've imagined the worry. "He told me his money's on me."

"That's great, baby. What else did he say?"

"That they were here to listen to two lectures—he's here with someone from the West Coast—and then he'd make an announcement. I'm going to the final party with him."

"Wow." Dan toasted his glass against hers. "Did he say who the competition was?"

"Oh, yes he did." Ann grinned. Champagne bubbles threatened to spill over the edge of her glass in her excitement. "And I know he's not supposed to tell."

"Well, who is it?"

"Reinhart."

"Reinhart? You mean Adam Reinhart?"

"Yep." Ann curled herself back onto the bed, inhaling the warm scent of Daniel's skin. "Adam Reinhart's my competition. And he's married. Newly married."

"Which is why you'll get the job and he won't. He'll take a sabbatical when the first kid is born. He'll miss all those classes and committee meetings, and when the second kid is born, he'll miss all the same classes a second time."

Ann knew all the arguments and knew they were right. She'd seen it happen over and over at Duke and in graduate school and even as an undergrad. Still, she didn't particularly care, at least not as much as Daniel did.

Besides, she thought, maybe she'd beat out Reinhart on merit alone.

"We have to celebrate," Daniel said.

"Good idea." She brushed aside her consternation and set her glass on the nightstand. "And I know just how to do it." She pulled him toward her, one hand on the snap of his chinos.

"Wait." He lifted his champagne glass so she wouldn't spill it. "I have a better idea."

"Better than this?" She pulled off her panties. "I've waited too long."

"No. Put your clothes back on. I'm taking you someplace special."

"The most special place I know is the bed."

"Please. You'll love this." He turned his back completely toward her as he fumbled through yet another bag.

Suddenly, she caught a glimpse of his reflection in the huge mirror. He pulled a ring-sized box from one of the larger bags and put it into the pocket of his chinos—and she wasn't sulking any longer. He was going to propose.

She'd have to tell him the truth, and she had to tell him now. "Daniel, there's something I have to tell you, and I need your help—"

"Ann." He gathered her in his arms. "It can wait, can't it? Just an hour. Let me take you someplace. You can tell me there." The ring box in his pocket bumped her thigh, promising a happy ending.

And what could she say? The vials could wait an hour, couldn't they?

4

Inhaling the warm salt air, Ann waited as Daniel locked the car. He'd chosen the beach.

The full moon hung low over the Pacific, lighting the waves with its ethereal magic. Starlight sprinkled the velvety blue darkness, and the rhythmic sound of the surf hitting the shore made her heart pound with its intensity. She could hear the waves lapping the shore on the bay side of the beach, too.

This was the moment her mother said would never happen—not for her kind. An ache jolted through her heart, a loneliness that surprised her with its intensity. Fighting to take a normal breath, she wished she could talk to her mother, just for another second, just to share this moment.

"It's beautiful, isn't it," Daniel said.

"I can't imagine anything more breathtaking."

Daniel had found the most deserted stretch of beach she'd ever seen. No cars cruised Silver Strand Boulevard, and city lights didn't spoil the darkness. She thought of him on bended knee, offering her the ring, and fear wrapped around her lungs.

What man would accept her as a wife, and what man would let his fiancée fuck a predator?

"Hey." He took her hand as if he sensed her nervousness.

She swallowed, grateful for the contact. "Hey." Would he help her fight the predator and get the vials from him?

"Your hand is so cold," he said.

"Cold hands, warm heart."

He pulled her against him. "I know how to warm you up."

"Hot sex on the beach?"

"That, too." He held up a small cooler he'd taken from the trunk. "I brought some wine and cheese—and chocolate."

"Chocolate? Yum."

"Champagne truffles."

"Sounds perfect." She tried to control her pounding heart. He bought these in advance, to celebrate. Even if she didn't get the Harvard job, he'd bring their relationship out into the open with the ring. No more hiding. "Sounds absolutely perfect."

"You're perfect."

And although his words were mawkish, their sentiment should've bound her closer to him, melted her heart. Instead, they brought her fear to a head. If he were coming out of hiding, she'd have to, too.

What was the worst that could happen? He'd never reject her. He loved and accepted her. She trusted him with her life. He'd understand what she had to do with the predator.

"Let's take a walk." He led them toward the water. In the distance, she heard a vireo's chirruping call. The warm scent of the ocean filled her nose. Underfoot, the sand shifted as they walked in silence for a few minutes. "What about here?"

Ann looked around, ignoring the bright lights of a lone car as it passed them. A few yards to the east, an oversized green shell moved over the sand. The giant sea turtle began to dig a hole for its eggs. She felt blessed by the turtle's choice. "It's perfect."

"It is, isn't it?" Daniel asked. Against the dark sky, she saw the white of his teeth as he flashed a grin. "I know how to give you exactly what you want."

"You do, do you?" Her nervousness made her flirtatious remark come out like a challenge. How would she tell him her dark secret?

Daniel didn't seem to mind her edginess. Maybe his own roiling emotions left him impervious to hers. He set down the cooler, took out a blanket, and spread it on the sandy knoll. "I brought your sweater." He pulled it from his basket and handed it to her.

The last time she'd seen it, she'd packed it in her suitcase while in North Carolina. "You went through my bag." The man was about to be her husband. He knew a lot more about her than the contents of her overnight case. Why did it feel like he'd invaded her privacy?

Because she was about to tell him the truth.

"I hope you don't mind," he said. The fine lines around his eyes deepened. A normal woman wouldn't be able to see them. If she were normal, she wouldn't be bringing mortal danger to their marriage. "I wanted to surprise you tonight, and I didn't want you to be cold."

"Oh, Daniel." She stepped into his arms, wishing with all her heart that she was a normal woman. "I'm sorry. Of course I don't mind. It was thoughtful of you."

He brushed his lips over her temple, wrapping his arms around her. "Ann, I love you."

"I love you, too." She relaxed in his arms, inhaling the clean citrus of his scent, so different from the predator's dark fragrance. Then the sharp edge of the ring box in his chinos pressed against her thigh.

"Here," he said, perhaps noticing the contact. "Let's sit." She let him pull her down to the blanket, and he pulled a bottle of wine from the cooler. The cork popped out, and he set the bottle aside for a minute. "We'll let it breathe."

"Did you remember wineglasses too?"

"Yes." He chuckled softly against her ear. "I've been planning this moment for a long time. For months, it seems. Maybe years."

"And what moment is that?" The pounding surf nearly overwhelmed the sound of her ragged question.

He didn't answer. Instead, he took her in her arms, kissing her neck. Over the surf, she heard the swoosh of the turtle tossing sand for her nest, preparing for her future.

"Will you still love me when you're a famous Harvard professor?" he asked. "Will you still love me when you're on every animal program showing how you've stopped the mustang culling?"

She laughed. She'd always love him. "Will you still love me when you're the most famous wildlife veterinarian?" That wasn't the question at all, she knew, but she couldn't bring herself to pose the real question, reveal the actual truth. "Oh, wait. You are. And you do."

He chuckled, shielding her eyes from the sudden glare of another passing car as it rounded a turn. "I thought we were far enough away from the road for this nonsense."

"I don't care about the cars." And she didn't, but instead of hearing the vehicle complete the coastal turn, the engine stopped in the distance, and the car door closed, softly. She thought about leaving, finding a different knoll, but if other people saw the beauty of this perfect beach, so be it. "This is lovely."

"Now where were we?"

"Let me remind you." She pushed him onto the warm, blanket-covered sand and pinned him beneath her with a lascivious giggle.

"Mmm," he answered. His lips met hers, taking before she could give. Not that she minded. The heat of his tongue traced the edge of her lip, and she nipped in return, sucking his lip into her mouth. She savored his taste.

Rolling across the blanket, he nibbled the back of her ear, making the hairs on her neck ripple with pleasure. He kissed the side of her neck slowly as his cock pressed against her thigh.

Ann tilted her head to the side, inviting more kisses, yielding. Sliding the thin straps of her dress off her shoulders, his palms caressed her bare shoulders, and his hands traveled lower, to her upper arms. The backs of his fingers brushed the sides of her breasts, almost on accident. Ann arched her back as he slid the straps over her shoulders, pressing her tight nipples into his palms.

"That feels so good. In this moonlight, you look like a goddess." Then he kissed her. "Diana of the Hunt, maybe."

Heat raced into their kiss, and nervous fear fell to the background. She ran her hand through his hair, enjoying the purr of delight he gave. That pleasure was nothing compared to the pleasure she felt when he pressed his chest against her breasts.

Ann lay back in the warm sand, inviting him, tugging with her hands. "Please, don't stop."

He did though. He sat up and took her hand in his. "My life—" he started to say, but then emotion seemed to choke him. "My life," he said more clearly, "hasn't been the same since I met you. You make me—" He stopped with her hand on his chest.

She couldn't let him finish. She had to tell him the truth. "I—"

"No." He pressed a finger against her lips. "Let me finish."

She'd wait. She curled around him, resting her cheek against his naked chest. The pounding of his heart echoed the sound of the surf. It couldn't possibly be pounding as loudly as her own.

"You've made me happier, more content, and more inspired than I've ever been," he said.

With her heart in her throat, she felt his hand sneak between them and into his pocket. She knew what he was about to ask.

"I can't picture the rest of my life anywhere but by your side."

Ann stared at him, trying to memorize the moment. The empty beach spread around them, and the moonlight gleamed in his hair, turning its rich gold into silver. His eyes were hard to read, even for her, but what could be in them except devotion and love?

"Will you do me the honor of marrying me?" He handed her the now-opened box.

She wanted to jump up and dance around the beach, but she managed to control herself. "We won't have to hide anymore!" She clapped her hands.

"So, will you marry me?"

She accepted the box as if it were fragile, as if it might break into a million pieces. The moonlight glinted off the huge marquise-cut diamond, and it glittered like one of the stars above them. "It's beautiful."

"I hope you'll say that when you can really see the ring." He touched the box gently but didn't take it from her. "I looked at so many, trying to find the one I could see on your finger. I wish you could see it."

"Daniel." She had to confess now. "I can."

"Of course you can, but when you get it into the light—"

"I mean, I don't need the light to see it. I—" Again, words failed her. "I'm not—" She stopped.

"Ann?" He said her name so softly.

"Yes?"

"Do you accept? Will you marry me?"

She ached to say yes. "I have to tell you something first. I won't be a coward and keep this from you."

"There's nothing you could say that'd change my mind."

His words sounded sincere, but the tiny muscles beneath his eyes tightened and his eyebrows came together.

"There might be." She wanted to tell him. She did. Still, she couldn't shake the feeling that something calculated lurked just below the surface in his gaze.

"What is it?"

She didn't answer. It wasn't just her life she was putting in his hands—it was the lives of all her kind. If he ever let her secret out, she and her family would spend the rest of their lives as guinea pigs in the basements of laboratories—just like the aliens at Roswell, poor souls.

"Tell me your secrets, baby. You'll feel a lot better when you do. And I'll still love you." He planted a kiss on her nose. "I promise."

A paranoid thought hit her out of the blue. Had he planned this entire proposal not to take her hand in marriage but to hear her secret? Maybe that's why she didn't want to tell him?

Absurd. Her fear was normal, not based in anything creepy. She tried again. "It's just that I . . . I don't always look like this."

"I've seen you with bedhead, baby. You're gorgeous then, too. Even without the bun."

"That's not what I mean."

"What is it, then?"

Soft footfalls intruded just then, to the south and in the scrub roses. "Someone's coming."

"How could you know that?" In the dark night, his eyes didn't seem like cobalt—they seemed like steel. Why did she have such a bad feeling about this?

"Someone parked a car up the beach a few minutes ago, and he must have walked over here. He's in the roses over there, the ones with the pink flowers."

"How can you know that?" His eyes were locked on hers.

He wanted an answer. "The color of the flowers? Where some-one's standing? How could you know that?"

"That's what I'm trying to tell you." It was time for the truth. "I'm not hum—"

"Daniel!" Rage vibrated through the intruding voice.

"Who's there?" He squinted into the darkness, his shoulders bunched.

"Daniel, goddamn it." The woman flicked on a huge spot-light, the kind people use when night hunting. She pointed it right at them. "Daniel Hallock, how dare you?"

5

For a moment, Ann froze, her breasts naked, the skirt of her dress fluttering. "Do you know her?" Ann's voice croaked with doubt, but she knew the truth.

"It's not what it seems."

"Do you know her?"

"No, I don't." He touched his hair, straightening it with deft fingers, and for the first time in their relationship Ann knew with absolute certainty that Daniel lied.

"How dare you?" The woman's voice shook with controlled fury. "How dare you?"

Ann's lover—her ex-lover—shot Ann a wild expression, his eyes wide and eyebrows high. The moonlight caught the black of his irises. "I've never seen her before in my life."

Shock had been protecting her, Ann realized, but that cocooning layer fell gently away now, leaving her naked and raw. Without a word, she stood and slid the straps of her dress over her shoulders, the surf pounding in her ears. Or was it her heart? Not until she tried for a third time to get the silky straps to stay where she put them did she understand her hands were shaking.

"Oh, my God." Her words trembled. She'd been sleeping with a married man? Certainly an attached man. "I just—" She wrapped her arms around her chest, wanting to hold onto something solid. "Oh, my God."

"Ann, listen." Daniel tried to get her attention, touching her shoulder, but he was lost to her. She jerked away from him like his hands were poisonous, as poisonous as a rattlesnake.

"Ann, listen to me."

The flitter of hope that he could explain this, that he could make her believe his wife wasn't real, lived—but only for a millisecond. "Go away, Daniel." Her voice had no emotion. "Leave me alone."

"Ann!"

She straightened the bodice of her dress as the wind whipped the skirt. "I want no part of this. Or you. I can't believe you dragged me into this. You sullied me—and yourself." She looked at the resolute woman standing in the sand and added, "And her."

"I don't know her," the bastard insisted. Ann saw a shifty look in his expression, a momentary flash of anger that he quickly mastered. The subsequent tightening around his eyes made him look like a cornered dog. "I've never seen her before this."

"I don't believe you. And I don't want to see you again. I—"

"You don't know me?" the woman said to Daniel. She put her hands on her hips, pointing the spotlight downward into the sand so that it highlighted her black sandals. Some weird part of Ann's mind saw that the woman's toenail polish, a deep purple, was chipped. "We've been together for more than ten years, and you don't know me?"

"Listen." He took a step toward her, his muscles tight. "Get out of here before I call the cops."

The woman backed away, clearly unnerved. A breeze whipped through the night and blew her dark hair into her face. She might have followed them here, but Ann didn't blame her for moving away from Daniel now. The tension in his shoulders, the hard set of his face, gave him a feral look.

"That's right." He took another step toward her. "Run home. Leave us alone."

"I won't leave—"

Daniel didn't let her finish. "We don't want you." He took another step closer. "We don't need you."

The woman took a third step back and stumbled in the sand, dropping her gear. The spotlight flung crazy shadows over the dunes as it hit the sand, hurting Ann's eyes.

"Stop it." The stumble seemed to have bolstered something in her, solidified her resolve to see this confrontation to the end. "I'm not in the wrong. You are."

"No one believes you." Daniel's voice growled like an angry dog's.

"I believe you." Ann found her boots and started to put them on. "And I'm so sorry."

"Ann." Something in his tone made her pause. "Ann!" Daniel took another step toward the woman.

"Leave her alone, Daniel. I never want to see you again."

His eyes didn't leave his wife's face. "This woman's raving. She's a lunatic. Don't listen to her." He flicked a quick glance in Ann's direction, but Ann knew he was mostly blind in the moonlit night.

"Should I show her pictures, Daniel?" The woman reached for a handbag she'd dropped in the sand. She didn't sound crazy at all. "You and me in the Bahamas. You painting the garage."

"Shut up!"

"You can look and explain it yourself to the blond floozy."

Floozy? Ann wasn't a floozy. Was she? "I'm so sorry," Ann said, but the woman didn't seem to hear her apology. And what good would it do anyway?

"I have the love letter you wrote me just last week." The woman turned toward Daniel as she fumbled with the handbag. The light from the spotlight illuminated the sand rather than anything useful for the woman.

Daniel stepped into the light, his hands in fists. "I'll call the cops and have you arrested so fast you won't know what hit you."

"Go ahead." She quit searching inside her handbag, and a preternatural calm seemed to settle over her, as if nothing on this beach could touch her. "Call them."

Daniel hauled back his arm and started to swing a round-house punch at the woman. She tried to turn away, her arms in front of her face, but she couldn't protect herself.

Ann could, though. She let her biology take over.

She pulled power from the earth and shunted it to her arms and fists. Before she could blink, she shoved Daniel with the in-human strength only her kind could channel.

"Daniel!" the other woman cried, flinging herself in his direction. Was she trying to protect him?

The sound of his elbow cracking into the woman's face reverberated through the night, and then the woman gave a reedy shriek. She clutched her face and fell to the sand with a terrible moan.

"What have you done?" Daniel pulled himself to his feet. "Is she okay?" He looked at the woman he'd been about to punch, and Ann realized she had never known this man. "How did you do that?" he asked.

"You've lost your mind." Ann went to the unconscious woman's side. The coppery scent of blood filled her nose, tugging at her, calling to her magic.

"You threw me into her. You did this." He punted the spotlight across the sand with a kick. The bulb exploded as the light hit the ground, and Ann saw bits of white glass shower the sand like wedding confetti.

And Ann knew the truth. She *had* done this. She'd ruined the relationship the woman had had with the man she'd thought of as her husband, and now Ann had ruined the woman's face.

"You have no idea what was at stake. If I bring you in I can—" Cutting off his own words, he stalked to the blanket. "I was protecting you," he snarled.

"I don't need your protection." Because unless he had planned to help her fight a predator he didn't know existed, she didn't need *his* help—the magic coalescing in her blood saw to that.

"You have no idea," he repeated. He stood unmoving as a black cloud skittered in front of the moon, leaving them in darkness for a heartbeat. Despite the blackness, she read his expression. He showed no emotion, no fear or remorse. In that moment she realized if she were a normal woman—a human woman—she would be afraid.

Regardless, she wasn't normal. Ignoring him, she kneeled in the sand beside the woman. Even without her powers in full swing, she knew the woman's left cheekbone was crushed and her eye already swelled shut. The hard cartilage of her nose sat at an odd angle, and blood poured from her nostrils.

Ann watched blood trickle from the victim's ear and faced an ugly, ugly truth. Her own denial had caused this. She should've paid more attention during their courtship, realized she'd been cast in the role of the "other woman." Even Daniel's perennial unwillingness to truly make love to her should have keyed her into the truth.

She'd have more time for regrets later. Now, she needed to fix this.

Squatting next to the woman, Ann reached for her purse, wanting her phone. She needed paramedics now, but her hand found nothing. "Where is it?" She scanned the sand where it must have fallen.

"Wanting this, babe?" Daniel dangled her cell in front of her. His smile mocked her.

"Let me have the phone, Daniel."

"I think you can heal her. You should do it."

The words should have chilled her, but anger boiled in her gut instead. She pointed at the woman. "You're crazy. She's bleeding from her ear. You're a vet. You know what that means."

"Then do your magic." He nodded at the woman. "They told me you have special powers. Use them."

What? "She needs paramedics now." Or healing magic, like Daniel suggested. "Don't rob her of her life." *Who'd said she had special powers? What nest of snakes had her mother stumbled into?*

"I'm not robbing her of anything—you are, if you just stand there. I can protect you. Let's see you do your stuff."

Devils would dance across the beach in figure-skating dresses before she showed him anything. "Call 911, and I won't tell anyone you did this. We'll say we found her like this."

"No." He shook his head and his blond hair gleamed in the moonlight. "I think you need to tell me what you were about to say before she interrupted." He loomed over her as he said this. The moon threw crazy shadows over his shoulder, but Ann wasn't intimidated. "Tell me now."

"I've no idea what you're talking about." How could she get this woman to the hospital? "You need help, Daniel, but she needs help more. Just give me the phone."

"You were telling me about your extraordinary hearing and your amazing vision." His white teeth glittered in the odd light.

And Ann realized he was right. She'd been just about to tell him her secret.

With a growing disgust, she realized she'd been just about to accept his marriage proposal. Dear God. How pathetic could she be? "You would risk her life for some crazy idea?" she asked. "You'd wait for me to heal her like I'm some wizard from another realm rather than call a doctor?"

"You're not human, are you?"

"No, I'm an alien from Mars."

"I knew it!" Harsh glee filled his voice as he jerked his hand back and pitched her cell into the crashing Pacific waves.

"Oh, for God's sake." She stood so that he didn't lurk over her. "You're out of your mind. Do you still have your phone, or did the little voice in your head that sounds like Cthulhu tell you to chuck that, too?"

"I have something better for you than a phone, babe." He walked over to the cooler and squatted, rummaging through the wine and cheese. What was he going to do? Start a food fight? She considered jumping on his back and taking the phone—but the pistol stopped her.

"You're going to shoot me?" Incredulity rippled through the intellectual part of her mind.

Except her animal self believed the threat. Magic began swirling through her blood, licking her veins. Ozone crackled through her hair, and she focused so her power didn't whip from her control.

"I'm going to bring you in. There's a huge bounty on your head if I bring you in alive." He centered the weapon at her heart. "Don't be scared, though. I can keep you safe. I love you."

Time to state the obvious. "People don't usually use pistols on people they love."

"It won't hurt you. It's a dart gun."

Her nose caught whiff of a chemical—Telazol. She'd used it herself to knock out wild horses. He was going to tranquilize her, which just might work, if she stood here and did nothing.

Unlikely. "Good luck with that," she said as she moved away from him.

"I don't need luck, babe." He pointed the pistol and started to pull the trigger. "Not tonight."

She didn't stop to think; she acted. Her biology worked its spell, and hot lust surged through her veins. Unfocused desire woke in her, imbued every cell in her body with a dark craving. Her lips ached for a lover's kiss. Her neck yearned for the caress of a skilled tongue. Her breasts and nipples craved a skillful stroke, a hard touch.

And for the first time in years, it wasn't Daniel's face and mouth and hands she longed for. Detective Atlanta's slow smile flashed though her mind, searing its way through her veins— but that gave way to an image of the dark-haired stranger, the predator. And she wanted him.

Yes, her body said. *Him.* The predator.

She ignored the urge to fuck, relying on years of purposeful changes, the strength originating from resisting that temptation.

And even as her cells pulled strength from the earth, even as her mitochondria pulsed with energy while forming iridescent green tendrils and wrapping them through her breasts and hips, she ran toward the roses, her human feet still clad in boots.

Her fingertips craved the feel of hard muscle beneath them like a junkie craves heroin; her mouth craved the searing kiss of a magnificent lover, even her ex-lover—but all that desire was beside the point. Her rational mind craved secrecy, and it won the battle.

Never in her life had she let anyone see her change, and she wasn't about to let this pustulant asshat be the first. Foliage crackled beneath her feet as thorns ripped her thin dress.

A flash of yellow whizzed past her face just after she heard a crack. She needed a heartbeat to register the truth: he'd shot at her. The glow-in-the-dark yellow was the tranquilizer dart.

Only the ineffectual workings of the human eye in the darkness had saved her—Daniel was a great shot. She herself had watched him bring down her wild horses, one after another.

Ignoring the jagged thorns, she crouched into the thicket. Her breasts ached for a rough caress. Her clit longed for a hot tongue, skilled fingers—and her hands and feet gave way to hooves. She channeled breath-stealing lust into power, shunting the desire throbbing in her core into muscle tissue, storing away the excess energy until she needed it, until she could use it.

Waves crashed on the shore, and her thighs morphed into gaskins and stifles. Toenails and fingernails gave way to coronet bands. The scent of crushed roses filled her equine nostrils, mingling with the odor of blood in a way not possible in her human form to detect. Her equine hindquarters formed, and her tail sprouted. Her neck elongated and her mane tangled in the thorny branches—but she didn't care. Daniel wouldn't hurt her. He couldn't. And she'd see to it that he'd never hurt anyone again.

Another yellow dart flew past her with a cracking explosion. It missed her.

Her ex-lover might know where she was, but he didn't know what she was, not for certain. By the end of the week, the man would be locked in a padded cell and labeled insane.

"Ann!" Daniel called. She heard him reload the pistol, knew he had plenty of Telazol darts. "You can't hide from me," he called.

Hiding wasn't what she had in mind. Concentrating her strength into her haunches, she sprang from the thicket, her mane and tail flying, her ears pinned back.

"Dear God, it's true," Daniel gasped. She heard him pull the trigger as she blasted toward him, and she felt the loaded dart fly past her neck. "We're going to be famous!"

Fucking bastard.

She galloped a long distance past him, not because she was afraid—she wasn't—but because she needed speed for her plan to work.

Damp sand sprayed over the beach as she slid to a stop and spun around. Pouring the excess energy she'd collected into her legs and pulling more from the earth as she caught her bearings, she focused on Daniel—and then barreled toward him.

As her nostrils dilated, salty air filled her lungs and oxygenated every one of her cells with an efficiency Secretariat would've envied. She ran faster than any racehorse, and her hooves slammed into the sand, channeling more energy to her veins.

She'd smash Daniel into the sand.

But even as her head bobbed in tandem with the pounding of her hooves, even as the wind whipped her mane flat against her neck, she saw him adjust his aim.

He trained his pistol right on her chest, and Ann realized her white coat must shine in the full light of the moon.

"Ann," he called across the beach as she closed the distance between them. "Just hold still. I won't hurt yo—"

She didn't let him finish. Within two heartbeats she slammed her withers into his chest, and he hit the ground with a thud.

6

Ann considered her options as Daniel Hallock lay in the sand, gasping for breath like a netted fish. If she could've questioned him, she would have. Who had a bounty on her and why did he think—no, know—she could heal? God, she'd love to ask what he knew about the predators.

She'd have to find some other way. Right now she needed to neutralize the threat he presented—and she didn't mean that in an FBI way. The bastard needed a head injury. Not something life threatening, tempting as that was, but something no one could ignore. Something that would make listeners doubt every word that came from his mouth from this day forward.

When he started talking about shape changing, she wanted people to ask him about fairies and dragons. And aliens. And yetis.

"Ann." His voice came out like a frog's croak as he lay on the ground and stared blindly into the sky. With audible effort, he inhaled. "I love you." He gasped again. "I love . . . everything about you."

She snorted through equine nostrils. She couldn't believe she'd let this bastard go down on her just an hour ago. What had she been thinking?

"You can . . ." He inhaled with a disgusting, snotty noise. "Trust me."

Bullshit. His wife thought she could trust him too, no doubt, and look what that got her. Anger roiled through Ann's veins, pounding more heavily than the Pacific surf on the beach sand.

"Ann." He held his hands above his head, and she saw his breath was coming easier now. She didn't have much time. "I knew you were magic the first time I saw you. I . . . knew it."

She snorted again and pawed the sand.

"Don't hurt me." He lifted his head to plead with her. "Please. You can trust me. Together we can knock science on its ass. You're real! We'll get our names—both our names—in *Science* and *Nature*. We can rewrite all the rules of biology and evolution."

Ann had a different kind of history she wanted to rewrite. Slowly she walked toward him, her ears pinned flat against her head. She concentrated her fury into her legs and neck, into her chest. She didn't need magic for this.

"Don't hurt me," he said again. His features wrinkled as he tried to gather his arms behind him and sit. "Please, don't hurt me." His hand crept toward the pistol at his side. He was going to shoot at her again.

She stepped back and snapped her forefoot. Her hoof hit his skull with a disgusting thud, and he passed out cold. Blood poured into the sand from the gash.

Killing him would be so easy. Another lash of her forefoot, a slam of her back feet. She could grab his neck between her teeth and crush his trachea. She could shake him, break his neck. Or hell, she could drag him to the water and let him drown.

Still, death wasn't hers to give. Her ears flicked toward him, and she listened to his heart pounding solidly in his chest. The breeze whipped through the tall palm trees.

She had a choice at this point: she could heal Daniel's wife, or she could find Daniel's phone and call 911. This woman—who'd done nothing but confront her husband's lies—lay smashed at her feet. Under the care of the best American doctors, she would endure years of reconstructive surgery, and she'd still be scarred from that smashed cheekbone.

No real choice existed.

Ann turned toward the woman, and her hooves churned the damp sand. Swiveling her ears in all directions, she listened for intruders. Nothing.

Standing on the beach where the sea pounded the sand, Ann noticed something she'd only registered in the back of her mind earlier: the earth's power in this spot was stronger here than in most places where she had worked her magic. More power coursed through her veins here than in the Sierra Nevadas. Perhaps the energy released as the water slammed against the beach gave her something additional to harness?

She didn't have time to care. Taking a deep breath, she focused on the earth's strength, letting it connect to her hooves and pour into her veins. She locked that air in her lungs for several heartbeats, letting the earth's might infuse each and every one of her cells, into each mitochondria and into each ribosome.

Another huge wave crashed on the shore, and her magic coiled around her heart, through her veins. She controlled the lust that accumulated as she'd changed shape now. She would stay in control of it until she slipped back into human form—unless the predator tracked her out to this empty beach. Then control was a less certain thing.

She released just a touch of lust and shunted it to the coalescing magic. Desire licked through her veins.

She was ready.

Ann dipped her head toward the prone woman and positioned her horn just above the smashed cheekbone. The tendrils that had wrapped around her heart flowed like water to her forehead, and then ethereal wisps spiraled around her horn, slowly at first and then with increasing speed. Power raced through her veins toward her horn and concentrated there.

Finally, the magic coalesced, becoming nearly solid. The tendrils dripped down toward the woman's cheek. The green evidence of Ann's magic pooled on the woman's face. The deepest puddles formed over the injuries, flooding the left side of the wound in a saturated, moss-green plasma.

Within seconds, Ann sensed the healing, her horn registering every microscopic movement in the woman's injury. Shattered bone fragments found mates and knitted together, stronger than before; broken blood vessels wormed back into their natural positions and reattached themselves, rejoining torn neighbors. Newly grown cells shunted blood from the injuries back toward the woman's kidneys, and the bruised flesh healed.

Within minutes, Ann's magic had restored the woman's health.

"Where—" the woman started to say. "What happened to—"

Sleep, Ann commanded the woman's body. *You're safe here. Sleep.* And the patient obeyed.

As Ann surveyed the woman, her dark hair fanned out around her; guilt snaked through her guts and suffocated her heart. She had caused the woman's heartache and pain and demoralization.

If she were in this woman's shoes, she'd be questioning her very being, her femininity and attractiveness. She'd look in the mirror and see the normal changes wrought by time and stress— the crow's-feet and laugh lines, the gray hair. She'd look at a forty-year-old woman and see a sixty-year-old crone. And she'd blame herself for her husband's infidelity.

Ann could help this anguish.

She absolutely shouldn't—but she could. The last time this type of healing had been used, her mother had broken all the rules and done it. Why? Because Ann lost control.

Still, if ever there'd been a time in her life to break a rule, this was it. She owed this woman.

Ann took a deep breath. Aging wasn't an illness, but it was

biological. She would repair the cellular damage. The woman wouldn't need to doubt her femininity, and Ann could free herself of at least some guilt.

She dipped her horn again and let her healing suffuse the woman again, lengthening the telomeres in the woman's cells and washing away all but the necessary free radicals. She repaired all the random mutations in the woman's DNA, washing the cells in antioxidants.

The effects wrought by years and stress evaporated. The veins in her hands shrank; the flesh of her face tightened and lines vanished. Her hair softened and regained a richer hue. The strands became thicker. The curves of her hips, the flatness of her stomach returned, mirroring the beauty the woman had had at the peak of her loveliness.

Ann walked slowly back to the blanket, hooves dragging in the sand. Cold starlight caught the diamond of her supposed engagement ring, and it sparkled on the checkered beach blanket. It'd been such a beautiful thing. It would've looked gorgeous on her finger. She would have cherished it and the man who'd given it to her.

If she'd belonged to the human race. If she'd been normal.

As she changed back to human form, her heart bleak, the memory of her happiness hit her in the chest like a truck. When she'd seen Daniel smuggle the ring into his pocket back at the hotel, no woman alive had ever been happier.

What had she done?

Her hooves gave way to human feet, still warm and dry in her boots. She caught her breath as her breasts became human—and filled with lust. Her bra felt too tight, too constraining, and her core ached with desire. She stumbled with her need—and then pushed it aside. She had no time for this.

She leaned over Daniel's prone form and fished into his pocket, trying not to cringe at the proximity of her body to his. She took out his cell phone and pulled Kai Atlanta's business card from her purse.

"Hello." His deep voice rushed through her, lighting up the neurons kindled by her shape-changing. Lust had a physical taste, she realized, a palpable flavor. Her mouth watered for the salt of his skin.

"Kai." Her voice was too husky, but she couldn't help it. "This is Dr. Ann Fallon. We met at the hotel—"

"I know exactly where we met." The deliberate way he spoke, his deep tone, these made her catch her breath. "Your face isn't something I'd forget."

His words might've stoked her innate lust under normal conditions, but now . . . so close to her change . . . she'd be tempted to fuck him silly if he were here.

"I, um—" She paused, wishing she'd thought this out a little better. "There's a man lying at my feet—"

"Lucky bastard."

Again, that unwanted lust twined between her thighs. All doubt was gone. If Kai were here, she knew she'd fuck him. Forget that squeaky-clean appearance, she'd teach him to play dirty. "Seriously, Detective Atlanta." Her voice sounded steadier than she thought it should. "He's bleeding."

"I apologize. I'll call an ambulance."

"That's a good idea, but . . ."

"But what?"

She concocted a plausible story on the spot. "But I was walking on the beach, and I saw him attacking a woman."

"Where is she?"

"Also lying at my feet."

"Bloody?"

"Umm," she hedged. The woman had been bloody, but now . . . "It's too dark." This implied she couldn't see but didn't actually say it.

"So . . ." He apparently searched for the right words. "You're surrounded by two bloody bodies?"

"Bodies?" She laughed, but it was a nervous sound. A guilty sound. "No. They're alive."

"How do you know?"

"I took their pulses."

"So if he attacked her, why is he unconscious?"

Ann had had enough of this. If he kept giving her rope, she'd hang herself. "I don't know. I don't know anything. I just know that when he wakes up, the woman here might not be safe."

"And you know this how?"

"Maybe he has a gun?"

"What makes you think that?"

No way she'd answer that one. "This seems like something for the cops, doesn't it?"

"It does. Where are you?"

"The victims are at . . ." She looked at the road, making out the mile-marker signs with an ease a human would have found impossible. "They're at mile-marker 5 on Silver Strand Boulevard." She turned and her eye caught the rough-hewn wood building in the distance. Gigantic palms waved by its darkened doors. "South of the Silver Strand State Beach."

"You called them victims?"

"Well, the woman isn't moving and something attacked the man, for sure."

"What?"

"I don't know." She gave a low chuckle. "I'm not a detective."

He didn't laugh. "Was it you?"

"Me?" She didn't fake her surprise. How'd he suss out the truth so quickly? "This man's twice my size."

"I'll be right there with an ambulance. Wait for me."

"I won't be here. I'm leaving."

"You can't leave a crime scene."

"I'm reporting it, which is all I'm required to do. You have my cell and you know where I'm staying." Except it occurred to her to wonder where she'd be staying, exactly. Not in Daniel's room, that's for sure. If he'd been hunting her, and if the predators had been hunting her . . . Jesus, what was she going to do? "Just call if you need me."

"If you're not guilty, why're you running?"

Ann knew goading when she heard it. "Why would I stay alone on a dark beach in the middle of the night where people have just been attacked?" She clicked off the phone before he could answer.

Her pleasure at having such an unassailable final word lasted a nanosecond. A person who belonged to the human race would sit in the car. An innocent person would wait. She couldn't though. Not in Daniel's car. Not for the cops. Not even for Kai Atlanta.

She had to find the vials.

In that moment, she realized her future was ruined.

Her fiancé had been hunting her for bounty and was essentially already married—and she had missed all the classic signs of his betrayal. The secrecy? She'd bought it, hook, line, and sinker. His utter refusal to let anyone know about their relationship? She'd fallen for that too.

Why had he done this to her?

No, she thought. Why had she let herself be fooled? She hadn't missed classic signs; she'd ignored them.

It was time to start putting her family first—really first. She needed to find the vials and destroy them, and then she needed to help her mother destroy the lab.

She stepped away from the beach blanket, face to the wind. The salt air rolled over her tongue and filled her lungs. Ann knew why she'd done it, why she'd pulled the wool over her own goddamned eyes. She'd wanted the dream too much. Tired of running and hiding and scheming, she'd wanted a so-called normal life so badly that she'd spurned her heritage and embraced what this man had to offer.

Which was lies.

A gust of wind rolled over the water and hit her in the face, chilling her. Fuck this, she thought to herself. Just fuck this. She planted her feet deep into the sand and ripped power from the earth, giving herself no quarter. Her equine form took hold fast, too fast. Muscles tore and ligaments shredded themselves as her human form gave way—but she didn't care. She deserved the pain. She craved the pain, but it couldn't last. Her biology healed damaged tissue as quickly as it ruptured.

So she ran.

She ran like a hurricane roaring over the ocean. Sand flew from under her hooves as she thundered over the turf, waves licking her ankles. She put her head down and let the strength of her legs dominate her spirit. Soon she heard nothing but the pounding of her heart and the wind in her ears.

She ran for ten miles, then twenty. Then she quit counting. The naval base had a huge fence, and she cleared it without trying. She sped past a homeless guy, then a couple walking on the shore. They didn't notice her. She burst past a virgin, a young woman just shy of maturity. The girl woman saw her, saw her horn, but even her sweet perfume of innocence failed to stop Ann. She'd run until—

The fragrance washed through her like a deluge, the kind that rushes through Southwestern arroyos and leaves them barren.

She knew what she had to do right now—before her job talk in the morning, before she found a safe place to spend the night.

Ignoring the wind rippling through the tall palms, Ann looked up the beach and saw the bright lights curving along Glorietta Bay. A shell crunched beneath her boot as she began to walk toward the hazy crescent of the Coronado Bay Bridge.

Where was he? Her mouth watered for him. Her thighs craved him. She'd do now what she should have done earlier.

The predator had become prey.

7

Her human feet made no noise on the red pathway winding through the gardens of the Hotel del Coronado. A dim light illuminated an ornate park bench where he sat, but her nose found him first. The fragrance swirled around her before her eyes adjusted to the lights.

"Hello, gorgeous," the deep voice said. The tiny woman sat silently beside him, her black dress clinging to her athletic curves.

"Erik Sutherland." She let his name hang in the air. The moon shone from behind the huge beehive turret of the hotel, casting a jagged shadow over them, and his scent was already beguiling her. Like her own magic, his brooding perfume looped around her ankles and saturated her blood. His sensual lips, the smoldering desire in his eyes, those matched the hunger in her. At least she wouldn't betray her fiancé by going to this man's bed. "Are you enjoying the conference?"

"Not as much as I'm going to," he paused, his eyes scanning her body. Her nipples hardened as his gazed flicked back down to her breasts. "Ann."

She arched her eyebrows, wondering if he could see it. Getting her mind around the fact that the man sitting before her was a mere human with a vial of compelling fragrance was proving difficult. It was too easy to imagine her death in his eye—but if he were just a man . . .

"I know more than your name, Dr. Ann Fallon." The predator let his voice roll over the syllables like whiskey rolls over ice. His arm dangled over the armrest, and his fingers slowly caressed the spiky red petals of a bird-of-paradise. "Duke University. Harvard's new darling." He paused. "Maybe."

"How nice to meet someone as well informed as you." Could he tell how much she wanted to taste the salt of his skin?

He smiled then, a slow, deliberate smile that promised a very certain kind of pleasure, a pleasure that came with a cost. "Would you care to join us?"

Magic licked through her, begging her to acquiesce, begging her to taste his mouth and offer him her neck. She needed to find the vials, but tasting him might be . . . okay. Getting her hands in his pockets—around his cock—would be a delight.

"Yes," Ann said. "I'll join you."

A sardonic smile crossed his face then, and he turned toward the other woman. "Go. I don't need you right now."

The woman nodded and left, the yucca plants towering over her small figure as she followed the walkway to the stairs.

"Sit," he commanded after the other woman was no longer visible. Ann obeyed. Would she have been able to refuse if she wanted?

"Were you walking alone through this secluded garden just to find me?" His powerful fingers slowly followed the curve of the red flower in his grasp. The spiky bloom looked like a weapon in his hand. "Like Little Red Riding Hood looking for the wolf?"

"Yes," she breathed. And the vials—but her aching breasts

and the deep hunger between her thighs made it hard to focus. "Although I have no hood."

"I wonder, how did you find me?"

He released the bloom and touched her neck then, sliding his fingertip from her ear to her shoulder. The pleasure was exquisite, and she squirmed against the hard park bench. Once she admitted the truth to him, she couldn't go back. Once she told him the truth, they'd both know the rules: He was the predator and she was the prey—and she'd have to go to his bed.

To find the vials.

"I smelled you," she said. They'd play the game.

"Is that so?" He leaned in so close she could see the dark stubble across his chin.

What would it feel like as it abraded her flesh? Knowing she'd discover the answer in a heartbeat made her skin long for his touch. "Yes." She barely breathed the word.

"And how do you find me?" His lips were so close to hers she could feel his breath heating her skin. She moved in closer. She couldn't help it.

"Irresistible."

His kissed her then, if such a brutal thing could be called a kiss. He wrapped his hand around the back of her neck and pulled her to him. He slid his lips over hers with such force she had no choice but to open her mouth.

His tongue wrapped around hers. His mouth sucked her breath. And his scent made her crave him like the desert craves the rain.

He pushed her away, but she couldn't read his expression. "Do you belong to me?" he asked.

She was prey. "Yes."

"Are you sure?"

"Yes."

"Strip for me, then. Show me your breasts."

Was this a test? Did he doubt his hold on her? Ignoring the

sound of laughter just a few feet away, she slid the thin strap of her dress over her left shoulder until her breast was bared to the cool night air.

And to his mouth. He leaned over and licked it. She could feel his hot breath on the wet, sensitive skin. The sensations bewitched her.

He roughly caressed her back, her arms. He surrounded her with his touch as he ravaged her.

She lost herself, her desires and needs. He left her with an awareness of only him—his teeth, his tongue, his fingers and palms. She shivered at the sensation running through her, the deep throbbing desire that made her ache for him. Against her will she moved against him, wanting more. She grew increasingly willing to accept whatever he would give.

She arched her back in pleasure. A long sound of delight escaped her. Other people in the park must have heard, but she didn't care.

He flicked his tongue across a taut nipple, and she shuddered in pleasure. Her delight grew. She squirmed in his arms, gasping. "Please," she said, begging for release. His hand crept up her bare thigh, and she felt only anticipation, excitement.

Finally, finally, he reached between her legs and oh so gently stroked her.

His mouth traveled up to the tender spot behind her ear. He bit her earlobe as his fingers slipped over and around her throbbing clit.

She fought back a moan and the urge to press against him. Enslaved by the delicious ravishment that overwhelmed her senses, Ann yielded. If he stopped now . . .

She couldn't control herself any longer. Ann began moving rhythmically against his hand and shifting to show him exactly the right angle.

He added more fingers. Suddenly it felt like he had a fingertip slithering around every slippery centimeter.

Her body stiffened and she knew she was so close. He didn't miss a beat. Suddenly, she cried out. She knew everyone in the park heard her, and she didn't care. Her muscles pulsated against his fingers, and he expertly pressed against her, satisfying her.

Finally, she fell against him in exhaustion, and he grinned. "You are mine," he said, and horror zipped through her, freezing her against him. She realized he was right.

She hadn't made the smallest attempt to find the vial.

"My room is this way," the predator said.

The slide of her silk dress over her thighs heightened her awareness of her desire as she followed the predator down the hotel hall. Even as Ann held her breath, the seductive bergamot wafted around the predator, clothing him in the promise of pleasure and enchantment.

Ann knew she'd have to breathe eventually, just as surely as she knew the predator would hurt her, trap her, maybe kill her. But it was easy to forget that as she followed him into his hotel room, watching the muscles of his back play beneath his thin shirt, watching the muscles of his ass move as he walked . . .

He believed she'd be helpless to do anything but follow, and she had to keep him convinced of that. She waited silently as he opened the door. He entered first and she followed. Did she still have control of herself? Could she turn away now if she wanted?

She thought she could.

But she'd been wrong just moments before.

"Close the door," he said, and she obeyed, trembling at the sick way her body yearned for his. She craved his mouth and hands and fingers in a way that swept away all other thought—almost all other thought.

She would discover the truth of her strength—could it withstand the predator's lure? She'd know when she found the vials. His back was to her as he unknotted his tie. Would he have a vial in his pocket?

Yielding to his power—hoping that the capitulation was temporary—she walked to him and pressed her silk-clad breasts over his back, purring in his ear.

"You hunger," he said.

"Yes." She hungered. She slid her hands over his chest, over the pockets there. She could lose herself in the heat of his skin pouring through the cotton. She buried her nose in his black hair and imagined the high of snorting coke. It would feel like this. Beneath her fingers, his nipples hardened, and she ran her fingernails over them.

She didn't find a vial in his breast pocket though.

The subtle bergamot and jacaranda imbued her blood now . . . carrying the hidden pheromone with it. She ran her fingertips over his hips and thigh . . . into his pants pockets.

When her hands grazed the side of his throbbing cock, she forgot what she'd been looking for. Or, rather, what she'd found excited her. Ignoring the small item in the right pocket that might be a vial, she imagined the taste of his cock, the way it would slide over the roof of her mouth and back toward her throat, filling her, making her whole.

Nothing would taste better than his cock.

She ran her hands over the length of him, searching not for a vial but for the buttons, for the zipper. She needed to taste him, to lick him, to suck him. Now.

"I knew you'd be hot." He jerked her around, his dark eyes molten with desire.

Holding her lower back, he grabbed the low neckline of her dress and tore down with one fierce movement. The red silk fluttered to the floor like a dead bird, but her aching breasts were now bared for his hot mouth. And she craved his mouth on her breasts like she'd never craved anything before this.

The hand on her back pulled her hips tightly against his, but he didn't need to force her. She arched her back, offering her breasts to his hungry mouth.

"I want you to touch yourself." His voice commanded, and she couldn't resist. "Make me want your breasts."

His cock pressed hard against her thigh. He already wanted her—and she couldn't refuse him, not with his enthralling hold on her. And if she *could* refuse him, now wasn't the time to make that obvious.

She palmed the weight of her breast, teasing her nipple with her thumb. The feel of her own flesh in her hand delighted her.

"More." He pulled her hip harder against his. "Rougher."

She grabbed herself and pinched the nipple. Bathing in the scent of his magic, the sight of her fingers against the pale flesh of her breasts gave her a sense of power. Desire left her too weak to stand. If he hadn't been holding her back, she'd have crumpled at his feet.

Still, her body didn't crave her own touch or even the pleasure of watching herself—it craved his touch. Her eyes craved the sight of his muscles, his flesh.

She pushed her breast toward his mouth and arched her back, drinking in the power of his neck and arms, the feel of his hand on the small of her back. *Here*, her body said. *I am yours.*

And he claimed her.

He didn't use his lips. No quarter from him. No gentleness. The predator's teeth found her now, and nibbled—no, bit—the tender flesh around her nipple, imbuing her blood with heat.

He grabbed her breast and it hurt—but the punishing roughness was exactly what she deserved. For what she'd done to Daniel's wife, for what she'd done to herself, she deserved it.

And then she let the brooding fragrance work its unnatural spell. She yielded to its siren call and gave herself wholly to it. *Fuck control.*

The predator's tongue flicked her nipple. She wanted to get fucked, and she wanted it now.

No one satisfied like a predator. She'd seen the fulfillment on the faces of her sisters and cousins.

"Look," he said. He pivoted her hip so she stood square to the huge mirror above the hotel's low desk. "Look."

She did. Wearing her tiny pink panties and her high-heeled boots, she looked like a Playmate.

"Do you think you're beautiful?"

She knew she was. She also knew what answer a predator expected. "If I please you, then I'll believe I'm beautiful."

The predator's rough fingers grabbed one of her breasts while she watched, and he sucked hard and long. Teeth brushed over tender flesh, seared delicate nerve endings. She inhaled through the pain, letting his scent anesthetize the jagged torture tearing through her.

Only his magic didn't exactly anesthetize—it beguiled. It made her crave what *he* wanted.

It made her crave the pain.

"Now." He released her and looked at his handiwork in the mirror. A bright red spot rose on her breast just above her nipple. "Now we can see the lushness of your breasts, the way your hips scream fertility."

And he was right, she saw. The red mark highlighted the beauty of her skin, and she wanted him. She ached for him, for the way he'd claim her and make her his own. She took a deep breath. Could she walk away?

"Now you're beautiful." He bent over her and licked a trail from her breast to her hip. His hot tongue delighted her flesh, and she wrapped her fingers through his thick hair as his lips reached the line of her panties.

She shifted her legs, opening for him.

He ignored her offer and stood. "Come with me." He opened a door she hadn't noticed, and she saw the adjoining room. She followed him through the doorway. He pointed to the bed, an oversized king, and she walked to it.

Before she could sit, he touched the soft flesh of her stomach and caressed her as gently as he might stroke a kitten.

Ann couldn't help herself. She moaned with the pleasure of it. Skating on the edge of death, knowing he held her life in his hands, knowing the danger was as real as the bed behind her. The desire to fuck was stronger than anything she'd ever felt.

Then he dipped his hand into her panties and stroked her clit. As swollen and wet as she was, the sensation left her dizzy with need.

"You please me," he said.

The traitorous part of her mind glowed with the praise. She pleased him. She felt chosen. She longed to rip his clothing from his back as he'd done to her. She'd fuck him so hard the hotel guests would complain. She'd scream the glory of his name so the women in the lobby would hear and feel the wretched claws of envy.

The small part of her mind that still belonged to her realized she had two rooms to search now.

A brutal kiss stole her breath, and he pushed her onto the bed so that she leaned against her elbows. "Don't move."

As his fingers reached inside the thin pink silk panties, separating her ass from his flesh, she realized the last thing she wanted to do was move . . . unless it was toward him.

Then she spied the small woman who'd been on the predator's arm earlier. Only she wasn't on his arm now. Instead, she was directing the oversized lens of a video camera, pointing it toward the bed. The tiny woman had taken off her formal dress but still wore her bra and panties.

As the predator unbuttoned his shirt and pants, Ann knew the camera should bother her, but the sight of the predator's huge cock, his massive thighs, blotted out her mind, erasing the questions. His scent had worked its dark magic.

Even the scent of death and ruin wouldn't destroy her pleasure tonight.

The predator turned toward the bed with the controlled rage of a stallion scenting a mare. He grabbed Ann's hair and pulled her to a sitting position. With his fingers wrapped around the bun just above her neck, he controlled her. He pulled her chignon back and exposed the length of her neck. His palm shoved her breast toward his cruel mouth.

And he smelled like heaven.

She wouldn't stop him now even if she could. Pleasure twisted around pain and grabbed her. Wet desire ripped through her as he sucked her breast hard enough to raise a second welt—and she moaned, hating herself for molding her body into his hot palms, hating herself for wanting his touch more than she wanted her life.

"I knew you'd be like this." The predator grasped her thigh and nipped her erect nipple. The pain was exquisite.

So was the pleasure.

She tilted her head back farther, hoping he'd bite her neck, grab her breast again.

He ran his face from her breast toward her ear, inhaling. His unshaved face abraded tender flesh, but the pain wasn't enough, not nearly enough. When he reached her earlobe, he kissed it, brushing his hot tongue across that soft spot behind her ear. And before the pleasure of the kiss wrapped itself around her brain, he caught her lobe between his teeth and bit her hard, crushing her thigh between his massive fingers at the same time.

With cruel hands, he pushed her toward the camera and ripped off her panties. Shredded pink silk fluttered to the carpet.

The brutality, the feel of the predator's skin and mouth against hers, it left her wild. She belonged here. A prey belonged to a predator.

"Spread your legs." He didn't touch her. "Now."

And she wanted to. That was the scary thing. With a small moan, she obeyed, knowing the camera would record the glistening proof of her desire, her cries of pleasure. The welts, proof of her pain.

"Good girl." He licked her ear. "I can reward you for your

obedience." And without letting go of her bun, he dropped his mouth to her breast and kissed her as gently as a kitten licks its paw. His tongue lapped her areola as his hand caressed the nape of her neck. His lips found her nipple, bathed it in warmth, in soft warmth.

After his cruel teeth and rough hands, these gentle caresses felt like silk. She'd been good, his touch said. She'd been so good. She deserved his kindness.

"You like that?" He lapped her areola.

She couldn't answer, not with words. Instead, she spread her legs farther, unashamed of the camera. She curved her hips toward him, answering his question.

And he heard her. Keeping his lips on her breast, he traced the length of her spine with hot fingers, caressed the curve of her hip. His fingertips looped through her pubic hair as he sucked harder now, crueler.

She tilted her hips farther up, toward his fingers, begging for their touch. She thought he might refuse her, tease her, maybe even chastise her boldness.

Instead, his fingers plunged into her, burying themselves deeply inside her. A brutal thumb slid over her clit, ripping a shocked gasp from her. The camera caught it all, she knew.

"This is what you wanted, isn't it?" He voice held no affection, no gentleness, but she didn't care. She was his prey. She belonged here.

She arched her breast toward him, begging him without words to suck harder, to bite, to fuck her with his hard fingers.

"Yes," the predator breathed. "You love this."

And she did. As his finger slid over her clit, she truly did.

Deep inside her cunt, she began to tremble with the impending orgasm. She knew it would rip through her like a storm and she'd be helpless when it finished.

She didn't want that relief yet. She didn't want this to end.

As if reading her mind, he pulled his fingers from her, leaving her empty. "You want to taste her?" The predator turned toward the auburn-haired woman behind the camera. "Taste her cunt?"

"If you wish it."

The arcane phrase snagged Ann's attention—the woman had all but implied *lord.* Then he sucked hard on her breast, inhaling her completely. His muscles beneath her palm felt as hard as his cock pressing against her thigh.

The woman walked over and knelt next to the edge of the bed. She moved with the cool efficiency of a panther, and a jagged bolt of fear ripped through Ann.

She'd never played with another woman, not like this. Still, she'd always been . . . curious. The predator pushed her to the edge of the bed and spread her legs, spread her cunt.

"Lick her."

Ann froze as the woman's tongue touched her clit. Would she like it? Would she hate it? Would she even be able to tell the difference?

The woman obeyed the predator and licked—like a cat laps milk. Her tongue slid so gently over her that Ann quivered in his arms. And when she thought of what the camera was catching—this dark-skinned woman with her perfect curves clad in black panties and bra, this perfect woman with her head buried between Ann's white thighs while the predator held her arms behind her back—when she thought of what the camera was catching, she almost came right then.

The slow-building spasm began, and Ann moaned, bucking her hips toward the woman, sliding her breasts against the sides of his arms. She needed a cock inside her, and she needed it now.

"Enough," the predator said to the woman. His voice was as husky as a porn star's. "Check the camera."

"No." Ann squirmed with her dissatisfaction. "Don't stop."

The muscles of his arms tightened with her words, and for a moment fear sparked through her. Would he punish her?

Instead, he chuckled. "I'll give you something better than a pussy-licked pussy." A wicked grin crossed his face as he roughly slid his fingers into her, his eyes locked on hers. "I'll give you something a woman like you will enjoy much more than that." His fingers slid more deeply inside, and only a shiver of fear kept her from coming in that instant.

And fear made the delay that much sweeter.

He wrapped his fist through her bun, twisting it so she couldn't move in his grasp.

"Hand the whip to me," he told the other woman. "Now."

"Whip?" Ann said. "I don't think—"

"That's right." He took the braided leather crop in his powerful hand. "Don't think."

"I—" She was about to say she didn't like pain, but that would make her a liar. He'd been hurting her since she'd fallen into his bed. And she definitely liked it.

She deserved it. She needed it.

"You what?" He rolled the textured braided edging over her nipple.

That trembling need deep in her cunt started again, and she thought she might come like this, without a cock anywhere near her. He rolled the leather over her nipples again, harder this time, and she didn't answer.

"This hurts," he told her.

"Yes." She breathed out the word and cupped her breasts, pushing them together, inviting him to taste. To bite. He slid the crop over her nipples, and she saw they'd turned red—but they ached for more. She ached for more.

"Do you want me to stop?"

"No." She arched her back, pressing her breasts into the brutal leather. "Don't stop."

"You'll do as I say." He took the whip away from her breasts and let the dangling leather straps tickle her stomach, her hip, the curve of her waist.

A small mew of disappointment came from her lips, and she knew it'd been caught on film. She didn't care.

"You want to play harder?" He sucked the top of her breast so hard she knew he must have left a welt.

"Yes."

"No." Dropping the whip, he rolled her over onto the bed and kissed her. A butterfly landing on a mimosa flower couldn't have been lighter than his lips on hers. "I can be nice. I can make you crave this more than your life."

"Yes."

She lay alongside him, and she could see in the camera lens how much bigger than she he was. He released his brutal grip and gently touched her tongue with his. His lips felt warm and soft against hers, but she knew they could turn hard and vicious in a heartbeat.

He retrieved the whip, and she thought he might strike her—and she didn't know if she'd cry in pain or joy.

He didn't spank her though. Instead, he pulled her thighs apart and slid the thick braided leather between them. He rolled the leather over her clit, making her arch in pleasure.

Next to her, his cock pulsed, and as she squirmed she watched it throb. He wanted her.

The thick nub of the whip slid over her clit, and then he slid the thing inside her. Her second orgasm began to tremble with its promise. Now, she needed to fuck.

"No." She rolled off him and tossed the crop on the bed.

"You can't refuse m—"

She cut him off by slithering down his chest, wrapping her mouth around his cock, and sucking. She slid him to the back of her throat, caressing him with her tongue. Before he could object, she sucked, sliding his cock further down her throat, and his cock throbbed in her mouth. The salty taste of pre-cum told her he was as close as she was.

Here, in this bed, she wasn't an anomaly. She wasn't an outsider. Releasing him, she straddled the predator, pinning his wrists under her hands. She started to slide his cock inside her. As he filled her, the shuddering began. The intoxicating pleasure of her orgasm enthralled her. She'd die for this. She'd—

As if she weighed nothing, the predator flipped her off him and onto her back. She whimpered with need. She needed him inside her more than she needed to breathe. She wanted him more than her lungs needed air.

His knees pinned her legs open. One of his massive hands pinned her wrists to the bed, as the other wrapped around her throat. Exhilarating fear seared through her. She lived only at his command.

She didn't fight him. She wanted him to use her, take her and fuck her until the taste of him filled every cell in her body.

His cock pressed against her cunt, and his hand trapped hers to the bed. She wrapped her legs tightly around his hips, pulling him inside her. Their bodies connected, as did their mouths and hands. His cock slid over her clit, and he thrust himself inside her with one fluid movement.

He didn't stop there. He wrapped his hand around her throat. With every thrust, his fingers tightened, bruising her skin. Still pleasure built, and his power reminded Ann of the ferocity of a wild animal. Pleasure built and blossomed.

Together, their breathing became shallow, quick. He roared as the orgasm tightened his body over her, but she couldn't scream her delight. The hand around her throat . . . she couldn't breathe.

And she wasn't sure she wanted to.

Then the orgasm grabbed ahold of her, pounding through her coiled muscles. The fingers around her throat loosened.

And then . . . and then . . . and then wave after wave washed over her, shook her, until she cried out, until she cried out in shame.

"You're mine now." His deep voice caressed her even as his fingers stroked her stomach.

"Yes," she answered. "I'm yours."

And she wasn't sure if she lied.

8

As Chiron drove, he clicked his cell phone closed. The hairs on his arms and neck didn't actually creep, but they thought about it.

Ann Fallon was trouble. He'd known it when he'd first seen her, and he knew it now. There'd been something about her at the conference . . . He couldn't put his finger on it, but she hadn't been straightforward there either. How could a mortal woman remind him of the Earthmother, of Akantha, of magic long gone from this world? Yet she did.

Chiron opened his phone again, and he started to press the numbers for his squad sergeant. His boss would send the black-and-whites and the ambulance to the beach site. Protocol.

Then his fingers stopped. *Earthshaker's balls.* He couldn't call his boss. Because his gut told him something else: He knew Fallon would've called 911 if the victims needed it. She wouldn't let people die. Right or wrong, she wanted him at the beach. Probably wrong, but he had to go.

With a sigh, he put the phone on the passenger seat and circled the car around. He'd check out the beach—even if it landed him in the broiler with his boss.

After twenty minutes of highway, the lights of the naval base slid past his window. Nothing but empty road and black ocean before him now. He cranked Nickelback to fill the emptiness, but it didn't help. The singer howled about graves and death and beds.

Lyrics like that shouldn't remind him of friends, but they did. Nessus had been better with a bow than any centaur alive, and that was saying a lot. He could hit an acorn from the top of an oak. Good to have him at your side during the Wars. Pholus had loved to fuck, and his blue eyes and charm brought even goddesses to his bed—not that that was generally a good thing. When Aphrodite had given him that jar of wine, for instance. Not good. And Eurytion. His voice would rival a Siren's. If he'd sung with Nickelback, everyone who heard it would just lay down and cry.

And they were all gone. In the grave. Dead.

He pumped up the volume. The guitar screeched up the scale, and his chest ached like some long-dead claw reached from the vast beyond, wrapped its cold scaly fingers around his heart, and squeezed.

Akantha.

Nickelback started singing about staying alive just to follow his girl home. He'd never follow her home. Not while he lived—and he'd live forever.

He sped past the green mile-marker sign, the white number refracting in his headlights. This was it, Fallon's beach. By Earthshaker's balls, she was almost to the estuary. The hairs on the back of his neck crept like an army of red ants.

Akantha's death had started with a phone call from the beach . . . a phone call just like Fallon's. From a beach just as isolated as this one.

Something weird hung in the air—something that reminded

him of the gods, the ancient ones, the ones who were old before Hera and Zeus. He had to kick back the urge to shift into his native form and gallop across the beach.

Suddenly, he was glad Fallon hadn't waited out here for him.

He gunned the Crown Vic to the breakdown lane, and braked. If men like Sutherland could bring down goddess-touched Akantha, what would they do to a mortal like Fallon? He slammed the transmission into park.

"Fuck." He hated this feeling of helplessness. He fished his Maglite from under the seat. "Fuck," he said again, remembering to grab his phone. He slammed the car door shut and walked toward the beach, smashing a beer can under his foot.

Climbing the short guardrail, he clicked on the flashlight, scanning the sand for footprints or weapons or condoms or bottles—anything that hinted at what these people were doing at the beach—what Fallon had been doing on the beach.

The beam of his light caught a ripple in the sand. Not a ripple, he realized—a print, a set of prints that took him back to a different time. For a moment, he could almost hear the clank of a legion's armor, the creak of wooden wheels as heavy horses pulled heavier wagons over cobbles and through sand.

A lone car sped up the boulevard, and he regained his grounding. Something in the night air was strange . . . ancient and unsettled. He squatted and inspected the prints.

The twenty-first-century hoofprints ran north, toward the hotel. The prints weren't large—no warhorse made them, but they weren't small either. A saddle horse then. The rhombus layout of the prints told him the animal had been galloping, and the depth of the prints said the beast had been galloping hard.

Chiron stood and shook his head. In all likelihood, the hoofprints weren't related to Fallon. If he went back to the car and turned on the police band, no doubt he'd hear about a farmer or schoolgirl missing a horse.

Following the tracks south for no other reason than they

were there, he headed down the beach, toward Mexico. The Maglite flooded the sand ahead of him, but when the edge of the beam hooked on something, he centered the light.

The something was metallic and black—a firearm.

The pistol reminded him of a snake. It sat in the sand unmoving but deadly all the same. Fallon could have been shot— that was his first thought. *Help me!* Akantha's last words echoed through his mind.

Then the cold logic kicked in. A spent CO_2 cartridge lay next to the weapon. The gun didn't belong to a killer; it belonged to a paintball fanatic.

He trained his light on the beach, looking for spent paintballs. Colorful as Mardi Gras beads, they shouldn't be hard to find in the pale sand, but they were. He couldn't find any. Not red ones, nor purple, nor blue.

Instead, a small Day-Glo yellow object sat in the divot of a hoofprint. He knelt in the sand. What was it? A toy? But then the beam of his flashlight glinted off an evil steel needle: it was a tranquilizer dart.

"Fuck." Fallon had said the man might have a gun, but she hadn't said it might be a tranquilizer gun. A medicinal scent clung to the humid night air, and he knew it was loaded.

"Fuck," he said again as a second thought struck him. Where were the victims?

He stood, careful not to touch a print with his knee or shoe. As he shined the beam down the beach, along the trail of hoofprints, he saw that the horse had galloped north hard, slid to a stop, then ran back south . . . And the trail led him to the exact scene Ann had described—two bodies laying on the sand.

Someone must have been tranquilized with the gun, he thought as he walked toward the victims. At least no one was dead, but the darts themselves raised a question. Who'd have such a thing? The conference was full of geneticists and biologists. Maybe a wildlife vet would have a dart gun.

That was a whole different spin. Fallon knew more than she'd said on the phone.

He carefully followed the prints to the bodies. Odd how the hoofprints went directly to the beach blanket. Had one of the people here brought the horse? Maybe they'd ridden here and the shot scared it off. A well-trained horse might circle around looking for its rider.

A small groan, a feminine groan, came from one of the figures. Still avoiding prints, he approached her. "Don't move, ma'am. I'm Detective Kai Atlanta. Are you okay?"

"What happened to me?" Her voice sounded clear enough to belong to a Monday-morning DJ. "Where am I?"

He didn't want to alarm the woman. He didn't want to tell her she'd been shot with a dart gun—especially if she hadn't— but he needed to assess her health. "I apologize, ma'am. I need to shine this light in your face."

She squinted as he did, holding her hand over her eyes. She looked about twenty, and she was gorgeous. Ice-blue eyes and hair as black as crow feathers.

"May I see your pupils, miss?"

"I don't—" She cut her own objection short as she removed her hand, trying not to squint. Both black pools dilated immediately, and they both appeared the same size. No obvious brain damage. No concussion.

"Is that blood under your nose, miss?" he asked. And then he saw a dark trickle beneath her left ear. More blood. He took his phone from his hip. Ambulance time.

Her next words stopped him.

"I feel better than I've ever felt in my life." Her dark hair blew in the breeze. "I don't feel forty-five—I feel twenty-five."

"Miss, I believe you're in shock." He knew the words fit the situation, but when he inspected her, she didn't look like she was in shock. In fact, she looked great. Her skin was smooth and clear, even in the harsh beam of his Maglite. The blood beneath her nose and ear seemed dried, almost like it'd been painted there yesterday. Her hair could have belonged to a teenager. If she were forty-five, he'd sprout wings.

Of course, maybe the head wound made her think she was forty-five.

"I dreamed an angel healed me," she said. "A glorious angel with all this blond hair." She waved her graceful hands around her face to show what she meant.

"You're in shock, miss. I'm calling the paramedics."

"My name is Rachel. Please don't call me 'miss'—and I'm not crazy."

"I—"

"I know no angel healed me. I'm just telling you my dream."

"Why don't you tell me what happened here tonight instead." The fingers on the buttons of his phone paused.

"That man." She pointed to the other figure. "I ran into his elbow." She ran her tongue over her perfectly formed teeth. "Are my teeth okay? I know I smashed them. I remember tasting one. And I broke my nose."

"Your nose—"

"Don't tell me," she said, shaking her head. "I know my nose isn't broken."

"It doesn't look like it." Why was there blood under it, and why was it long dried?

"It was." Rachel's tone had an undeniable certainness. She believed what she said.

"I'm sure you're right, miss."

"I can tell you don't believe me." She laughed in a self-deprecating way. "I heard the bone crunch under his elbow—the cartilage, I mean. It made a sound you just don't mistake."

He decided to drop the issue, at least for now. "You know this man?" He shined the light on the man's face and squatted next to him. His fingers found a strong and steady pulse.

"His name is Daniel Hallock, and I thought I knew him,"

Rachel said. "I didn't." She looked down and wrapped her arms around her chest. "We've been living together for ten years."

Since she was a teenager? This story didn't make any sense. "Why'd you run into his elbow?"

"I found him with another woman." Her words were simple, but her tone was bleak. "He was cheating on me. He was going to attack me, but the other woman stopped him. She threw him across the beach like she was the Incredible Hulk or something, and I tried to save him." She laughed in that subservient way again. "Only I got in the way instead."

He shined his light over the man's expensive shoes, his tailored pants. He didn't look like a wife beater—and the beauty next to him didn't look like a victim.

She didn't look insane, either.

Then his light caught the scalp wounds in the man's hair. "He's bleeding—a lot," Chiron told the woman, his fingers back on the phone. "You know anything about that?"

A quick glance at her found her shaking her head. No telltale signs of a lie crinkled the corner of her eyes or worried her lips. "I don't." Her dulcet voice could have belonged to a teenager.

"How'd he get hurt?"

She shrugged. "The last thing I remember is running into his arm, his elbow. Then I dreamed of the angel. She had a long silver horn, and when she played it, the world became so beautiful."

Chiron stood. He'd seen a lot of things in his overlong lifetime—but he'd never seen an angel.

Shaking his head, he called the ambulance. When he finished telling the team where to find them, he turned back toward Rachel, still confused. He knew the simple answer: Rachel found her man with Fallon and clubbed him. He got in a punch before he fell.

She didn't seem injured, and what about the dart gun? Dried blood under her nose, under her ear? It looked faked. His colleagues on the SDPD would ignore it, and that gave him freedom to ignore it, too. Ignoring the information didn't sit easily with him.

"Rachel," he started to say, but then he stopped. How much trouble was Fallon in?

"Yes?"

"Who was the other woman?"

"I don't know. I never learned her name. Daniel was so secretive, I never would've figured out he was cheating if it hadn't been for the package—someone hand delivered a package. Who hand delivers a package?"

"You saw her, right? Here tonight?"

"Yes."

"What did she look like?"

"She had hair like—" Rachel held her hands behind her head, outlining a chignon, but a groan from the blanket at his feet interrupted them.

"The horse," the man moaned. "Where's that goddamned horse?"

What kind of man woke up worrying about a horse when his woman just found him cheating? Nothing made sense here.

"Stay down, sir." Chiron walked over to him. "You've got a head wound. You've lost a lot of blood."

"The horse. Is it here?"

Chiron looked at Rachel. "Do you know what he's talking about?"

Rachel shook her head, the sea breeze wrapping her dark hair around her face. "I never saw a horse. I saw an angel."

"I tried to tranquilize it." The man sat cautiously, fingering his temples.

"You shot the angel?" Rachel asked.

"No." The blond man scowled. "The horse."

"Why?" Chiron took out his notebook.

The vet paused for a minute—from the pain or to concoct a story? Chiron couldn't tell. "I couldn't let it run up the highway, could I?" the man asked. "People get killed when they hit a horse. It's worse than hitting a deer." He paused. "The stupid animal wouldn't let me catch it."

"And you just happened to have a tranquilizer gun and loaded darts?"

"I'm a wildlife vet. I'm helping the staff bring down some Przewalski's horses at the wildlife park tomorrow."

"That doesn't explain the pistol tonight."

"He takes that gun with him everywhere," Rachel said, as Chiron shined the light on her face. "It makes him feel manly. Makes up for his other . . . shortcomings."

"Rachel!" the vet said, gasping. At first Chiron thought he was outraged at the slur to his cock size, but that wasn't the case. "What happened to your face?" he asked.

"You happened to it." The bruised expression in her eye would have been hard to fake. "I ran into your elbow, you big—big—"

She didn't have time to find the right word.

"But you look twenty years younger!"

"Something hit you on your head too, you ass." Her voice cut through the wind. "Were you going to leave me?"

"Rachel." The vet didn't sound angry. He sounded disappointed.

"Excuse me." Chiron pulled out his pen. "Can I get your name, sir?"

"Daniel Hallock. Doctor Daniel Hallock."

"What were you doing at the beach tonight?"

"Look." Hallock reached across the blanket—and swooned. Apparently swooned, at least.

"You've lost a lot of blood." Chiron pushed him back, assuming the near faint was real. "Please. Don't move so quickly. In fact, don't move at all. EMS will be here in a minute."

"I was here to propose to her." The injured man picked up a box. "Look. Here's the ring."

"That wasn't for me," Rachel said, angry and . . . hopeful. "It was for that other woman. The one with all that—"

"Rachel, love, I brought it for you. I brought you out here to propose. Don't you remember?" He gestured to the blanket, which had all the trappings of a romantic interlude. Crystal glasses. Strawberries. An opened bottle of wine, which had been knocked over in the melee.

"I remember perfectly. You gave that ring to the other woman."

"What hit you on the head, sir?" Chiron wasn't getting anywhere with this conversation.

"The horse. It kicked me. I was trying to shoot it—I wouldn't have killed it. Just knocked it out cold."

"A horse attacked you?" Chiron knew more about equines and their relatives than most people—especially modern people—had forgotten. And horses rarely attacked people. Evolution designed them to run from predators, not attack them. Horses were prey, and they acted like it.

"I've never seen anything like it," Hallock said, perhaps sensing the weakness in his tale. "I've seen a lot of things in the wild, but never an attacking horse."

Chiron shined his light on the wounds. The blood soaked the man's scalp so much that he couldn't see the shape of the wound. Was it—no, were *they*—shaped like horse prints? Chiron couldn't tell.

Rachel took a step away from the men. "He didn't propose. I wouldn't have forgotten that. I saw another woman here, and he got down on his damned bended knee for her." She gave a small sob. "He never did that for me. Never!" Her voice came out with tears. "Even though I kept his house, put him through school. I worked in a diner for three years to pay for his damned vet school." She pushed her long black hair out of her face again. "And this is what I get in return."

"You were drinking too much, love," Hallock said. He nodded at the bottle. "You know what wine does to you."

"I'm not drunk!" the woman said. "I've never been more sober in my life. You cheat!"

The black-and-whites pulled up next to Chiron's Crown Victoria, the ambulance right behind them. Never in his life had he been happier to see them.

"Over here," Chiron called as the cops opened their car doors, their flashlights swinging over the sand.

"Be right over," one of the men bellowed.

"Do you want to press charges, ma'am?" Chiron asked Rachel. "For assault?"

"I—" She was speechless for a moment, and Chiron knew why. How could she press charges when she had no injury?

"Rachel," Daniel Hallock said, falling to his knees before her. "I love you with all of my heart. I love the life we've built together. You make me a better man, a more complete person. Will you marry me?" He offered her the ring box, blood trickling down his neck, soaking his shirt.

"I—" She stuttered. "Those are the same words you said to her."

"You're confused, my love."

Yet he was the one with the head wounds. What was going on?

"I'm not confused," Rachel said, but Chiron could see the indecision in her eyes. Her eyebrows were raised, and she seemed . . . happy. Maybe the woman was delusional. He'd ask the black-and-whites to do an alcohol test on her. Maybe a drug test for both of them. And a check on the wineglasses for her prints. And on the pistol.

"Will you marry me, Rachel?" the man asked.

One of the uniformed officers arrived just in that moment. Chiron watched him glance at the bloody man on bended knee.

"Take him for illegal discharge of a firearm," Chiron said.

"What a night for the loonies," the cop said in a lowered voice, shaking his head.

"No kidding." Chiron moved away from the couple. "On one hand, she makes sense—but the evidence doesn't match, and better than that, she dreamed of angels. On the other hand, I don't trust a word that man says but all the evidence supports him. He was kicked in the head by a horse."

"Go figure," one of the cops said.

"It's the moon." The second cop laughed and pointed at the sky. "We just got a call from north of the naval base. Some teen-aged girl was walking on the beach with her dog and she swears—" The cop shook his head, laughing quietly. "She swears a white unicorn with a huge silvery horn just raced up the beach. Right toward the city."

9

She woke wearing nothing but her boots and a sheen of sweat. His dark scent called to her through her pain though, and lust simmered in her veins. Before she could grab control of herself, she rolled over, running hungry fingers from his thigh to his cock—and he hardened instantly.

The vials. The small part of her brain still belonging to herself begged. *Look for them!*

It was too late though. The predator's arm snaked between her thighs, and he slid his fingers around her clit, which was hot and swollen with desire. She couldn't sneak out of bed now.

Burning with desire, she wrapped her fingers more tightly around his cock and slowly moved her fist down. He throbbed in her hand, and she squirmed. She needed him now.

He didn't disappoint her. He moved as swiftly as a snake, pinning her hip under an immense hand. Ann couldn't move, could barely breathe. Then he forced his cock into her. Roughly.

So much for foreplay, but why would a predator need any? His fragrance guaranteed him a sex slave—but not for long.

He drove into her again just as roughly as the first time, and it hurt. Given the size of his cock and the way he'd fucked her just hours earlier, she wasn't surprised. The third thrust didn't actually hurt—not as wet as she was.

A dark glint from across the room caught her eye. The video camera again. The tiny woman operated it, keeping the lens on them. How could Ann find the vial with two predators in the room?

The predator's hand wrapped around her throat, and his dark eyes burned into hers. "Pay attention to me," he growled. "Not to her."

"Yes," she said, keeping her eyes on him as fear sizzled through her veins. Would a true slave to the scent be able to look away? Would a true slave care about the camera? To soothe him, she ran her palms over his muscled shoulders, through the rich hair at the back of his neck, and he groaned.

When she reached up to run her lips over his neck, he groaned louder. That sound and the salt of his skin sent a wave of desire crashing over her. She might not be a true slave, but she wasn't free either.

Ann relaxed into his rhythm, having no choice in the matter. He didn't spare her. Again and again he pounded, so focused. Why would a predator aim for tenderness? A prey belonged to a predator.

And that realization gave her hope. Would a true slave to the pheromone complain about technique? She could do this. She could overcome this man's hold on her, and escape the woman, too.

Ann lay back on the bed, staring at the headboard, as he drove his cock into her. Bypassing any rational thought, each thrust hit that spot. Each thrust made her want to scream in delight.

Ann blinked and clenched her teeth to drive away the heat growing in her belly. She would not come. Not yet.

The predator, still silent, began an even faster and deeper

plunging than before. Ann tried to resist, but the wild thrusting, a thrusting that became increasingly intense, made her gasp with bliss, despite herself.

Of their own accord, her hips flexed to meet his with each plunge. She bit back a whimper, pressing her nose into the hollow of his neck as the electric flash of her orgasm crackled through her.

Still he thrust, the power of his iron-hard cock strong and wild. Ann was beyond herself now. Denying herself was impossible. She met him stroke for stroke, and her belly quivered as the second orgasm laced through her body and mind, nearly blinding her. Still he pounded on, maintaining the same feral, unforgiving pace.

Through her numb mind passed the thought that the predator was not human. Maybe her mother was wrong. Maybe he was a demon who'd consume her orgasm by orgasm. Still he drove into her, again and again, and her clit was now so sensitive that each thrust nearly made her scream—in pleasure and pain. She became a torch whose source of fuel lay in her cunt, the light and heat burning through her whole body.

Ann lay helpless as his assault continued, and amazingly, she could feel yet another, even more ferocious orgasm gather itself. Fear and anticipation filled her. He had to come, too, for her plan to work. Sooner would be better than later.

Digging her fingernails into his back, she opened her legs wider, inviting him, begging him.

Then a screaming orgasm tore through her. Thankfully the same storm ripped through him. Her legs twined around his waist as spasm after spasm of pleasure coursed through her body.

His body shivered, too, and Ann knew her odds of success had greatly increased. The spasms slowed in intensity and frequency, but each time she quivered, he did too.

At least some part of the predator was relaxed and satiated now. Now, she could lull him into a comfortable haze of sleep.

With a big, noiseless yawn, she moved him off her. He might be human, but he was big. Then, with not-so-feigned fatigue, she curved her body around his. She draped a leg over his hip and pretended to sleep, burying her nose into the nape of his neck. How could any human smell as good as this one?

That's the trap! her mind screamed, and she knew it was true. Ann needed the vials. She needed her freedom.

Moments later, she heard his breathing deepen. She peeked at the woman with the camera. She'd collapsed into the over-sized chair and seemed to be asleep. She was probably as tired as Ann.

What about the predator? She jabbed him lightly. No response. She nudged him again while she studied his face. Nothing. He slept.

The vials. The time was now. If only she could convince her body, which wanted to do nothing more than roll over and fuck him again. She'd fuck him until she died and still not get enough.

She hadn't spent all those years learning to resist a predator's lust to cave in at this moment though. Taking a deep breath, she let the desire wash over her, riding the cascading waves rather than fighting them. Her breasts ached for his cruel mouth, and her cunt ached for his cock. She exhaled. She could live with this.

She needed to find the perfume vials.

The red numbers on the alarm clock blinked 3:14, and every part of her hurt. Her clit and breasts and nipples and cunt all throbbed in pain. The skin behind her ears and across her neck burned, and her ass felt like someone had set it on fire. Not to mention the headache. And the nausea.

You deserve this. She rolled over, trying to escape the vindictive sound of her own judgment, but it didn't work. *After what you did to Daniel's wife, you deserve this. For ignoring the needs of your own family, you deserve this.*

Then a wave of his insidious scent wafted over her again, and her cunt ached—not with pain but with desire. She wanted to look death in its eyes. And that helped her focus. The chain that kept her in the predator's thrall might be right here, in this room.

If she could break that chain just enough to accomplish her task . . .

She'd do it. She had to. If her mother could risk her life busting into some lab—and she still couldn't quite believe this awful spell came from a lab—Ann could accomplish her task. She could find the vials.

She shifted in the bed, and the heat of the predator's body begged her to touch it, to lick it, and she felt like such a slut.

But that wasn't true either. To whom did she need to be faithful? For a heartbeat she saw Daniel's diamond ring sparkling in the moonlight, and she remembered the taste of forever. It'd been replaced with the taste of sweat and semen—and fear.

Ann could flick her tongue over the predator's nipple now, and he'd roll her over and fuck her hard enough to make her forget everything else. In a sick way, she belonged here more than anywhere else in the world. At least here she didn't have to lie about what she was.

Stop it. She blew out a breath and kept it out. Could she walk away? She couldn't lick him now. She couldn't fuck him. She needed him to stay asleep.

And hadn't she felt one vial in the pocket of his pants?

She took stock of the room, wondering where he'd stripped off his clothes. Or had she stripped them off him?

As they'd fucked the moon had sunk toward the horizon. The tiny woman who'd been filming them had fallen asleep, Ann saw. Her gently closed eyes and pixie cut made her seem as waiflike as a child.

Ann looked at the video camera. What did a predator do with a film like this? Would he watch it on some cold, dark night? Would he use it to stalk others of her kind? Would he blackmail her with it?

Harvard. The word pounded through her like a Mack truck down a steep hill—she had to give the talk of her life in less than five hours.

Maybe the predator's venture into porn flicks would give him some sort of hold on her when she landed her job? Was that what this was about, a way to give the predators an in at one of the world's most influential institutions?

Not on her watch.

She looked at the camera with an eye to theft and saw it wasn't a video camera at all. She knew from her own fieldwork that this camera was a $50,000 movie camcorder, much better than the one she'd used to record her wild horses. In fact, it was much better than any car she'd ever driven.

The predator had money—lots of it—and a lab. What was he up to? Her mother had said the predators had been trying to capture her kind, that the deaths had been an accident, but why did they want unicorns?

She couldn't worry about this now.

It came back to her now, what had happened to his clothes. He'd stripped while she lay on the bed's corner, eyeing the camera. Which would mean that his clothes were on the floor at the foot of the bed.

She lay still for a moment, gathering her courage—but when she realized her heart was beating madly in her chest, she simply sat. No sense waking the man with her pounding heartbeat. Then, as silently as a cat, she rolled from the bed and padded over toward the camcorder.

His clothes were there.

She didn't stop to see if he'd moved, even though if he woke, she would die. She bent over and picked up his trousers as if she had every right. She slid her hand into the pocket, holding her breath.

And she found it. The small thing slid into her fingers like it belonged there—but as soon as she looked at it, her stomach heaved.

It wasn't a vial. It was a pocketknife.

Stifling a sigh of disappointment and fear, she checked the second pocket. Her fingers discovered a handful of change, nothing more. Carefully, she pulled out the coins anyway and looked at them in the pale moonlight.

Three quarters, a dime, a penny. Only the mundane. She was about to set the change on the carpet, but the moonlight glinted off something odd . . . a tiny cylinder, about the size of a perfume sample. And the cylinder was made out of silver. Jackpot. She'd found it!

A sudden shift on the bed made her freeze. If he woke, he'd know—no prey could leave a predator's side.

The predator just rolled to his side though, his muscled thigh a sexy temptation thrown across the bed. Maybe she should just fuck him again, make sure he slept really well.

No! She forced herself to look away from him.

The orange light of the camera blinked at her. She needed the second vial, but a bird in the hand . . .

On the right side of the camcorder was a rectangular panel, which she suspected housed the memory cards. To the right of that she spied a slide-lock button. She probably had to push that puppy down to get the panel open. Then she could take the card out and find the last vial.

She pressed it. Voilà. The panel opened without a sound. She tugged on what she thought was the memory card.

Nothing happened.

She tried again, tugging so hard the tripod wobbled beneath the camera. Still, the memory card remained in the camcorder.

She flashed a quick glance at the predator, who hadn't moved. His eyelids didn't flutter, and his breathing didn't change.

But looking at him was a mistake—a big mistake—because

the need to crawl into the bed and straddle him washed over her like a storm surge. The dark glow of his skin in the fading moonlight called to her, demanded that she come to him.

She had no choice but to pause then, close her eyes, and focus on her heartbeat. She let the blood-searing lust wash over her. She didn't fight it.

Her nipples hardened, but she didn't beat herself up. When her mind showed her the predator's mouth opening to taste her, she pushed her mind in a different direction. She imagined herself in equine form, racing over the beach, surf pounding at her feet. She didn't have to outrun the surf. She could let it lick her hooves. She'd survive.

And then the tide ebbed and she could breathe.

Keeping her eyes off the man in the bed—who was after all just a man with a maddening perfume—she turned back toward her task.

Without a sound, she bent over the camera and looked in the now-opened panel. A small button glowed red. It said: eject. She pressed it.

With a soft hum and click, the card came out. She pressed it again, and a second card came out. She didn't see a third memory card, but she pressed the button again just in case—and nothing happened. She was done with the camera.

Ann found her tiny purse on the floor and picked it up. Both memory cards and the vial fit inside. She settled the cold chain of her purse over her bared shoulder and looked up. Now all she needed was the second vial.

On silent feet Ann walked into the predator's room, the one he'd first taken her to. She glanced at the door, the route to freedom, and stifled the urge to run. Well, finding the fucking vial was more important than her freedom. The second vial would give her real freedom.

The room's minimal moonlight was enough to show her that the predator had left nothing on the desk, the table, the dresser—no files to paw through, no briefcase to rifle, no collection of wallet and keys and wristwatches to inspect.

Careful to keep her boots quiet on the small patch of tile, she walked toward the hall door and opened the closet. Wooden hangers. An ironing board. Nothing belonging to the predator or his minion. She opened the drawers beneath the oversized mirror, trying to remain as quiet as possible, but still, the swooshing of the rollers seemed to fill the room.

Hurrying, she peeked into the drawer. She found nothing. No change of clothes. No briefcase. Where were the man's belongings?

She went into the bathroom. No moonlight made its way here, but she managed to find a shaving case. She took it and dumped it on the bed, looking for a vial to match the one in her pocket.

Razor, tweezers, condoms—funny, he hadn't used them with her. She found a room key there with a logo for the hotel—and slid it in her pocket—but no tiny vials of perfume.

Damn. She shoved everything back in the case and returned it to the bathroom. No need to advertise that she was looking for something. But where was it? In the other room?

With the tiny woman and the predator asleep there, the last thing she wanted to do was go back. If she looked at the predator, his rich hair, his perfect body, his huge cock . . .

God, she had to return, if only to look at him again. Just look. She wouldn't touch him or fuck him.

No! This wouldn't do. Filling her mind with the image of the clean mountains, she exhaled and went back. The scent of sex wrapped around the tainted bergamot fragrance, but she kept her eyes on the dresser and tables, her mind focused on small silver vials.

She opened the drawer. Nothing. Nothing on the table. Nothing on the countertop.

Then she spied it. A briefcase sat open on the table. Wasn't that a vial in the back corner? She couldn't be sure, but Ann would have to walk past the woman sleeping in the chair to get to it.

If she woke the woman? If the woman woke the predator? The thought chilled her blood, but she had to take the chance. More than her life was on the line.

Only a few inches spanned the distance between the woman's knees and the bed. Moving at turtle speed, Ann turned sideways and crept past her, glad that her high-heeled boots made her legs a little thinner.

Ann moved closer to the table, and her heart pounded. The vial sat right there! She reached for it, moving as soundlessly as she could—and a slight movement caught Ann's eye a heartbeat later.

Fuck.

She shot a look at the predator, holding her breath and steeling herself against the imminent lust and the effect it had on her mind—but the predator hadn't moved. He wasn't stirring, not even an iota.

Then she saw it again—the movement as slow and graceful as a floating butterfly. The woman's eyelids fluttered . . . and then opened.

The two women stared at each other for the space of a breath. As Ann gazed into the depths of the woman's eyes, she wondered whether the petite woman was predator or prey.

The woman's expression was very self-contained, almost blank. Since Ann had seen the predator's fingers wrapped around the woman's neck at the cocktail party, she'd been imagining her as Sutherland's victim, another prey enthralled until he tired of her—and then consumed.

But now, for the first time, Ann doubted the relationship. Lust didn't give her eyelids that drowsy expression. This woman could leave if she wanted to. Couldn't she?

Then the woman raised one languid hand. Graceful fingers

pointed toward the bed. "Erik." The woman's voice sounded as loud as a fireworks finale. "Wake up now."

His muscled form shifted in the bed, and fear covered Ann's entire body in cold sweat. The woman and the predator stood between Ann and the door.

"You don't belong anywhere but here," the predator growled. And the cloying scent of bergamot tantalized her, woke that aching need in her—again.

Ann didn't answer. Grabbing the vial, she jumped over the woman and leaped toward the door, wishing she could shift form right now—but horses can't open doorknobs.

The high heel of her boot made her ankle twist when she landed, but the cold metal of the knob filled her hand.

"Lying bitch!" The predator launched himself toward her with a speed she couldn't believe.

She had the door open, but he swung a punch at her, catching her shoulder. Her stunned arm dropped the vial, but she still had her purse. Naked save her boots, she bolted into the hall, the predator right on her heels.

She shifted to unicorn form as she ran, pulling the earth's strength through the hotel floor. Its strength should have been diluted, but it wasn't, and Ann was grateful. Four hooves ran faster than two feet.

She galloped down the long hall, and within heartbeats, she turned the corner.

He pounded after her, and fear crashed through her veins. She turned another corner. She might be faster, but she couldn't get off this floor—not without hands.

She turned another corner, following the red EXIT sign. Maybe some drunken fool had left a door propped open. But when she came to the stairwell, she saw she was out of luck. The door was shut, and the predator was close.

She ripped power from the earth, changing into human form quicker than she'd ever done in her life. The lust from the shift and from the predator's scent threatened to undo her. Some part of her wanted to turn around and throw herself into his arms.

Instead, she tore the door open as soon as she had hands, and she launched herself down the stairs. On the first landing, she paused to shift back to equine form—just as the door above her slammed open.

In unicorn shape, she easily jumped down the stairs and around the curves. The predator took much longer. By the time she hit the ground floor, she heard his footfalls at least three floors above her.

Thankfully, the final door didn't have a standard doorknob. It had a narrow lever to push, and Ann did that with her muzzle. The door opened into the parking lot, and her hooves clattered over the pavement as she headed to the gardens.

She'd escaped.

As she galloped exhausted over the red pathway toward the beach, her relief was short lived. When she changed back to woman form, she'd be completely healed, which was good. Every abrasion, muscle ache, and hickey would have vanished with her shift in forms. On the downside, when she changed back into a human, she'd be wearing nothing but boots and a tiny purse, she had no place to sleep, and the computer she needed to give the talk of her life was locked—with her clothes—in Daniel's room. The predator might very well be lurking just outside—or inside—Daniel's room.

What the hell was she going to do?

10

The sound of his cell phone buzzing at four in the morning zapped Chiron awake. He picked it up, squinting in the dark to read it: Daniel Hallock.

That couldn't be right. It rang again. Hallock was in jail. Besides, the last call he'd received from this number . . . He put it together then.

"Dr. Fallon," he said after pressing the green button. Maybe she'd blame the huskiness of his voice on the early morning. "You're up early."

"Detective Atlanta?"

"Yes." The wobbly sound of her voice made him sit straight up. "What's the matter?"

"I need your help. Can you meet me?"

"Of course." He slid out of bed without missing a beat. "Where are you?" He pulled on his jeans and shirt, taking a second to snap his holster and pocket his badge and handcuffs.

"At the hotel," she said, her voice still shaking. "On the parking level."

He grabbed the car keys and headed to his garage. "I'll be there in five minutes, okay?"

"Yes."

"What kind of help do you need? You need an ambulance?" The garage door opened as he started the car.

"Not exactly. But . . ."

"Is someone chasing you now?"

"No!"

"Explain, please." He gunned the car through the automatic gate and onto the street. Her caginess made him wonder for the hundredth time what exactly had happened on the beach last night. Attacking horses? Angels? All on the same beach where he'd last heard from Akantha? Too much coincidence for him. "What's happened to you?"

She didn't answer. The call had been dropped—or she'd hung up. Or someone had grabbed her.

As he sped down the empty streets, the sky barely lightening with the impending dawn, he kicked back his fear. Whatever had happened last night, Ann Fallon was alive. At least, she was alive when she made the call.

She was still alive when he pulled into the parking garage. He found her almost hiding behind a thick concrete pillar near the front gate.

He rolled down his window as he parked. "You okay?" He could only see her face.

"Yes." She came out from hiding. She was wearing a blue-striped shirt from a parking attendant's uniform and high-heeled boots. The shirt was smeared with grease, and it didn't look like she was wearing panties.

It was easy to see why she was hiding.

"Are you hurt?" He closed the car door. The odd feel of ozone charged the early morning air.

"Not—" She waved her hands in a futile gesture. "I need my clothes. My computer. And I don't have any place to stay."

"Where're your things?"

She paused and looked at her boots. "In Daniel Hallock's room."

Chiron understood what he'd only suspected before—Fallon was the other woman Hallock's wife had raged about. Funny, Ann didn't seem like "other woman" sort of material— but that just went to show: even after four thousand years of living, a man could be wrong. "Don't you have a key?"

She opened the tiny purse he'd noticed earlier and pulled out a piece of white plastic. "He's on the concierge level."

He stood for a minute, confused. "Any reason you didn't go use it yourself?"

She nodded. "I was afraid."

Weird. The woman he'd met in the hallway didn't seem like the kind of woman to be afraid of a pompous ass like Daniel Hallock. He sighed. "Daniel Hallock's being held on a weapons charge. He's not coming back tonight."

She blinked at him, in what? Confusion, maybe? Then she said, "Could you just go with me to his room?" A pause. "Please?"

It would take a bigger man than he to say no. He held out his arm to direct her toward the elevator as he made a supreme effort not to look at the naked curve of her ass peeking out from under the shirt.

"So what happened to your dress?" He pushed the button and the doors opened immediately.

She cut a glance at the stairwell before she got into the elevator and shook her head. "I don't want to talk about it."

"I didn't find it at the beach." He looked at her feet as the elevator went up. "Although the prints I saw all around the beach blanket looked like they'd match your boots."

She looked at him. Despite her clothing issue, her hair was in perfect array, the bun straight and not a stray tendril anywhere. "I didn't know about the other woman." She swallowed, and the hollow expression in her eye made him realize she was devastated. "How could a man propose if he were living with someone else?"

Chiron didn't have the answer to that. Her vulnerability did something to him. He wanted to wrap her in his arms and tell her everything would be fine.

He didn't though. Something about her nudged him, or maybe it was the ozone hanging in the garage. Somehow, she reminded him of Akantha—and her death. He asked, "Why'd you two go to that beach? There're a lot to choose from. Why there?"

She shrugged as the elevator door slid open on the concierge level. "He picked it. He had the entire proposal planned. Ring, wine, blanket, and everything."

Which meant Rachel had told the truth, he realized, as Ann stood looking at him. He put his hand on the door so it stayed opened and nodded for her to go—but she shook her head, peering around the corner. "Will you go first?"

He looked down the hallway, his hand on his Glock—but saw nothing. "You know Hallock's locked up. He's not here."

She nodded and followed him out, but she still seemed nervous to him. She didn't seem to trust the emptiness of the hallways, and it was four in the morning.

What was going on here? More than meets the eye, that's for sure. "Where's the room?" he asked. The ozone charge seemed to have followed them up here.

"There." She pointed to her left with the key in her hand. "Room 352."

He led the way. When he got to the door, he took the key and opened the room without stepping in.

The place was set for seduction. Jazz played on a laptop, expensive champagne sat in buckets, and the lights were dim. Bags of lingerie were dumped on the floor next to the bed. "You want me to check out the room?"

"Please." She nodded, and he kept his hand on his holster as he went inside.

He looked in the bathroom, in the closet, under the bed. "No one's here," he said, relaxing. Not a lot of places to hide in a hotel room.

"Thank you." Her shoulders relaxed marginally, and she walked toward what he supposed was her suitcase. The expression on her face wasn't particularly encouraging though. She still looked scared as shit. "I need to get dressed."

That was definitely true. "I assume you're going home tonight. Can I drive you to the airport?"

"Home?" She stopped her rummaging and froze.

Something here really didn't make sense. "You seem upset, and this is just a conference. Why don't you fly home? I'll even call the airline for you."

"I can't. I really can't leave until tomorrow and I probably shouldn't leave until the next day."

"What could be so important?"

"A job at Harvard." She grabbed jeans and a shirt. And he couldn't help it then. When she stood to go to the bathroom, he eyed her ass. He wanted to grab it. Her bare flesh called to him. "I have to give the talk of my life in the morning."

"I don't want to offend you, Dr. Fallon, but if I had to guess, I'd say you were just a victim of sexual assault. I—"

"What are you talking about?" She turned and looked at him. The high boots accented the length and leanness of her thighs.

"You're scared. You're hiding. You're almost naked." He held up his hands. "Most women I know who show up with those symptoms have been assaulted."

"I'm fine."

"I know." She was strong—he had to admit that. "I'm just saying you don't look like you're ready to give a lecture." He shook his head. "Press charges on the bastard so he doesn't assault anyone else—I'll help you—but don't torture yourself with a lecture tomorrow."

She didn't answer. Instead, she went into the bathroom, presumably to change.

He stalked around the room, taking in the piles of gifts the veterinarian had bought for Ann. How much money did a wildlife vet make anyway? Enough to lavish a mistress and keep a wife? He'd get the desk jocks to check. "I get the feeling you're not listening to a word I say."

She opened the door, dressed in jeans and a simple shirt. Without the boots and the man's shirt, she didn't look like a pole dancer—and the caveman part of him was disappointed.

She pulled a pair of sneakers from the suitcase. "You don't understand what's at stake for me. I absolutely need the job."

"Talk to your would-be boss. Tell him something came up." He took in the dark smudges beneath her eyes. "Tell him the truth."

"Detective Atlanta, you just need to trust me on something—we need to get out of this room." She tied her shoes. "And I can't talk to Stoller. Harvard's too competitive. They don't want to hire a problem. I cannot be a problem." She looked up at him. "Too many people are relying on me."

He met her gaze, the steady sea of blue green behind those glasses. "Even if you've been assaulted?"

She closed her eyes and took a deep breath. "I was not assaulted."

"Then what are you afraid of?"

She paused, and he thought she might be considering telling him the truth, but instead she said, "I'm afraid I won't have a place to sleep tonight. I was afraid I wouldn't have clothes for my lecture for tomorrow." She gave him a small smile. "So, thank you for that, but I won't stay in this room."

Chiron picked a random small box off the floor. It looked less glamorous than the other packages, and someone had handwritten Hallock's name on it. "I think you're afraid of something else—and I also think you should tell me."

She took the box from him and tossed it to the floor in exasperation. "Will you please book a room for me here? I'll pay you back. I just don't want the room in my name."

She didn't want anyone to find her. She *was* scared. "It's not a good idea," he said.

"Please?" She gave the same look she'd given him in the garage, and he knew he must have "sucker" tattooed on his forehead. He knew he wouldn't leave her side, not until he knew what scared her—but he wasn't going to sell himself cheaply. "If I do it, will you tell me what really happened on the beach tonight?"

The muscles in her face tightened. "What do you mean?"

"I mean, how does a wildlife vet armed with a tranquilizer gun get attacked by a horse? Why does a woman think she's twenty years older than she looks? What is that same woman talking about angels?"

"Angels?"

"Don't try to change the subject, Dr. Fallon. If you want my help, you have to tell me what really happened."

As she followed Kai Atlanta's broad shoulders down the hall, Ann knew she was taking advantage of his cop nature, but she couldn't help herself. If the predator got close to her, she'd give in—even thinking about him made her core soften in desire. The pleasure of that fuck . . . she pushed it from her mind. Because she also knew he'd hurt her. He'd do more than hurt her.

The expression on Sutherland's face as he'd lunged toward her could only be described as rage. She knew this new seducin pheromone wasn't supposed to drive the predators insane, but she'd seen her death in Sutherland's expression, and she didn't want to die.

So when Detective Atlanta opened the door to the room checked out in his name while carrying her bags, the guilt she felt took a backseat to gratitude.

"Thank you," she said as he set the bags down. And the strange sense of belonging didn't hurt either. There was something about this man that made her more comfortable than she'd ever been with her scientific colleagues or school friends. In fact, there was something odd about him, a subtle scent of equine about him that soothed her. Maybe he was an equestrian? "I can't thank you enough."

"You're welcome." He looked at her, and she wanted to touch his lips, feel the shape of them under her fingertip. Maybe it was leftover desire from the predator.

"You want to meet for lunch tomorrow?" She'd tell him about the beach then, or at least some version of it.

"Lunch would be fine." He stretched out on one of the two queen beds, the muscles of his upper arms defined. He stopped a minute to adjust his holster.

She froze. "What are you doing?"

"Serve and protect." He adjusted a pillow under his head, the bronze of his hair shimmering in the light. "That's our motto."

"That may be true, but I don't think most people have San Diego's finest sleeping in their rooms," she said. Which was sad for them, really.

"Most people haven't called on one of San Diego's finest while wearing nothing but someone else's shirt and a pair of hot boots."

Ann sat on the bed. "You don't have to stay. I can handle this. All I needed was a room."

"An anonymous room." He looked at her, and she saw the same core of sorrow she'd noticed at the reception party. His eyes held something so bleak.

"You can go," she said softly. She didn't want him to go, though. There was something so comforting about having him lounging in the bed that she just wanted to curl up with him.

"I can't let anything happen to you," he said. "That would

be the protect part." He gave her a wicked grin. "And I don't know you well enough for the serve part."

She threw a pillow at his head to cover her embarrassment. This wasn't a fight she could win—and she didn't want to. Ann turned off the light and looked at the gorgeous man lying two feet away from her. She felt nothing but relief.

Okay, she also felt desire—which she had no right to at all.

11

Ann had twenty minutes to get to her lecture, and she felt nauseous. Taking a quick look in the bathroom mirror, she reminded herself to breathe. She looked fine. In fact, she looked better than fine. She looked wholesome and smart and earnest, which were accurate descriptions on most days.

She felt like a home wrecker, though. She felt like a tramp. She felt dirty and scarred and used. In the three-hour nap that counted as her night's sleep, she'd dreamed about the predator's scent, dreamed about his mouth, his tongue, his hands, his cock.

It was all she could do to keep from throwing herself at Kai in the middle of the so-called night to get any relief she could find, but that wasn't right. He was wounded enough without her callous needs, and while his warm presence tempted her, the predator called to her. No. He screamed for her.

Oh, God, how would she escape him? Now that he'd given her a taste of his skin, how could she walk away? She should take Kai's advice, just get on a plane and get out of here. She'd find someplace else to hide her family.

Pull up your pantyhose. She needed this job to save her

cousins and siblings and aunts and uncles. Her mom might need help with whatever dark plot she was hatching for the predators—Ann couldn't leave her. And besides, if Daniel was right and someone had a bounty on her, running wouldn't help. She could hold it together until they defeated the predators. Then she could go back to the security of her own apartment, away from the predator and the haunting presence of Kai Atlanta.

You can't leave for another reason, the dark side of her mind added. *You haven't found the second vial yet. Maybe you'll have to go back to the predator's bed.*

The lust from that thought made her choke, and she pushed a stray hair back into its bun, looking for visible flaws, something she could fix. Something she could fix now. She'd healed all the abrasions on her body—and *in* her body—and she'd healed the dark circles under her eyes. A shift to unicorn form and back again had seen to that. With her cream suit, scant makeup, and sensible shoes, she didn't look like the kind of person to break up a marriage. She didn't look like a porn star either.

She looked like a Harvard-professor-to-be. Now all she had to do was become one.

"Your talk is in the Admiral Room?" Kai's deep voice rolled over her brooding thoughts and washed them away.

"Yes." It scared her that he cared.

He sat up in bed, and she caught his warm scent. His skin held the trace of something like cedar, and she knew that under different circumstances, she'd find him very attractive. In fact, even under these circumstances she found him very attractive. The lean line of his thigh would have tempted any woman. "I'm coming with you," he said.

"What?"

He shrugged out of his holster and walked toward the bathroom. She left the small area—he gave off the vibe he might strip off all his clothes right there to make his point. "I know the jeans and T-shirt might not fit with the academic crowd, but they're clean. I'll look like a student."

"It's not your clothes." Jeans were the official uniform of biologists. "But don't you have to go to the office or something? I don't want you to lose your job."

"I'm doing my job."

"I don't need a bodyguard."

"I think you do." He pulled off the T-shirt, and she couldn't help but admire the perfect muscles of his chest and stomach—not over-the-top Conan style, but definitely noticeable and mouth watering. "You still haven't told me what scared you last night or what happened on the beach."

"I don't have time." She looked at the clock. "I have to be down there in fifteen minutes."

He held up his hand. "I'm not rushing you. I'm just not leaving you alone." He turned on the shower and steam began to fill the room. "Until you get on that plane back to North Carolina, I'm staying by your side."

The predator wouldn't be at her job talk, but she wouldn't mind knowing Kai had her back. "Can you meet me down there?"

"You said you had fifteen minutes." He gave her a wicked grin. "Do I have to leave the door open to keep my eye on you? Maybe you'd like to join me?"

"I think I'll . . ." Ann swallowed. "I think I'll just look over my notes."

When they entered the Admiral Room on the main floor, a tall, thin man in his early twenties came toward her, winding through the line of the empty chairs with apparent purpose. His kinky black hair was cut close to his scalp.

"I'm Brad Scrimshaw," he said, ignoring Kai and grinning like a fool. He stuck out his hand while he fingered his name tag, and he looked down at it like he had to check its information. "I work at the National Zoo? Maybe you've heard of my advisor? Doctor Zim White?"

"Of course." She knew his lab. "You're mapping equid microsatellites."

His eyes lit up. "Yes." His eyes slid down to her breasts and then quickly—guiltily—up. "I wanted to talk to you about your work?" He blinked nervously. "I can't believe I'm really meeting you."

"Zim says great things about your research."

"He does?" She didn't need to be a genius to recognize his joy at this recognition.

"He says you can ID the paternity of any horse," she added. "You can even tell full brothers apart, he says."

"That's right! Your work is amazing." Brad slid his eyes more boldly over her tits this time. "What's your secret? How do you get so close to your wild horses?"

Her smile wanted to come out tight, but she forced it to appear easy, even flirty. "I'll never tell," she said. And she wouldn't. Not in a million years.

"I'm moderating the talks in this room today. Can I get you some coffee?"

And leave her jangling nerves in peace? "That'd be great. Thank you."

Brad pointed to a computer at the front podium as Kai found a chair. "Load your presentation there." He ran his hand over his hair in a self-conscious gesture. "And hope to God it works because the IT guy is swamped, and we're on in ten minutes."

"Okay." She walked over to the computer and tried to insert the flash drive. It jammed, and the memory of the predator's camera filled her mouth with the tang of fear.

She swallowed it though. He couldn't hurt her—not with blackmail. She'd stolen the video cards back. And with Detective Atlanta here, the predator couldn't hurt her physically either. She knew Kai wouldn't let him touch her—or her touch him.

"Oh, good." Brad came back carrying three cups of coffee, and he pointed to the screen with his elbow. "You got your program running."

"I did, thanks."

"I didn't know what kind of coffee you drink." He set the cups on the podium. "This one's black. This one has cream and sugar. This one just has sugar." He looked at her and laughed, touching his hair again. "I would've got one with just cream, but I couldn't carry it."

She laughed, trying hard not to be too flattered. "You didn't have to do that." She took the one with cream and sugar. "Still, it's very sweet of you. Thank you."

He shrugged apologetically. "I have to go. I have to help the other speakers, but I'll be back to watch your talk. Zim'll be here too. I bet all the big guns will be here. Everyone's been dying to hear your research."

"That's great." Ann refused to be intimidated.

When he left, she slipped into a chair and picked up the remote, glad that Kai was both here and silent. She needed just a minute to concentrate. Flipping through her talk for what must be the hundredth time, she found each slide familiar.

And she relaxed. She could do this.

She set down her notes and walked to the lobby. Kai walked to the lobby too, but kept his distance. No one would know he was there to protect her.

As she poured herself some water, a group of professors walked toward the Admiral Room. She was worthy of them. The scientists with whom she'd studied had trained her well. These people had read the papers she'd published and thought they were good. Feeling comfortable back in her role as scientist, Ann joined the growing crowd.

"Ann." Dr. Carl Stoller touched her shoulder as he joined the entering throng.

"Good morning," she said. He looked pale and fragile, and

were those age spots on his hand? They kind of looked like lesions. Had they been there yesterday? She sure hadn't noticed them.

"Glad to see you look so refreshed this morning," he said, and she wished she could return the compliment.

"Thank you, Dr.—" but she caught herself with a small laugh. "Thank you, Carl." She gave him what she hoped was a confident-but-not-brash smile.

"Do you know Dr. Sutherland?" He motioned behind him. "My colleague from the Brode Institute?"

Dr. Sutherland? She froze. It couldn't possibly be the same man. "I don't think so." Except she inhaled his brooding scent—and thought she might pass out right there in the Admiral Room.

A bland smile crossed the predator's face, and her fingers and knees went numb. "No," she said. "No."

"He's the second member of the search committee," Carl Stoller said with a kind smile. "He's here to help Harvard select the best candidate."

Sitting in the back corner of the Admiral Room, Chiron watched the scientists fill the chairs. The scent of coffee hung in the air, and some of the scientists were yawning. He guessed Ann wasn't the only one who'd had a late night.

A group of young women walked in, serious with their notebooks, pens, and neatly pinned ID tags. Two men, one really tall, accompanied them. They kept looking at the women's asses, but they weren't laughing or flirting. Chiron guessed they were trying their best to be as serious as the women, and he wished them luck.

When Ann walked in, Chiron froze. She looked like shit, and she hadn't looked like shit when they'd left the hotel room.

What the hell?

When civilians found dead bodies or their houses burned to

the ground, they looked like this. When they identified the corpses of loved ones, they looked like this.

Before Chiron could stop himself, he was on his feet, walking toward her. What part of her world had just crashed?

"What happened?" He kept his voice low as he came behind her.

She looked at him a moment, and he watched her expression waver between fear and trust. Something she saw in him must have reassured her. Her expression settled on trust, easing his heart.

"I—" She shot a glance to an older man in a tweed coat. He stood next to another man. Sutherland. What the hell was he doing here?

"What'd he do to you?" He knew if he touched her, her skin would feel cold. Shock did that to people.

"He—" she started. "I—" She couldn't seem to form the words, but a sick feeling churned through his stomach. Had she gone from the beach to Sutherland's bed last night? Was that the reason for the scared look in Ann's eye?

"You fucked him, didn't you?" His tone surprised him. He sounded accusatory. Which he guessed he was. Even though he had no business caring about whom she fucked. "Did he hurt you?" Like he had hurt Akantha.

She didn't seem to hear him. "He's the other member of the search committee."

"Search committee?"

"For the Harvard job."

"Erik Sutherland says he's Harvard faculty?" Chiron had been illegally tailing Sutherland since Akantha vanished, and he knew the man hadn't been to Massachusetts. He hadn't left San Diego in two years.

"Brode Institute." Her voice was almost a whisper. "Harvard's West Coast research lab. Genetics and longevity."

Chiron understood in that moment how Fallon's world had

crashed. Or how she thought it had. She'd fucked the man who'd decide whether she'd get a position at Harvard.

"Ignore him." He pressed his shoulder lightly against hers. "Give your talk to the old guy."

"Old guy?"

"The one in the tweed jacket who looks like crap. Pretend Sutherland isn't here."

"Stoller," she said. "The guy in tweed is Stoller, and he's the chair."

"Give your talk to him."

"I can't ignore him. Erik *is* here. I—" Someone dimmed the lights, and the moderator, a young kid with dark skin and really short hair, went to the mike.

As the kid began to speak, Chiron glanced at Fallon. Every muscle in her face and shoulders was rigid, and the line between her eyebrows was furrowed. Earthshaker's balls, what had Sutherland done? Would a normal fuck have done this to the strong, self-assured woman he'd met yesterday? The moderator began to introduce the session and the people in it, but Ann's face didn't relax.

Chiron subdued a strong urge to wreak mayhem. The ancient centaurs would have raged. Eurytion would've thrown chairs, bellowing like an enraged bull, and maybe the old ways should make a comeback. Right now. Chiron could take Sutherland out in the melee. Beat him to a bloody pulp. He could—

The audience began clapping, and Ann walked to the podium, her shoulders hunched. The room darkened as someone dimmed the lights further.

And then her title slide illuminated the screen. The audience quit talking. Chiron didn't blame them. The camera had caught a dozen wild horses and froze them in time, mid-stampede. Manes whipped the air midflight. Legs churned dark earth midstride. In a sea of color—black, gold, sorrel, bay—dark eyes met the camera and gleamed with spirit. The photo caught the essence—the glory—of wild horses.

It filled him with a longing that left him stunned. He'd denied his animal side for too long, tried too hard to civilize it. Looking at this slide, he wanted to break free of his life, of his need to protect. He wanted to run in unfettered joy.

"I'm going to tell you the story of the horses of the Sierra Nevadas." Ann's voice filled the room, and the quaver Chiron expected to hear wasn't there. He heard authority and assurance, and when she continued that way for several minutes, he relaxed. She flashed bar charts and statistics without cutting a glance toward Sutherland.

"In conclusion," she said, "I have a video that shows exactly how mothers react during the culling process." She clicked a button with the mouse to play the video, and Chiron's eyes locked on the screen.

Except horses in the mountain field didn't take flight as he expected—instead, porn filled the screen, complete with cheesy music.

"No." He watched Ann frantically move the mouse to the "stop" button, but nothing happened. The camera panned across a pair of exquisite breasts and flawless thighs, spread. An auburn-haired woman licked the clit of the woman with the perfect breasts, and the sound of moaning floated over the music.

For a heartbeat, Chiron didn't understand what he was watching. Had Ann accidentally played a private video? The camera cut to a different image. A man slid a riding crop deep into the woman with the perfect breasts, and she seemed to enjoy it. She was wet and swollen with desire.

"Stop this!" Ann's voice cut through the room like a fire alarm. She quit trying to click the "stop" button and grabbed at the memory stick protruding from the side of the computer. "Damn!" She ripped it out and sent the room into dark silence.

But not before the camera showed the face of the woman with the perfect breasts and the swollen clit—Dr. Ann Fallon herself.

12

When Ann looked at the video and saw herself cast as a porn star, she felt like a jellyfish full of stingers had moved into her throat. She couldn't speak. She couldn't breathe. Living hurt.

She wanted to be anywhere but here. She wanted the safety of her mother's arms, the sanctuary of her own apartment. Even the solace of her hotel room would be preferable to this hell.

She also wanted to kill Erik Sutherland and his nasty little accomplice—and that hatred dislodged the jellyfish.

"This is ridiculous." Detective Kai Atlanta's no-nonsense voice rang across the mayhem, and everyone shut up. "Could someone turn on the lights, please?" The request was polite, but his voice rang with authority.

Brad nodded to the professors near a switch, and light filled the room—then she caught Dr. Stoller's measuring glance, his pale eyes hooded and watchful.

She'd given a damned good talk, and the predator had ruined it. What was Stoller thinking right now?

She wouldn't give up that easily. Forcing a tight smile on her face, she turned toward the crowd. Zim White was watching. So was the man who'd discovered the double-helix nature of DNA. They'd all seen her fuck the predator in wide screen, complete with porn music, crop, and some girl-on-girl action. Damn.

Ann took a deep breath. "It's amazing how well a digital image can be altered, isn't it?" She scanned the audience, refusing to be embarrassed or daunted as she let the implication float over them. The video hadn't been digitally altered, and she hadn't said it was—but she'd certainly put the idea in their minds. "How many people are so talented with PhotoShop?"

Brad Scrimshaw picked up the cue. "I haven't seen a job talk sabotaged before this, and I'm sure the Association will investigate it."

The tiny brunette in the seat next to Erik Sutherland's smirked at her, and Ann's stomach churned. What was the little bitch up to? Why were they doing this to her? Why were they humiliating her and ruining her chance at landing this job?

Ann shoved her shoulders back, pushing to the back of her mind the image of the crop sliding into her wet vagina. "Does anyone have any questions regarding the scientific nature of my talk?"

"I have a question." The tiny brunette turned toward Carl Stoller, whose rheumy eyes widened. "What's Harvard's policy on hiring a nymphomaniac? That good for PR?"

"Nymphomaniac?" Stoller asked. Then he cleared his throat and narrowed his eyes. "I'd question any person who brought an accusation like that against another in a public forum rather than in private." He shook his head. "I think you should leave, ma'am." He gestured toward Brad Scrimshaw. "Young man, I think you should call for security. I believe this woman should exit right now."

Ann watched in horror as the brunette stood with a saucy roll of her hip. The predator stood right behind her, his official name tag banging against his chest. His scent curled through the room and crept into Ann's blood.

"I can prove Dr. Fallon is a nymphomaniac." The woman touched her throat with her fingers and filled her voice with mock sympathy. "Poor thing should find treatment some-place."

"Get her out," Stoller said to Brad, but the grad student was gone, presumably to find security.

"I'll escort them out," Kai said. He took hold of the tiny woman's shoulder, flashing his badge to the crowd.

The tiny woman was leaving, but it was the predator who scared the crap out of Ann. He sauntered right toward the podium, and his eyes were loaded with dark intention.

"Watch!" The tiny brunette squirmed in Kai's grip to face the audience. "She'll throw herself in anyone's arms. Just what Harvard needs!"

It might be true. The lust engendered by the predator's scent made her mouth water for his skin, the rough touch of his hand on her breast. As she stood, frozen in fear, her core quivered in sick desire. She belonged to him.

He moved into her space. Desire and fear cemented her feet to the floor. He swept his hand behind her bun and brought his face to hers, and she still didn't move. She was proving to the audience, to her peers, that she wasn't a slut. She'd didn't have a choice.

"Come to me, Ann." His soft words barely traveled the distance between them as his warm breath touched her cheek, her lips. "You are mine. Show them."

"No." She breathed the answer, but she couldn't move away. Even with her fellow scientists watching, she couldn't deny him. She'd tasted his magic last night, and now she craved him. Her training hadn't prepared her for this.

"Oh, you're mine." He smiled that sardonic grin, and his dark eyes gleamed with power. "Kiss me now. You want to."

She moved closer still, even as the rational part of her mind screamed. Her job! Her family! She couldn't betray them.

Still, his scent twined around her like a lover's caress. The bergamot and vetiver called to her, and she yielded, craving the sanctity of his kiss.

Her lips slid over his, and her tongue sought his. She *was* his.

"Ann!" Kai shoved the brunette out the door and moved toward her.

Kai was too late. The heat of the predator's kiss hypnotized her, ruining her life—but it didn't matter. She'd die for him. She'd die in his arms.

"Ann, stop!"

She didn't want to stop—but that tight core of training inside her heart broke through, shattering the spell like ice. Kai's voice helped. It rang with power and concern, and she rediscovered the strength she'd developed through years of denying herself—and stepped back.

It was too late. They'd seen her kiss him. The eyes of her peers felt as heavy as weights around her ankles—but she was free of the dark spell. She took a second step back. She might have lost the respect of every scientist in the room, but she was free.

Detective Kai Atlanta ushered her toward Dr. Stoller. "Get her out of here," he told the old scientist. Then Kai grabbed the back of the predator's shirt and dragged him away from the podium, which was no mean feat. Sutherland was huge.

As Ann extricated herself from Stoller's embrace, Brad Scrimshaw gave her a quick wink and began to clap, a loud deliberate sound. "Great talk!" he told the crowd, but no one in the audience joined in, and she wanted to burst into tears.

A hand landed on her shoulder, its heat permeating both her suit jacket and shirt. Lust spiraled through her veins, and she knew who it was. The predator. "Run to your mommy, little girl," he said in his panty-dropping voice.

She pulled away from him with a quick twist of her shoulders, and Detective Atlanta pushed him toward the door. "Keep your hands off her," he growled.

The predator didn't move though. Ignoring the audience, still hushed in apparent shock, his eyes raked her body. "You have something I want."

"What? Tits?"

"Very funny." He moved in so close that she could see the flecks of dark brown in his almost black irises. "The vial. I need it back now."

The surprise she let show on her face wasn't faked. In that heartbeat she remembered she hadn't destroyed the vial like her mother had asked. "Vial? I've no idea what you're talking about."

"Let's step outside, shall we?" Chiron gestured Sutherland toward the door at the end of the lobby. He could see the gleaming blue pool through it.

"I don't talk to cops without my lawyer." But Sutherland moved toward the door anyway.

"You sound guilty of something."

"You're obsessed."

"With keeping people safe, yes." Chiron opened the door, and Sutherland walked through it. The scent of chlorine filled the morning air.

"She kissed me. It's hardly a crime."

Which might have been true—if the whole thing hadn't been a setup, if someone hadn't played a porn video starring the job applicant, if Fallon hadn't somehow been mesmerized to kiss her enemy, and if said enemy hadn't killed Chiron's beloved.

"And what about Akantha? Was that a crime?"

"Why don't you just drop it, detective?" Sutherland walked

toward the water, his wingtips looking out of place against the textured cement of the patio. "What was that woman to you that you can't let this go? Your wife? Your girlfriend?"

"What *was* she to me?" Past tense. More evidence. "You ask a lot of questions," Chiron said. "Thinking of a new career as a detective?"

Sutherland snorted. "Fat chance." The pool was as blue as the ancient Greek skies. "You've been hounding me about her for years. Makes me think you have more than a professional interest."

Surprised, Chiron didn't answer. A young woman with two small kids set an armload of towels on a chaise and started to put bright orange floaties on the smallest child's arms. How was it that this scum from under Earthshaker's balls didn't know Kai was Akantha's beloved? "I keep people safe, Dr. Sutherland. It's my job."

"Not a job. An obsession."

"I can't find Akantha, I ask questions. You assault Dr. Fallon and play questionable videos, my suspicions rise. An intelligent man like you ought to be able to understand that."

Sutherland didn't answer, and Chiron watched him eye the woman's ass as she bent to take off her daughter's sandal.

"Akantha's such a strange name." Sutherland said this slowly, as if hypnotized by the idea—or the woman's ass. "Don't you agree?"

"Depends. Some people might think 'LeBron' is strange. Doesn't seem to bother basketball fans."

When the woman gave Sutherland a look from under her lashes, he turned to Chiron and smiled. "I looked it up. It's old. And weird."

"I assume you mean 'Akantha.' Not 'LeBron.'" Alarm rippled through Chiron.

"Yes."

Chiron turned. "Jacob's an old name. Sarah's an old name. What's your point?"

Sutherland shrugged, his eyes drifting back to the woman. "I don't have a point. Just an observation."

Was Sutherland implying he knew Akantha's true age? She'd never have told that secret. Even if she'd been tortured, she would never have told their secret.

Of course, if she'd been tortured, someone might have seen she was immortal. Not many people grew back new fingernails after the originals had been pulled out.

He watched the young mother shrug out of her wrap, and a terrible thought occurred to him. If Sutherland knew Akantha's secret, he might discover Chiron's. "If you look on Facebook, you'll find a dozen Akanthas," he said finally.

"Akantha's name is older than the Greek language."

"Who knows that?" Chiron asked. "Who can tell how old a name is?"

Sutherland shrugged, and Chiron watched the woman by the pool eye his suspect. He had a way with women—apparently all women. "Linguists figured it out," Sutherland said, keeping his gaze on the young mother. "Here at UC San Diego."

"Hard to believe even linguists know how old a name is."

"They look at ancient documents and oral traditions. You know, they figured the Noah's ark story is ten thousand years old. Maybe it's a retelling of the flooding of the Tigris-Euphrates Valley." Sutherland shrugged.

"Fascinating."

"You know Akantha long?"

"Yeah." He filled his voice with sarcasm. The bastard was on to him, had been after Akantha for more than her perfect ass. "I've known Akantha since the beginning of time. Methuselah was our father."

Sutherland stopped for a moment, his gaze tearing away from the woman to focus on Chiron. Then he laughed, his white teeth gleaming in the sun. The sound boomed across the pool, and the kids stared at him. "A cop with a sense of humor. I love it. You want to donate your DNA to the project?"

The non sequitur surprised him. "My DNA? Why?"

"We take donations. We study them."

"Interesting." He couldn't imagine what Earthmother had done to make him live forever at the height of his strength. Who knew how her magic worked? But Akantha's murderer was the last person he wanted to answer that question. "I don't think so."

"Craig Venter did it. So did James Watson."

Chiron had only the vaguest idea who Venter was, but he wouldn't have cared if Muhammad himself donated DNA. It wasn't going to happen. "No, thank you."

The woman in the pool told her kids to stay in the shallow end as she walked over to the diving board and bounced. She launched herself into the air with the grace of a bird and executed a perfect pike, her knees straight and a tight bend at her hips. Her body looked lithe and powerful.

"Why not donate?" Sutherland asked. "It's a kind of immortality, you know."

Like he needed more of that. Suddenly, a thought occurred to him. "Did you ask Akantha to donate?"

"Back to Akantha again. And here I thought we were finally having a civilized conversation."

"Did you?"

Sutherland pulled a cotton swab from his pocket as he shook his head.

"What is that—" Chiron started to ask. Sutherland's fist connected hard with his face before he could finish, and Chiron's head spun. Blood sprang from his nose, filling his mouth with that coppery tang. It poured down his shirt. Chiron balled his fist and swung, but Sutherland hit him again, right on the nose.

"Hey!" the young mother called. "Hey! Security! Hey!" Her kids started screaming, and the shrieks bounced off the concrete. She gathered them up and ran.

"You bastard," Chiron said. The pain blinded him. "What was that for?"

Sutherland didn't answer. Instead, he reached the cotton swab toward Chiron's bloodied nose. Through the lights dancing behind his eyes, Chiron realized the fucker was taking his DNA.

Not a chance. He jerked his knee up and lashed his foot out. The toe of his shoe connected with Sutherland's hand, and the swab went flying.

"Asshole," Sutherland snarled. He reached into his pocket for a second swab as he grabbed for Chiron's collar. Chiron ducked away and shot out a punch of his own, catching Sutherland in the ribs. "Oof," Sutherland said, but Chiron showed no mercy. He rushed him.

Pain slowed Chiron, and Sutherland managed to grab the top of Chiron's hair. Sutherland waved the swab toward the blood on Chiron's face.

No way. He grabbed Sutherland's shoulders to throw him into the pool.

Unhampered by pain, Sutherland jerked his elbow back into Chiron's face, connecting straight-on with his nose. Chiron saw stars in waves of exquisite pain, but he wouldn't let Sutherland get a blood sample, despite the fact that it was dripping down his arms and chest now. He hauled off and slugged Sutherland in the gut.

"Motherfucker," Sutherland said, staggering back. He managed to keep his feet though. Then he spun around and planted a leg between Chiron's. The hand with the swab came right for his face.

Chiron threw himself into the center of the pool. Water lashed into the air, splashing the woman and her kids. It washed all the blood off his face, off his hands and arms. The water diluted the DNA.

"Fuck." Sutherland watched him from the side of the pool, shaking his head. "What'd you do that for?" He sounded genuinely confused. "No one cares about DNA."

"If no one cares about DNA, you wouldn't have sucker punched me to get it." Chiron spit out a mouthful of water and pushed his hair from his eyes. Already the tiny fractures in his cheekbones were knitting themselves together, faster than he'd ever healed before, but he didn't have time to think about it. "I'm going to arrest you for assaulting an officer."

"Fuck you." Sutherland pulled a third swab from his pocket. "You've been harassing me for two years. I'll get you knocked back to uniform, detective."

Chiron slipped his shoes off and let them sink to the bottom of the pool. His clothes dragged him down. His cell phone would be ruined, too. Stupid bastard.

At least the asshole didn't get his blood.

Sutherland turned his back to him and squatted. Only then did Chiron realize what Sutherland was doing with that third swab. He was mopping up Chiron's blood from the tiled pool edge.

Chiron couldn't swim fast enough to stop Sutherland, not in wet clothes. Instead, he jerked his hand back and shoved a huge wave of water that hit the floor with a loud slap. The water hit Sutherland's back, drenching his clothing. It also washed away the crimson puddles.

"You stupid bastard," Chiron said. "I told you I don't want you to have my DNA."

Sutherland stood and smiled. He held up his prize. The blood on his swab seemed as red as a jewel.

Again Chiron shoved a wall of water toward Sutherland, but his enemy stood just out of range. Sutherland held the swab too high and too far away.

"Thanks for the sample," Sutherland said. He took another step back, and the palm fronds waved as he brushed against them. Chiron lurched toward the edge of the pool, fighting the drag of his clothes. He was still a foot from the edge when Sutherland pulled a small glass-looking vial from his pocket and dropped the swab in it. "Can't wait to see what this tells me." He flashed a cold grin at Chiron. "And after you went to all that trouble to protest, I can't help but think it'll be interesting . . . just like Akantha's sample."

She turned toward Dr. Stoller. Tension simmered low in her gut. She may have lost any chance at landing this job but wouldn't go down without a fight.

"What does Dr. Sutherland do?" she asked Dr. Stoller. She needed clues. "What's he work on?"

"Pheromones." Carl's wild gray eyebrows rose. "His work's quite remarkable, but you need a drink."

A drink with the man who'd just watched her fuck a crop? God. This was not how she'd imagined her talk—but if she weren't still in the running, why was Stoller talking to her?

He directed them toward a booth in the back of the restaurant, grabbing a waitress's arm. "I know it's early, but do you have any single malt?" he asked.

She nodded. If she were surprised at an order for scotch at nine-thirty in the morning, she didn't show it. "We have Glen—"

"Just bring me four shots of one of them."

"Yes, sir."

"And quickly, please."

"Yes, sir."

Ann sat in the booth, staring at the man. The lines around his eyes bespoke his age—but also his sense of humor. He looked like he smiled a lot.

"I don't—"

Carl held up his palm. "No. Don't say anything. We'll drink the scotch and then talk."

The waitress appeared right then, four highball glasses balanced on the tray. Each was filled with amber liquid. She set them on the table and placed a glass filled with ice in the center. "The bartender said the second drink will go better on ice, sir. Especially in the morning."

"And the bartender is quite right. Thank you."

She left, and Carl pushed one of the glasses in front of Ann. "This one's for you."

"Thank you."

Carl picked up a second glass and drank the shot in one swallow. "You gave a wonderful talk today, Dr. Fallon." He put the glass back on the table. "Very solid science. Great field site. Remarkable photography." He smiled at her. "Of course, you know all this." He shook his head and clinked the second glass against hers. "Still, Harvard can't hire you."

"My talk was sabotaged. How does that disqualify me?"

"You want the second shot?" Carl pushed a full glass toward her. "You still look like you need it."

"I need it." The heat from the scotch spread from her throat across her chest. "I'm sure I could sue."

"Sue?"

The scotch make her upper arms tingle and gave her a slightly giddy feeling. "The second member of *your* search committee seduced me, recorded it, and played it before my peers, thereby destroying any chance of me landing this job. Sounds like a lawsuit to me."

"Did he play it, Dr. Fallon?" He lifted his grey eyebrows.

"What do you mean?" She caught her glass between her fingers. "Of course he did."

"Maybe you did it to dig into Harvard's deep pockets. You'd never have to work again, Dr. Fallon, if your lawsuit met with success."

She subdued her anger, homing on the flaw in his logic. "That assumes I knew beforehand that Dr. Sutherland was on the search committee." She downed the second scotch. "And I certainly didn't."

The sudden expression on Carl Stoller's face scared the shit out of her. The muscles around his eyes were tight, and he'd pressed his lips so closely together they'd turned white. The lines around his lips seemed deeper now, and she knew she wasn't getting this job or any other at Harvard. He was pissed. He was beyond pissed. "You will not besmirch Harvard's reputation," he said.

"We'll see." Ann started to stand, but Stoller gave a sad little laugh and touched her hand. The anger faded from his expression. "You misunderstand me."

"I did not misunderstand—"

He waved his hand in a self-deprecating way, and an oily purple lesion above his wrist caught the light. "Youth doesn't last nearly as long as one might hope. Would that I had gathered more rosebuds." He stared at the table for a second.

"I should go." She stood.

Carl touched her wrist, and his hand seemed to shake a bit. Ann realized the old man wasn't completely healthy. "I apologize for my anger." He shoved the glass aside with a controlled movement, the lesion catching the light. "In my youth, I would have taken Dr. Sutherland behind the woodshed for his disregard of your reputation." Now she saw sorrow in his jaundiced eyes. "Those days are gone, though—my arm isn't what it used to be."

"You look pretty strong to me." She sat.

"You're kind." He nodded with a wry smile. *But you wouldn't want to go to bed with me,* his expression said.

"No, I—"

"Don't pity me." He raised a glass. "The clock cannot be turned back, and I wield Harvard's mighty power instead." He

flashed her a quick grin and raised his hairy eyebrows. "Th
isn't all for the bad."

Ann didn't know what to say. She wanted to apologize, but for what?

He clinked his glass against hers again with a resigned twist of the lips and finished the last of his scotch. "What if I give you exactly what you want?"

The tingly feeling from the scotch had traveled to her knees. "Just what is that?"

"The field site."

Suddenly, her mouth dried. It tasted like she'd been drinking paint thinner, not scotch. "Why would you do that?"

"So you don't sue, of course."

Her mind raced, because of course she wanted to field site under Harvard's auspices more than she wanted anything—but how in the world could he know that?

"I think I'd need more than a field site, Dr. Stoller." She chose her words carefully. "I earned that position—unless my competition gives a better talk tomorrow—and your committee member ruined my reputation."

Carl Stoller smiled and met her gaze. "Harvard can't hire a harlot."

"Harlot!"

"You should call someone for moral support," he said. His expression was nothing but solicitous. "Your mother, perhaps?"

13

"God damn it." Ann grabbed her suitcase from the floor and smashed it onto the bed. She was going home, now. She was a harlot and a slut, at least in the eyes of every scientist who mattered in her field. Even scientists who hadn't seen the video—or seen her kiss Erik Sutherland—were getting messages about her on cell phones and computers. Her career was over, even if she sued Harvard and Sutherland.

She didn't fool herself. Sutherland wouldn't get blamed for this, despite the fact that he'd made the video and approached her at her talk. Despite the fact that he'd seduced her, which no member of a search committee was ever supposed to do to a potential employee. She was the woman—and the slut. He was a stud. What jackassery.

She grabbed her toothbrush and makeup from the bathroom and threw it amongst her unfolded clothes. If her mom didn't try to contact her before her flight left—she needed to call the airline, she reminded herself—she'd try the mindlink herself. She didn't want to desert her mom if she needed help, but Ann sure as hell wanted to get out of this hotel and away from these people.

She grabbed her jeans and T-shirt from the suitcase and tore off her suit, stifling the urge to toss the cream jacket into the trash. She wanted no memory of this day. In fact, what she really wanted was to find her mother and cry on her shoulder. She did *not* want to drink consolatory scotch with another Harvard professor.

A knock on the door interrupted her rant. She gave a startled yelp, feeling really alone all of a sudden. What if the predator was at the door? She froze. Where was Kai Atlanta? He'd said he wouldn't leave her side until she boarded that plane, and she'd never been more ready to get on a plane than this second.

Someone knocked again, louder. "Ann," a masculine voice said. "It's Kai Atlanta. You in there?"

It sounded like him, and oh, did she want it to be. Still, she couldn't move. What if the predator had more tricks up his sleeve?

Then the door's lock mechanism whirred, and her biology went into overdrive. She couldn't smell his dark fragrance, but she knew it was the predator. Her body started to suck energy from the earth through the hotel floor, and green tendrils wrapped around her ankles. Ozone filled the room as her body prepared to change shape and kill the asshat.

Then the door opened as wide as the swing bar allowed. It wasn't the predator's scent that accosted her.

Kai's face peeked in, his hair hanging in his face. "Oh, you're here!"

The green tendrils of her magic evaporated immediately, and her ankles regained their full human shape. It *was* Kai. She unhooked the door guard and swung it open. "Sorry," she said. "I thought—" She waved her hand, not wanting to discuss how afraid she'd been. "I'm glad you're here."

And it was true. With him here, she didn't feel nearly so vulnerable. He walked into the room making an odd squishing sound, his eyes soft and relaxed. There was something about this man, something different. And it wasn't just the kind look in his eyes. He was . . . unique, an outsider in a way that reminded her of her own isolation.

"Thanks." He ran his hand through his hair and it stood on end. "Do you mind if I get a towel?"

Only then did she see past his eyes. His shirt was plastered against his chest, and his hair was wet. He smelled like . . . a swimming pool? "Detective Atlanta, what happened to you?" She grabbed two big towels from the bathroom and handed them to him.

Ignoring her question, he rubbed the towel over his bronze-colored hair and face. And his strong jaw. "I need to ask you something."

His tone brought her up short. He'd saved her skin last night and helped her out this morning. She was in no position to deny him—but she wanted to get the hell away from this conference, preferably with huge dark sunglasses and a big hat. She did *not* want to get caught up in cop crap—or supernatural crap. "Is this official?"

"No."

His tone suggested otherwise, and there were a lot of things she didn't want to tell him. "I'm going to the airport now. I'm taking the very next plane to North Carolina." She was shocked to hear her voice crack. Was she that close to tears?

"Please." The word was a plea. His eyes met hers, and the gentleness in them surprised her. Probably because every hot man she'd met in the last five years had been an asshole, and some part of her didn't expect him to be different. In fact, no part of her did. "There's no one else I can ask," he said.

She could feel herself caving. Pathetically wet men who looked—and acted—like heroes always did this to her. She wouldn't tell him anything she shouldn't, but . . . "What's the question?"

He pushed droplets of water from his eyebrow with a fingertip. "I want to ask about genetics. DNA fingerprinting. Genomics."

Genetics? A detective wondered about genetics and genomics? Not the direction she was expecting. "Okay."

"Thank you." The muscles around his eyes relaxed. He took a step back, and his shoes squished against the marble floor. "Can I order breakfast?"

"What about your burning question?"

He looked away from her, and she realized he was nervous. "I'll get to it. I haven't eaten yet," he said. "I'm hungry. French toast for you? Omelet?"

She wanted to say no, but the only thing she'd had was coffee and scotch. No wonder she wanted to cry. "Okay," she said. "French toast sounds good." She paused, wondering how wise it was to feel safe. "Did Sutherland see you come up here?"

"Not a chance." He picked up the phone. "I don't think anyone noticed me."

"Is that so, detective?" She shook her head. "You don't think anyone noticed a wet Hercules dripping into an elevator?"

"Hercules?" His voice sounded unnerved to her. Too tight. "I remind you of Hercules?"

"Should I have said Adonis?"

"No." He laughed, sounding more amused this time.

"Who then?" She turned around and sat in one of the plush chairs. "Eros? Apollo?"

"They hated each other."

She kicked a chair toward him. "I compare you to the hunks of the gods and you want to tell me they hate each other?" She had to stop blathering.

"I took the service elevator." He looked at the hotel information pamphlet for a heartbeat, then dialed. "Only the GM knows I'm up here."

"So you're denying you look like Hercules?" She needed to shut the hell up.

"Hercules had a brow ridge that'd make a Neanderthal jealous—and he killed his wife and kids." He met her gaze as he ran the soaked towel over his thigh. "So yes, I'm denying any resemblance, physical or behavioral."

She tried to laugh at his joke. Water dripped from the cuff of his jeans. The fabric plastered itself to his leg, highlighting every one of his thigh muscles.

Not that she cared. After he placed the order and hung up, she asked, "What was your genetics question, detective?"

He gave her a quick glance then went back to the towel. "I—" He held up the wet thing. "Do you mind if I take another?"

"Take them all. They're yours. Why don't you take off your wet shoes?"

"Thanks." He stood and went into the bathroom.

"What happened?"

"I was trying to avoid giving a DNA sample," he said from the other room.

"By . . . swimming?"

"Erik Sutherland punched me in the face first." His words echoed slightly over the chrome and tile. "I was bloody. He came at me with a Q-tip."

"So you jumped in the water. Good idea."

"In theory, yes." He walked back in, barefoot and holding a fresh towel. A distracted part of her mind noticed a few small coppery hairs covering the golden skin of his feet.

"Did he get a sample?" The more disciplined part of Ann's mind raced over this information. The predator wanted this man's DNA? What the hell for? Did it have something to do with the fragrance they'd been concocting?

"He got the sample." Kai unhooked his holster, slid it from over his shoulder, and put in on the table.

Even after that video, he trusted her enough to put his gun down. She tried to ignore what that did to her. "How?"

"From the blood on the floor." He paused and pulled his wet wallet from his wet jacket pocket. He set that on the table, too. "Unfortunately."

She picked up the computer, plugged in the Internet connection, and hit some keys.

"What are you looking up?"

"The answer to your question, I think: Erik Sutherland. I never heard his name before this conference, and Stoller told me he worked with pheromones."

"So?"

"Maybe that's why he wants your tissue."

"For pheromones?"

"Yes." The Web of Science site spat out a list of scientific papers he'd written, and she scanned them. Words like "protein pheromones," "lipid-binding," and "seducin" were common across a bunch of them. One title discussed the efficacy of something called enticin in attracting members of the opposite sex. "Maybe he wants to make one that works specifically for you."

"What's that mean?" Chiron asked from over her shoulder.

Ann looked up at him, into his gray-green eyes. Before she could answer, something odd struck her. Atlanta's skin wasn't bruised. No blood poured from his nose, although a faded reddish stain on his blue T-shirt might be blood soaked with swimming-pool water.

How'd he heal so fast?

She closed the computer and set it back on the table. "You said Erik Sutherland punched you in the face and that blood poured onto the floor." She tried not to let her unease reach her voice. "Are you okay?"

"My nose bleeds easily." He didn't look at her as he picked up the towel again. He dried the jacket plastering his arms.

A lie. "Okay."

"I'm fine." He touched his nose. "Really. Just a little tender."

"Mmmm." She pulled magic from her heart, and the damp hairs on his arms rose with the ozone charge of her working. She needed only the tiniest bit of enchantment to look at his bone structure, but too much power tried to pour out. *Weird*, she thought as she shoved it back.

"I had a friend like that," he said, toweling his other arm now. "Every time she sneezed, she bled all over the place." He paused, tapped the table. "Wonder when the food will be here."

"Mmmm," Ann answered, distracted. She blinked as she tried to process what she saw. Even now, his cartilage refitted itself. Skin and muscle cells regenerated themselves. Microfractures in his cheekbones reknitted as she watched.

The predator had pounded his face, smashed his nose . . . and he was healing.

The realization froze Ann in her chair. Who was this man? How did he heal himself? Why did she feel so comfortable with him?

"What is it?" he asked. "You're as pale as a ghost."

"Is that it?" The words came out in a shocked whisper. "Are you a ghost?"

"What do you mean?" He laughed. Too quietly. His eyes refused to leave hers.

"Sorry." She shook her head, trying to figure out what was happening here. Could he be one of her own? Male unicorns weren't common, but they existed. Had the predators run him out and sent him underground like all the others? "It was a bad joke."

Ann stood then, discharging the static over her own skin with a hand on the table. Vulnerability wasn't new to her. Moving through the human world, playing the human game, she understood vulnerability. Lying about who she was taught her vulnerability.

And she saw vulnerability now.

Kai kept his gaze on her. The sorrow she'd seen last night shined through, became almost palpable. Had the predator done this to him, too? Was he a unicorn? She had to know. Without a word, she stepped toward him, closing the space between them.

"What are you doing?" His voice was thick, but she didn't see lust in his face. She saw . . . hope?

Without a word, she peeled his wet jacket from him and set it on the table. With gentle fingers she pushed the wet T-shirt up his stomach and over his head. He stood before her, his chest naked. His brown nipples hardened in the cold—or maybe with desire. Something burned in his expression, something she hadn't seen even a heartbeat earlier.

"What are you?" she asked in a whisper. He was not a ghost. Beneath her hand, his flesh was hot, his muscles hard. She inhaled deeply, drinking in his scent. Was he one of hers?

"Ann." His Adam's apple bobbed as he swallowed. "What are you doing?"

She didn't answer. Not with words. Instead, she ran her fingertip over his eyebrow. His strength felt real. She inhaled. Slowly, deliberately she tasted the molecules of his scent. She had to know the answer.

His rich perfume filled her nose, delighted her. The pungent cedar scent of his sweat reminded her of ancient forests, of the feral horses that once ran there. His scent . . . it held a familiar flavor, something equine. "Who are you?" she asked again.

"Detective Kai Atlanta." His words were simple, but his tone was not. The melodious syllables of his name held such a deep sorrow, and a little fear—but it didn't hold an answer.

She inhaled again. His scent wasn't right for a unicorn. It

wasn't that she didn't like it, but he didn't smell like family. Did he? If he wasn't a unicorn, he knew one.

"Who healed you?" She stepped away from him, wanting to read his expression.

"Who healed me?"

Her arms yearned for the heat pouring off his body. "Yes." She stepped closer to him again, reaching her hand toward his cheek. She couldn't hide herself from him. She couldn't continue to live a lie, not with him. "Like this."

She imbued him with her magic, still not pulling enough of her power to form visible green wisps. Even as she subdued the physical embodiment of her nature—one of the embodiments, at least—she let him feel the truth of herself as she wrapped her power around the last vestiges of his wounds. Now, his tissue was healed. Completely. By her hand.

"What have you done?" He touched his nose, his eyes wide. "How'd you do that?"

"Who healed you first?" She refused to let his eyes leave hers.

He didn't seem able to speak. "No one." The words came out as soft as a caress. "No one did this to me. Who are you?"

"Please." She looked away, blinking back tears she hadn't felt coming. "I've been alone too long. Just tell me the truth. Who helped you?"

"But—" He touched her shoulder and forced her to meet his gaze. "I've never met anyone like you. No one healed me."

"I don't understand."

"It's true." He blinked, held his eyes closed. "I— I heal myself. It's a gift."

Could it be? Ann ran through the possibilities. He healed himself? He *healed* himself. The only creatures who healed themselves, at least at this speed, were . . . She balked at the conclusion, knowing the answer but needing to ask anyway. "Are you a unicorn?" Only human female wizards could run with male unicorns—and she found she really wanted to run with the man before her.

"A unicorn?" The suggestion seemed to puzzle him, and Ann could've kicked herself. The thought hadn't occurred to him until she put it in his mind. "No, I'm not a unicorn."

"What are you?"

He shrugged. His skin gleamed in the late morning light, complete with goose bumps. She picked up a towel and began to dry his chest, his arms. "I'm . . . me."

"Kai."

"I can't—" He turned away from her with a shake of his head. "I can't answer that. What if they come after you?"

"Come after me? The predators?"

"They killed her. Akantha."

"Who are *they*?"

"Erik Sutherland." He shrugged, and she felt the play of muscle beneath her hand. "And others. A lot of people work at the Brode Institute. They can do whatever they want."

"You were at my talk today, detective. Someone's already after me."

He nodded.

"Then you know I'm already in danger."

He nodded, and the resignation in his expression hardened. "What did you call him? The predator?"

"Erik Sutherland. Yes." But she didn't want to relive that old history. Not yet.

Because she'd just figured out his secret.

The Brode Institute wanted his DNA. Why? He could heal himself. Even if he wasn't unicorn, he was *not* human. "I know what you wanted to ask me," she said.

He stared at her a moment and swallowed. His eyes were haunted. Then he looked away. "I think this is a bad idea. I don't need answers."

She kept her hands on him, feeling the warmth of him, feeling his heart pounding beneath her palms. Was it fear? She wouldn't relent.

"What will they find when they examine your DNA?" she said. "Will the predator be able to tell the secret of your biology? That's what you wanted to ask me, isn't it?"

He closed his eyes for a heartbeat and then opened them. Beach-glass green. "Yes." He took a deep breath. "That's the question."

The trust he'd just laid at her feet left her speechless. She nodded and moved away from him, needing to think. What would his genes say about him?

"Do you know the answer?" he asked, his voice hushed. "What did they want with Akantha? What do they want with me, with you?"

He'd linked himself, Akantha, and her together—a group—prey to the predators. Kai Atlanta did not look like prey.

"They'd have to know where to look on the chromosomes—which is hard enough in most cases," she said, "and they'd have to know what to look for, which sequences of CATG's."

"I see."

Water from his wet jeans dripped onto the floor, but her fingertips longed to trace the lean line of his hips. "Do they know where to look?" she asked.

"You mean like various cancer genes?" He shrugged. "I have no idea what they know."

She found a T-shirt in her suitcase and gave it to him. "It's new. You need to pull off the tag."

"A blue devil." He unfolded the white cotton. "I always liked Duke. Thank you."

"Don't thank me. Thank Daniel."

"The vet. The one you were with the night an angel visited a female victim—that you called in, by the way." He looked up from the shirt and met her gaze. "And cops picked up a call about a unicorn running on the beach. Funny about all the hoofprints around the beach blanket."

Had something shifted in his eyes? She paused before catching herself. "Don't change the subject." Could he sense her heart pounding through her veins?

"I'm not changing the subject." He pulled the shirt over his head, hiding his golden abs, the planes of his chest.

"You are." The gift for Daniel—the cheating scum who'd wanted to turn her in for some sort of bounty—fit Kai a little too tight across the chest. Not that that was a bad thing. Hiding those muscles behind a T-shirt might be, though. She dug through the suitcase and found the pair of shiny blue track pants that went with the shirt. "We were talking about you."

"I'm talking about both of us—you and me." He shook his head, his hair nearly dry now, and he turned toward her. He was close enough now that she could see the gold highlights of his coppery eyelashes. "I'm telling you why I trust you."

"Trust me?" She stepped back toward the door. He might be gorgeous and sad and humble, but she didn't trust him. How could she? "Why? Why do you trust me?"

He moved toward her, not letting her escape. "You're not what you seem, either," he said, slowly taking off her glasses. "For instance, I bet you don't need these."

She froze. No one had ever guessed her secret. No one had guessed she'd *had* a secret. "I don't know what you're talking about." She did, though. The lie hung in the air between them, ugly and unnatural.

"You don't need this, either." This time, he slid his hand into her hair and loosened her chignon. Her hair tumbled past her shoulders and halfway to her ass. "You don't need to hide. Not from me."

And the frightening thing was, he might be right. She had

sensed it when she'd first seen him: he was different from other men. She could be her true self with him. If she dared.

Her breasts were inches from his chest, but her eyes had his attention. The fear lurking there pulled at him, and he wanted nothing more than to wrap her in his arms and protect her from the dark forces closing in around them, the people trying to discover her true nature—and his—for their own insidious purposes.

The room crackled like a summer night before a thunderstorm. Ozone.

With a start, Chiron remembered he'd felt the electrical scent in the hallway the first time he startled Fallon in the concierge-level corridor.

"I've been stupid." He moved away from her. Before he swept her up and kissed her. Protecting her was one thing, but taking her in his arms? Savoring the silkiness of her hair between his fingers? No. "I didn't see. I was too focused on myself. On Sutherland's past crime."

"Past crime?" Her voice was still too quiet. "What did he do to you?"

It was time to put the cards on the table. At least some of them. The woman standing before him was no ordinary woman—she had healing powers. Was she immortal? Was she an immortal centaur? "Erik Sutherland killed my . . . wife. We had a link." He touched the oak table, trying to draw strength from its stability. "Our minds, they were linked. It was part of the gift."

"Was she . . ." He saw Fallon searching for the words, or maybe sifting through questions. "Was she like you?"

How to answer that. "In some ways. She could heal herself." He shook his head, still unsure. He and Akantha had never shared their secret. Not in the four thousand years they'd spent together. To share it now . . . It seemed like a betrayal.

Then Akantha's face flashed through his memory, her smile. She wouldn't have wanted him to be alone for the rest of his life—and she wouldn't have wanted her death to go without revenge.

"Her name was Akantha," he said. "Akantha of Knossos."

"And your name? Your real name?" She gave him a crooked smile, heavy on the irony. "Hercules, Hercules of Olympus?"

He didn't answer. He couldn't. How could he tell this woman his name, his lineage, his deeds—all in one word? Could he tell her that Hercules had been his student, along with Achilles and Jason? "I can't tell you."

Except she gasped like he had. Amazement widened her eyes and sent blood to her cheeks. "Kai." She took another step back, her hands up like she wanted to ward him off—although he hadn't moved. "Kai-ron. You're Chiron. You're a . . ." She shook her head like she couldn't believe it. "You're a centaur."

He wouldn't deny it. He met her gaze and let her see the truth in his eyes—and then he slipped out of his wet pants. "It's true."

"What are you doing?"

"Trusting you."

"I don't think you need to get naked to make me—"

Then his transformation took her words away. Her eyes widened as his chest lengthened and broadened so that the planes of his human abdomen skated into the planes of his equine chest. His back elongated as she gasped, and the hooves of his hind legs hit the carpeted floor with a thud. Short sorrel horse fur spread over his flesh and his tail sprouted in a cascade of hair. The boxers he'd been wearing fell to the floor, ripped beyond repair.

He held up the jeans, still dripping with swimming pool water. "I didn't want to ruin them. How would I leave here? I'd be as trapped as you were last night."

With a dumbfounded expression, she held up shiny blue

track pants, the new tag still dangling from them. They matched the T-shirt. "You can wear these."

"Oh."

Without a word, she dropped the pants and walked toward him. She reached a hand toward his withers like she was going to stroke him, and then she jerked her hand back and looked at him. "May I?"

He nodded, his throat too choked to speak. Had he made a mistake here? After the Lapith wedding of Peirithoüs and Hippodameia, humans had hunted down and killed every centaur ever born—with glee. The scourge hadn't ended with the wedding attendees. The ancient humans had gone on a rampage then, killing all semihuman creatures. All satyrs and nymphs and Sirens, and all the other species forgotten in the sands of time.

Even his beloved Akantha had been reluctant to accept his race, nearly marrying a traitorous human prince rather than an honorable centaur. Why should Ann Fallon be different?

"Three thousand years ago," he said.

"What?"

"That was the last time I shared my secret with an outsider."

Her warm hand ran across his spine, down his hindquarters, and over his stifle. "I guess that means I'm not an outsider." Her fingers traced the planes of his shoulders, and he felt her shiver as she spoke.

"I—I guess not."

"I've never seen anyone so beautiful." Awe filled her voice.

Keeping his hooves in place he turned to look at her, looking for sarcasm, for some trace of repugnance at his animal self— but her expression held none of that.

"You're the most beautiful person I've ever seen," she said, her fingers tracing his gaskin. "The most beautiful by far."

He reached for her, wanting to touch her own beauty. He'd wanted her since the moment he'd laid eyes on her. As his hand touched hers, he willed her to . . . he didn't know. Believe him, maybe. Accept him as he was. "Ann, I—"

Polite knuckles rapped on the door. "Room service."

They kept their eyes locked for a heartbeat, and then the server knocked again. "Room service!" His voice was louder this time.

Ann gave him a playful grin. "I think I should get that, don't you?"

He nodded and headed to the bathroom, careful to keep his hooves from knocking against the floor.

"I bet you're as hungry as a horse," she said with a wicked smile, and she walked toward the door.

As he shifted back into human form, he heard her open the door.

"Dear God!" she said. "What are you doing here?"

14

As Chiron stepped from the bathroom—fully human and wearing the track pants—Brad Scrimshaw shoved a cart of food into the room and slammed the door behind him. He wore the white jacket of the hotel waitstaff, but his convention name tag bumped against his chest. He wouldn't have fooled anyone for long.

"Brad?" Ann asked. "What are you doing here?"

"What are *you* doing here?" He looked wildly around the room. "Isn't this the cop's room?"

"Yes, but—"

"Can I help you?" Chiron came to where the boy could see him.

"Look," Brad said, his voice vibrating with a tension that bordered on panic. "You've got to believe me. Everyone else will think I'm crazy, but you saw the guy. You know he's nuts."

"Brad, you need to slow down and explain yourself. Who's nuts?"

The lanky boy took a deep breath and straightened his white jacket, which was too short. His bony wrists stuck out from beneath the cuffs. "Okay. This is the deal." Chiron watched him meet Ann's gaze. "I heard the Sutherland guy talking, and he's going to do something terrible."

"Worse than what he's already done?" Ann asked. Chiron couldn't image she was happy to see any of her colleagues after that video show.

"Yes." Brad nodded. "Worse than that—or at least, as bad as that."

"What'd you hear?"

"Apparently the wildlife vet that everyone here uses—" Brad snapped his fingers trying to jog his memory. "What's his name?"

"Daniel Hallock."

"That's right. Hallock. Well, apparently Hallock was arrested last night." He met Chiron's eyes. "Did you know that?"

"Yes."

"Apparently he's gone mad, crazy. Like Renwick in *Dracula*."

"What?" Ann said. "He's eating bugs?"

"No. Weirder. He's saying you're a shape-shifting unicorn, so the man has obviously lost his mind. And he isn't just talking about it—he's ranting. He's screaming at anyone who'll listen."

"How do you know this?" Chiron asked.

"Sutherland said."

"Hallock's in custody," Chiron said. "He can't hurt anyone."

"That's what I'm saying." Brad hit the cart in front of him for emphasis. "Sutherland's going to break him out! He wants the man to come rant at the conference. He wants everyone to hear him say these crazy things about Dr. Fallon!"

It wasn't bad enough that every important scientist in her field watched her fuck a crop, now they'd listen to a madman spew her secret? Chiron felt Ann's pain. He felt it, and he knew he had to stop it.

"Sutherland can't get him out of custody," Ann said, her voice shaking as she looked at Chiron for support. "He's in jail. Who breaks someone out of jail?"

"Anything's possible." Chiron shrugged. "He's in the hospital for psychological evaluation. He was a little unhinged last night."

"What's that mean?"

"It means someone could bribe a nurse or convince a nurse he doesn't need restraints. If the psych nurse thinks he's not going anywhere, she might take the cuffs off."

"Exactly." Brad hit the topmost tray for emphasis again, and the smell of omelets and French toast filled the room. "You have to stop him."

"Wait a minute," Chiron said. "There are a whole lot of questions that need to be answered first."

"Like what?" His tone was incredulous.

"Like why are you dressed as a waiter? How did you get our food and find my room? No one knows I'm staying here. And most importantly, how did you hear this?"

"Just call your boss and make sure they keep a guard on the vet," Brad pleaded. "Then I'll answer your questions."

"This place is crazy. I'm getting on the next plane out of here." She flashed a glance in Chiron's direction. Was that regret he read there?

"You've got to stop this madman first!"

"Why are you so interested?" Ann asked. "That's the real question."

"Just call! Please!" He ran his hand nervously over his hair again. "Call me your knight in shining armor."

She didn't need another knight, but Chiron picked up his cell and shook the water off it before he pressed the green button. The number went through immediately. "Put the boss on the phone," he said, glad the phone still worked after its swim in the pool.

"Where the hell are you?" The boss was angry before noon. Never good.

"At the hotel with the witness from last night." He glanced at Brad, whose gaze bore into him. "Look, I got a tip that someone's going to break Hallock out of the hospital. Maybe we should keep someone on him. The guy here says Hallock's coming to the hotel to stir things up for the witness."

"What a coincidence." The sarcasm was heavy.

"Coincidence?"

"Yeah." The staff sergeant let out a long, exasperated breath. "Someone already busted Hallock out of Psych Eval. Can you bring that witness to HQ?" the sergeant asked. "We need to keep her safe. The fucker was positively ranting before he escaped."

"The unicorn thing?"

"Exactly—and he was nuts. You should have seen him. Practically foaming. Kept saying the witness made his wife twenty years younger. We got to keep these two away from each other."

Chiron glanced at Ann, and sudden fear raced through his veins. The woman had certainly looked twenty years younger than she'd claimed to be. What had Ann gotten into? He swallowed, remembering the way she'd healed him. Maybe the better question was: What had Ann done to the woman? Could she really make people younger?

If so, things were starting to slide into place. He and Akantha had immortality. Ann and her family could bestow the fountain of youth.

"Come right in, okay?" His boss made the order sound like an invitation, which was one of the reasons he made a great boss. "And bring the witness with you."

"What about the guy who gave me the tip?"

"Might be suspicious, but leave him for now. Get his stats. I'll send a couple of guys there to pick the nutjob up from the hotel—if he shows up there. We'll check into your tipper."

"Got it." Chiron clicked off the phone.

"Brad, you got your license on you?" After the kid handed it over, Chiron got his cell number and hotel room. "When you leaving?"

"Tomorrow morning, after the party and the tour, just like everyone else."

"Tour?"

"Yeah. Brode Institute. It's on the schedule."

"Brode Institute." He looked at Ann, but she shook her head. He understood she'd rather eat glass than go on that tour. "When's that tour start?"

"Bus leaves in an hour." He pulled at the lapels of his too-small coat. "And the party's at nine tonight. Formal."

"Okay." Chiron folded the hotel paper he'd taken his notes on—his notebook was wet from the pool. "You can go."

"But shouldn't I go with you, or talk to more cops or something? Maybe I should watch for the crazy guy by the door or something."

Chiron squashed the patronizing urge to laugh. "Why don't you go to the Brode tour? That's Sutherland's hangout, isn't it? Maybe you can learn something."

"You're trying to get rid of me. I'm not Shaggy."

"Brad, I've got to get Dr. Fallon out of here and to the station. I don't want anything slowing me down. The best thing you can do is what you would have done if you hadn't come in here to tip me off—including getting rid of that jacket."

Brad nodded, and Chiron saw he understood. "I'll go."

"Brad, thank you." Ann slid her hand over his arm. "I appreciate that you were trying to stop him."

"If he shows up here, I'm punching him in the face. He shouldn't have made that movie—and he definitely shouldn't have shown it. What an ass."

Chiron sighed as he opened the door. "Don't punch him, okay? Just call 911 if you see him."

"Okay."

Chiron closed the door after Brad left. "We've got to get out of here. Can you pack up your bag?"

"I'm nearly done."

"Look, let's take you to HQ. We'll talk the boss into sending someone as an escort with you on the plane, get you safely back home."

"You?"

"I'll try." She wanted his company, he realized. She'd seen his true form and didn't want to run—but would she tell him her true nature? "Tell me about the predators. What are we up against?"

"What do you want to know, exactly?" She folded her suit and laid it in the suitcase. He had the feeling she was avoiding his eyes. She knew he had all the information he needed to figure out her nature—and she was as scared as he'd been.

"How'd Sutherland make you kiss him?"

"Smell. I understand they're making pheromones in a lab that make them irresistible to us."

"You can smell them?"

"Yeah." She zipped up her suitcase and shouldered her backpack. "That's how they lure us to them. My mother told me yesterday that she thought she'd found the lab where they made the fragrance. When they wear the pheromone, we can't resist them."

"Like virgins in fairytales?" Would she deny it?

"Worse. Predators smell like . . . I don't know how to explain. Like if you're starving and you smell chocolate fondue or, I don't know, doughnuts. You want to eat it. You *have* to eat it, but you know it's not good for you, and you'll be sick to your stomach, and you'll regret doing it." She swallowed. "And still you do it."

"And virgins, what do they smell like?" He picked up her bag.

Again, she didn't deny the implication. "Imagine you're starving and you smell homemade bread baking in the oven. Wholesome. Delicious. And also hard to resist."

For a heartbeat he wished he'd walked through the bakery before he came up here.

"Let's take the service elevator to the garage." He opened the hotel room door for her and waited for her to enter the hall.

"Thank you."

Chiron found he couldn't leave the room, not yet. "Ann." She stood in the threshold, and he let her meet his gaze. "Tell me your secret."

She paused, and he saw her swallow. "Haven't you figured it out?"

Of course he had. She knew he had. "Show me."

She moved back into the room, and his heart beat in double time. "It's awkward," she said, and then she barely whispered. "Changing forms."

"Why?"

"Changing forms . . ." He watched a blush spread over her face. "It has a similar effect on our biology as scenting a preda- tor."

Meaning it made her uncontrollably hot? He let the door close again and set her bag down. No wonder she was hesitant.

"Be patient with me," she said.

"I will—" he started to say, but unnerving wisps of smoke or fog had begun to curl around her ankles. The tendrils were the color of emeralds. The ozone he'd noticed the first time they'd met crackled through the room.

And her legs began to morph into something more equine, something silvery and beautiful. Her mane cascaded past her withers. Her lines were as powerful as any Triple Crown hope- ful—more powerful.

And an opalescent spiral burst from her forehead.

Something about her magic was familiar. It reminded him of

something he couldn't quite put his finger on. He would have stroked her, felt the heat of her flesh beneath his hand, but she didn't give him the chance. Abruptly she changed back into a human, her body sucking in the green wisps. "I know you must take this ability for granted, but you are beautiful," he said.

"I've never changed in front of anyone before. Not any man."

"Not your fiancé?"

"He had no idea." Then she shook her head. "I'm wrong. He said there was a bounty on my head. I got the feeling he couldn't bring me in—or didn't want to bring me in—until he knew the truth."

She had touched him while he'd been in centaur form, and now he longed to touch her. "Now, neither of us are outsiders," he said.

The way her eyes shined when she looked at him told him she'd already come to that conclusion.

"We need to leave before Hallock shows up." He opened the door again, but she was standing there, flushed. The heavy scent of desire filled the short distance between them—and he understood what changing did to her. He understood in a visceral way, especially when he submitted to his desire and touched her arm.

She gasped in desire—and moved away from him fast. "I'm sorry," she said. "The change, it heats my blood. Unseemly. I can control this, but it's not easy."

Gesturing toward the service elevator, he said, "I'm sorry. I shouldn't have touched you."

"It only takes a few minutes to dissipate. When I was younger, I thought this was a curse." She approached the elevator and pressed the button. "But I changed my mind last night."

"Why's that?"

"It saved my life. My mother thought if I spent a lot of time shifting between woman and unicorn I'd acquire a sort of habituation, a measure of self-control unicorns don't generally have." The elevator doors opened, and he pressed the "P" button after they entered it. "She gave me that advice—to change frequently—just before we went into hiding fifteen years ago. She thought it might help me escape the predator if I ever found one again."

"Did it work?" The elevator moved down.

"I left the predator's hotel room last night. None of my cousins or sisters would've been able to do that." The flush had left her cheek.

"Feel . . . better?"

She didn't laugh. Instead, she touched his arm, tentatively, like a wild bird landing too close to a person for its own comfort. "Chiron, why are they doing this to us?"

Hearing someone new say his true name for the first time in thousands of years did something very odd to his knees—they felt . . . weak. "We'll head to HQ." The door opened to the parking garage, and he pointed in the direction of his car. "I suspect we'll be able to track down Daniel—"

"Hello, detective." The tiny, auburn-haired woman he'd seen with Erik Sutherland pushed off the side of the garage wall and sauntered toward them. Her jeans covered her thighs like a second skin, and her tight white tank top left little to his imagination. Black sequins made a heart between her nipple-sized breasts.

He felt Ann freeze beside him, but he didn't care. He had to get closer to this woman. He let go of Ann's luggage.

"You have me at a disadvantage." He held out his hand for her to shake. Anything to touch her. "We haven't been introduced."

She smiled. It was a cold smile. Feral. He didn't care. He'd never been the kind of man to rut like a stag, but he'd give anything to wipe that smile off her face with his own lips. All too easily he could imagine the taste of her mouth, the smell of her sweat, the sound of her voice panting his name.

"Detective, I am Meena." She took his hand, and her skin felt warm. Hot. Without any trouble he imagined her fingers wrapped around his cock, clever fingers massaging his balls—

What the hell was wrong with him? He jerked his hand back and stepped away from her.

"Detective," she said, again. "You know my face, perhaps?"

He'd love to know a lot more than her face.

She raised a dark eyebrow. "You will come with me. I have someone who'd very much like to meet you." Her voice held the faintest trace of an Italian accent. "You can trust me. You've seen me with Dr. Sutherland, no?"

Only then did Chiron have any awareness of Ann. She stood next to him, stiff and unmoving.

"I saw you at the lecture this morning," he said finally. And hadn't he seen her in the video, lapping the wet desire from between Ann's legs? Almost without noticing, he moved in closer to her and inhaled—and savored.

"What did you say your name was?" Ann's voice vaguely intruded into his pleasure. She grabbed his arm like she owned him, and she leaned back, not so much pulling him away as suggesting that he follow her.

"Meena," the woman said, and the accent was definitely Italian.

"We met last night," Ann said in a voice as hard as the concrete walls around them. "Meena."

"How could I forget such a pleasure?" the woman asked, but her eyes didn't leave his for a heartbeat. Her irises were nearly black, and silver flecks glinted within them.

"Is that Dr. Meena?" Ann asked. The sarcasm could have cracked the windshields around them. "From the Brode Institute perhaps?" He watched her step back and cross her arms over her chest. "Or maybe you're just the videographer—amateur, no doubt."

But Chiron didn't need to hear the answer. Desire burned in his blood like it never had before. Even when the Earthmother bewitched him and he lay with Akantha beneath the ancient stars he hadn't burned like this. He had to have this woman, this Meena, and he had to have her now.

He closed the distance between them with one stride. Her lips, as dark and tempting as blackberries, lay just before him. He'd just kiss her once. Devour her. He needed—

But fingers of steel grabbed his chin, his jaw, and pulled him away. The scent of newly mown grass swirled around him as she kissed him. The kiss wasn't the brooding thing he'd been craving. It was sweet and subtle.

Her lips met his, softly, gently, skin brushing against skin. He opened his eyes—and saw the turquoise of the Aegean Sea.

Not Meena. Ann.

What had he been thinking? He'd been wanting to kiss the auburn-haired woman? Had he lost his mind?

"Excuse me." Meena tried to invade their space, stepping too close for his comfort. She had one hand on Ann's shoulder, but Ann wasn't moving.

Her scent did something crazy to him. In that heartbeat he would have killed to fuck Meena. His body was already imagining what it would feel like to shove her against the concrete wall and rip those jeans from her skinny hips. He'd fuck her like a Viking or a pirate.

He started to pull away from Ann—but her tongue touched the tip of his lip, electrifying him.

"Detective." Meena's voice, hard now, echoed off the concrete walls. Her hand touched his shoulder now, and the heat of it raced to his cock.

A twisted part of him, a part he couldn't understand or completely control, wanted to reply. But Ann's lips couldn't be denied. The promise of her lips outweighed the dark temptation of Meena's.

Ann pressed herself more insistently against him and opened her mouth. When her tongue slid over his with the gentleness of a caress, fire coursed through him. If someone had replaced his knees with dry ice, he couldn't have felt weaker, less stable.

What she did to him.

The foreign hand on his shoulder moved down his arm in lazy circles. "You don't belong with her," Meena said. And then the darker seductive scents of oakmoss and ambergris invaded the safe haven Ann had created. The hand teased the soft flesh of his wrist. "Come with me." She flashed him a suggestive smile. "*Come* with me."

Ann didn't say a word. She simply caressed his lips again with hers. And the temptation to ravish Meena vanished.

He understood then. He understood just what Ann had done for him. She'd saved him. From a predator. Without taking his lips from Ann's, he reached back. His palm found the hard bone of Meena's chest, and he shoved her back. Hard.

Her three-inch heels weren't meant for this, and she wobbled crazily. Then she fell to her knees. "Goddamn it," she said, her voice echoing off the hard walls. "You stupid fucker. Look what you did to my hands." From his peripheral vision he saw scuffed flesh.

"Run to the car," Ann said, pulling back just enough to speak. Her lips still brushed against his as she spoke, and lust coiled through his veins. Faint green wisps floated around her face. Ann touched the bare skin of his neck with her warm fingers, and the desire fanned throughout his body. "We need to go. Now."

It wasn't his job to run—he had to protect her. "She's a predator, isn't she?" He didn't want to lose contact with Ann, and it wasn't fear of Meena that motivated his desire.

"Yes," Ann said. "You have your keys?"

He closed his hand around them and nodded, his cheek brushing against her face. Meena staggered to her feet, the black sequins on her tank top catching the fluorescent lighting.

"Hold your breath and run," Ann said. "I have to do something first. She has something I need."

"I'm staying with you." He didn't—wouldn't—let go of Ann's hand. Even as he pressed the remote start and unlock-door buttons, he kept hold of her fingers. He would let nothing happen to her. He'd die first—and immortals couldn't die.

Still, Ann refused to go to the car. She dragged him toward Meena with a strength that surprised him.

Ann shook off his hand with an annoyed flick. "Go!" she told him. "To the car!"

"What—"

But Ann had already wrapped Meena's hands in her own like they were lovers. Did this pheromone affect her, too? Did he need to rescue her like she'd rescued him?

As Ann's lips met Meena's, Meena tilted her hips until both women were pressed against each other. Meena's small breasts, barely constrained by her even smaller T-shirt, pressed against Ann's, and he could see the taut nipples of the other woman.

Chiron wanted nothing more than to throw both women to the floor and fuck them to oblivion. An image flashed through his mind—Meena's mouth on Ann's breasts, Ann's hands between Meena's thighs, one woman's hand on his cock, the other with her lips on his.

Only the lingering taste of Ann's lips in his mouth stopped him from joining the women. The taste of her mouth gave him that safe haven of common sense, and he did nothing. If Meena tried to hurt Ann, he'd act. Otherwise he needed to trust that Ann knew what she was doing.

As he watched, Ann released one of Meena's hands, and touched the woman's hip. Seductively, she slid her hand up, caressing Meena's stomach. She curved her palm over Meena's breast, and Chiron heard both women moan in pleasure. Or maybe it was his voice.

He slid behind Ann, wanting to press his body against hers. No, he wanted to protect her if Meena attacked. But Ann had a plan. She'd told him she was immune to the predators, and she'd been immune enough to save him. So he stood there and inhaled the wonderful fragrance of their lust.

Meena grew hungrier under Ann's fingers. Chiron saw the flash of white teeth as Meena grabbed Ann's lip. Her free hand cupped Ann's breast. Her fingers caressed Ann's nipple.

But Ann didn't seem to mind. She grabbed Meena's hip and pulled her tightly against her. Then she grabbed the other woman's ass. Their hips ground against each other as Ann's fingers dug into the woman's back pocket.

And then, as suddenly as she'd started this madness, Ann pushed Meena away, shoving her chest hard. The movement apparently surprised the woman, who once again fell to her knees.

"Run!" Ann told him, taking his hand in hers.

This time, they went together, him barely having time to grab her suitcase.

"Hold it right there, detective." Meena. As he reached his car, he heard a sound that couldn't be mistaken for anything else. The cold click of a safety release bounced off the concrete walls. "You need to come with me, willingly or otherwise."

"I'm going with otherwise." He didn't stop running. "Get in the car," he growled to Ann, but he heard the door opening even as he spoke, even as he opened his own door and threw the bag in back.

Meena fired the gun as he slammed the car in reverse. The silencer muffled the sound of the bullet's flight, but there was no muffling the sound of the bullet slamming into the Crown Vic's steel door.

"Oh my God!" Ann snapped her seat belt and looked at the

hole in the door by his thigh. Black plastic hung shattered by the armrest. "She shot us."

"That she did." He revved the engine. Meena stood on the pavement between his car and the exit gate. He needed to run her over or speed past her faster than she could shoot them.

He gunned it. The squeal of spinning tires filled the garage, and the smell of burning rubber mingled with the scent of nitrocellulose from the handgun.

"You're shot," Ann said, pointing at his thigh. But he ignored it, wouldn't have noticed the pain if she hadn't told him.

"It's fine." He floored the car toward the closed gate, thanking the long-dead Earthmother that it was automated and unmanned. "I heal fast."

"Watch out!" Ann touched him and pointed out the window. "She's still after us!"

Meena had the gun pointed right at his head.

Well, it wasn't the first time he'd looked his supposed death in the eye. In fact, adrenaline hardly laced his veins anymore, at least not when danger licked at *his* heels.

But Ann's heels were a different story. Danger and death were not allowed to lick them. Only he was.

"Hold on," he said. He swerved the car crazily, nearly smashing Meena in the process. Her heart must pump ice instead of blood. She didn't move. She didn't run. Instead, a huge spiderweb of cracks covered the windshield—a second bullet whizzed between him and Ann.

"That almost hit us." Ann looked at him. "Just as a reminder, I'm not immortal. Bullets to the head kill me as dead as anyone."

"I'll keep that in mind." He kept swerving the car as he passed the motionless woman, and the side of the Crown Vic scraped the automatic gate with a terrible shriek.

"I got the vial when I kissed her." She grinned at him. "From her back pocket."

He didn't have time to think about vials or make-out sessions—although he knew it was a memory he'd come back to on a cold, lonely night. "Watch out. I can't see." He smashed his hand through the shattered glass. The car tilted crazily as he hit the curb, but he corrected it before he flipped it.

For two heartbeats, three, they drove in peace, or at least without gunshots from madwomen.

"We made it." Ann laughed, and it sounded just a little hysterical as he turned onto Orange Avenue.

"Thanks to you," he said. "You saved me from the predator. Thank you."

"I—"

A third bullet burst through the rear windshield, exploding glass through the car like confetti. He took the next left, glancing out his rearview mirror as his tires squealed.

The bitch stood in the middle of the road with the handgun pointed right at them. Her legs were spread, and he saw no expression on her face. Any employee or hotel patron could see her doing her Trinity imitation. She didn't seem to care. The gate he'd driven through hung crookedly behind her, and he picked up the phone to call HQ.

"Jesus Christ," Ann said before he could press a button. She sucked in a breath, and he looked at her.

Her fingers were wrapped around her shoulder, and crimson blood seeped between them, staining the lines of her knuckles bright red.

"You're hit." The shock of it sent the blood from his face. For a heartbeat he felt numb, like his limbs weren't connected to his body, like his lips belonged to someone else.

He was supposed to protect her.

And she was shot.

"You're hit," he said again.

She gave a strangled laugh. "So are you." She pointed to his left leg. "Detective."

"But I'm—" His wound was already healing, he wanted to say, but the long honk of a passing car grabbed his attention. He'd crossed the centerline.

"It helps to drive on the right side of the road."

"I'm taking you to the hospital."

"Don't be absurd." She gave that strangled laugh again, and topped it off with a crooked smile. "I need someplace private. I can take care of both of us. At least she didn't shoot me in my head."

"I'm taking you to the hospital," he said again. She couldn't die, not on his watch.

"And what do you think they'll say when I turn into a unicorn on the operating table?"

She had a point. He looked at the street around them, the Starbucks and restaurants and boutiques. Nowhere would a unicorn have privacy around here. Then Chiron realized what he had to do. "I know where we can go. Just hang on a minute, okay?"

He glanced at her, but she didn't answer. Instead, she leaned her head against the black headrest, her face pale, too pale. So much blood had seeped from her wound that she sat in a crimson puddle of it.

He stepped on the gas and tore onto the highway. "You're not going to change form in the car, are you?" he asked, trying to tease her.

"I'll . . . try my best . . . to avoid it."

He needed to get her home. Now.

Her unicorn self screamed to take form. The wound was killing her. Lead was seeping into her veins while blood poured out. Her body wanted to push out the bullet and knit muscle and flesh together. Her true self fought for release.

She couldn't let it happened.

The green tendrils of her magic coiled from her heart down to her ankles, twining through her belly and between her thighs. Desire and pain wrapped around each other, hardening her nipples and leaving her gasping for breath.

With her mind, she jerked the healing tendrils back. There was no place for them here. If she let them start healing as a triage, Chiron would have a full-sized horse in his car. The damage was too invasive to keep her healing power at bay.

She tried to look out the window, tried to find something on which to concentrate besides the pain. But the landscape moved too fast to distract her, especially with the wind whipping in her face through the missing windshield. Everything seemed too far away, too blurry.

She focused on something closer. The black steering wheel. The leather texture of it. His fingers.

Ah, his fingers.

The thick strength of his hands, the curve of his thumb mesmerized her. He looked so powerful. Competent. That hand could shoot a gun and wield a longbow—if the timeless artwork on vases and in marble were to be believed.

That hand could hold a woman's. It had held hers, pulled her across the parking lot to the safety of his car. The supposed safety. It had snapped handcuffs around Daniel and kept him and his venom away from her lecture.

Coppery hairs rippled lightly over the golden skin of his wrists and hands as the wind whipped through the car. The California sunlight made the copper glow.

Copper. She mulled the word over in her mind. Copper. The copper scent of blood filled the car. Kai—no, Chiron—had copper hair. If he were a horse, he'd be a sorrel, a chestnut. Like Affirmed. Or Secretariat. He'd have hooves.

Could he run as fast as she could? In centaur form his chest looked like one of those Renaissance paintings. She could almost hear the pounding of his hoofbeats. Or was that her heartbeat? Or were her horses nearby? She could almost smell the clean, mountain air.

Her mind was wandering, she knew, loping in a delirious freeform path. But she let it gallop, encouraged it.

Because it put off sleep.

She just wanted to sleep. Just rest her head on a feather pillow and drift away under a blanket of down. But if she slept, she'd lose control.

Green tendrils wrapped around her ankles. At least she thought they did. She jerked them back into her heart where they belonged.

"Can you . . . ?" She looked at the centaur. She hadn't realized centaurs were shape-shifters. His strong jaw—covered in rough reddish bristles—distracted her. She wanted to touch it. She wanted to savor the roughness, but when she reached out, she discovered her hand wouldn't obey. "Can you . . . ?"

"Can I what?"

"Hurry?"

He nodded. That strong jaw nodded. Of course the sun glinted off his stubble. Of course, it was coppery.

"Why don't you have . . . an accent? You don't sound . . . Greek."

"Greek wasn't my mother tongue. The language I spoke as a child no longer exists."

"You don't . . . sound old."

He laughed. Did he understand she needed distraction? "I work hard at perfecting a neutral accent, getting grammar just right. When I get slang right, it lights up my brain."

"We have much . . . farther to go?"

"We're very close," he said. But if that were true, why did his voice sound so far away?

I heard a fly buzz when I died, her mind said. Or was it the wind whipping through the missing windshield?

The stillness round my form
was like the stillness in the air between the heaves of storm.

She hated Emily Dickinson. All her poems were dark and
brooding. A fly? Why hadn't the woman listened to a mocking-
bird or something? Why not listen to the halftime band as she
died rather than a goddamned fly?

Fly. Fly.

Chiron drove like a man possessed. He flew. But the stillness
around her, that remained . . .

Ann, she heard. *Anemone. Answer me.*

The fly buzzed.

She could rest. Let Chiron watch for a while.

Ann! Answer me right now.

She heard a fly buzz when she died. When she died. Healing
wisps floated through her blood, stemming some of the flow.
But not all of it. Not enough of it.

Ann.

Not a fly. Her mother. She paused, letting her mother's voice
float through her like fat snowflakes on the winter solstice.

"Ann?" Chiron touched her knee. "Are you okay?" His
gray-green eyes turned her way, and she thought she could get
lost in their beauty. Jade. Beach glass. Swirls of smoky agate.
She could lose her way in their depths. But he turned away,
worry etched in the lines beneath his eyes. "We're almost
there."

"I'm . . . fine." And she was. At least in a way. She couldn't
feel the pain. It couldn't touch her, not while she rode in this
fast car. Not while her mother spoke, caressed her with her
voice. "My mother's here with me."

"Your mother?" His eyebrows were furrowed with concern. "Is she safe?"

Ann mulled the question over, inspecting it from various angles. Why wouldn't her mother be okay? Why wouldn't she be safe? She sang lullabies. Lullabies weren't dangerous.

And then she remembered. Her mother. She'd been about to break into a lab. Brode. And Ann wasn't supposed to look for her.

Mom? she said. *Are you okay? Where are you?*

I'm fine. Don't try to find me—you gave me your word.

I . . . won't.

Why are you quoting that wretched Emily Dickinson poem? Her mother's words sounded angry. *What's happening to you?* Not anger, Ann realized. Relief.

I got them.

What?

The vials. Speaking was so much work. She wanted to sleep. Just a little nap. *I took one from a woman . . . Meena. I . . .* But Ann lost her place for a minute. She, what? *I don't think she knows I have it. I took it from her back . . . pocket. But it's made to work on men . . . or at least one particular man.*

That's great! Thank God. I can rest now. But her mother paused for a heartbeat. *Ann? Ann, why do you sound so weak?*

Someone—Meena, the woman predator—shot me. The tang of blood seemed thicker in the car all of a sudden. She wished she could shield her face from the roaring wind, but her hands seemed so far away. Did they belong to her body anymore? She couldn't remember. The best she could do was close her eyes.

Did she capture you? Her mom's voice sounded like a rock, and Ann held back tears, tears she hadn't felt coming until this very instant. How'd she lived all these years without her mom?

Capture . . . me?

Are you free?

No one captured me. I'm with— She looked at her savior, but of course, she'd saved him, too. *I'm with a friend, a centaur. Chiron. He's . . . lovely.*

Ann, there are no centaurs. Stay focused! With what did they shoot you?

A gun.

With bullets or tranquilizers? Her mother was exasperated now. Ann remembered. That's how her mom dealt with worry. She became angry.

Bullets—

Then heal yourself!

I'm in a car. He'll help me, Mom. He's taking me . . . someplace safe.

Don't trust anyone, Ann. Not even for a minute. Humans will sell you out. To a circus or a research institute or the news media or the highest bidder. Don't trust them.

The implication swirled around her brain for a minute, taking its time in forming. But then it did. *Did they capture you? Have the predators got you?*

Her mother didn't answer for a moment. Then she said, *Yes,* in a voice so quiet Ann might not have heard it. She heard a fly buzz. *Don't try to find me. I can still destroy them. I can still destroy the hold they have over us.*

The scent of blood was getting thicker, so thick. Then the car turned hard. Ann swayed and found she didn't have the strength to fight the inertia. Her cheek landed against Chiron's arm, and she gasped at her weakness. Forget the predator. Chiron smelled like heaven.

And then her shoulder hit his.

Pain flared through her like rockets through Florida skies. The purple stars glittering behind her eyes shimmered and popped.

Get help now, Ann. You need to heal yourself.

I will.

Ann? I have to ask this.

What?

Did you make a woman younger? I won't be angry if you did, but I need to know if the rumors are true.

I—

But a terrible shriek filled Ann's head. It was her mother's shriek. Something terrible had happened to her.

Mom?

No answer.

Mom!

But Ann knew her mother had lost her ability to speak with her. Had she been killed? Or maybe Ann had lost so much blood that she couldn't keep the mindlink working.

"Chiron," she said, cracking her eyes open.

"I'm here."

"They caught my mother. I think they just shot her."

"Shh." He touched her knee gently. "We'll deal with that problem next. First we need to take care of you."

Take care of her. That sounded good.

"Chiron?"

"I'm still here."

"I'm about to pass out. And then . . . you'll have to use the Jaws of Life to get me out of your car."

"We're here." The car halted. He leaned out his window, and pressed some button on a keypad. She looked through the missing windshield and gasped. Why had he taken her here?

A huge cream-colored mansion loomed before them. A winding staircase led to a huge carved oak door. A few lights were on, and she could see the place was gigantic. It must belong to a Hollywood mogul.

What was he thinking? Her mother's words still rang in her mind. Don't trust anyone.

She panicked. Had she escaped Daniel, who wanted her for a science experiment, and the predator, who wanted her for God knew what, just to land here, in the movies?

"I can't change here," she said, fighting the need. Her inner unicorn screamed for release as her blood poured down her back. Her magic tried to tear itself from her grasp as she spoke.

"You have privacy." As he drove around the front bend, past acres of grassland, he put his hand on her knee, grounding her.

"I'm not some sideshow freak." She felt blood trickle from her shoulder as her foot changed into a hoof. "I won't be in your film. Or your circus. Or whatever you have in mind. I won't talk to the news cameras."

"Ann." He said her name slowly, like a Sunday morning caress. "I'm not sure what you're talking about."

"I can't change here."

"You're safe here. It's my home, my house. *I* change here."

"Right." She thought of what he must make on a cop's salary. Not even Daniel Hallock would have been able to afford this. "Detective."

"I've had millennia to save and earn money, Ann. You can relax. No one can get in."

Ann breathed and let her fear float away.

Her mother might have been right about humans, but she didn't know Chiron. She didn't know anyone like him. Ann realized she trusted him with her heart—and her life.

Which was a good thing, because by the time he drove up the hill toward the garage, her hands were hooves, too. Gentle green mist shimmered through the car. She leaned her head against the headrest and gave in.

She couldn't fight anymore.

15

Chiron slammed the car into park and hit the button that closed the garage door and set the alarm. But before he could open Ann's car door, she began to transform into a unicorn. Her hands and feet had changed into white hooves. Her disheveled hair was giving way to a mane as he watched, and her magic filled his car with crackling ozone and an eerie emerald mist.

In that heartbeat, he remembered where he'd seen her kind of magic before: the Earthmother. He opened Ann's car door, trying to home in on the memory. The goddess had created a mist like this once. Her ethereal vapor had coalesced and enveloped him like a blanket, and then the Earthmother had changed the mist into fingers, delighting his flesh with them.

Akantha had been there too, but now wasn't the time for those memories. He had to help Ann. Now. If she changed into a horse in the car . . .

Ignoring his bloody thigh and the gaping hole there, he put his arms around Ann's still-human waist and behind her still-human knees. The soft hair of her tail pressed against his forearm, and her mane brushed his cheek.

He started to lift her, but a small moan of pain escaped her lips.

"I'm sorry, love," he said, but he didn't think she heard him. Her eyes were rolled back in her head, and her neck looked as limp as yesterday's flowers.

But when he lifted her again, sliding his hand over her ass and around her waist, she moaned again, louder and more piteous than previously. For a heartbeat, he hated himself for the hurt he knew he was causing, but there was no hope for it. He had to get her out of here.

"The vial." Her words were a whimper.

"Come on, love. Let's get you someplace comfortable." Like his bed.

"The vial."

"What vial?"

"In my back pocket. I can't lose it."

"I won't lose it, love. I promise."

"Or my backpack. It has the second one."

"I won't lose any of your things, love."

"Don't . . . My mother . . ." Her eyes didn't open as she mumbled the words.

"Tell her you're in good hands."

She didn't answer. Instead she rested her head against his chest, her blond hair pouring over his arm. "You're safe," he whispered to her.

He hoped that was true. Neither of them was in any shape to outrun, outthink, or outfight their enemies.

In his arms, she'd lost consciousness again, and he carried her through the door and up the massive staircase. No one alive knew this house belonged to him, and no one alive had ever seen him in it. He'd brought Ann here to the only place he himself felt safe enough to change between man and centaur form.

And as he carried her up the stairs, he couldn't help himself. He brought his face close to hers, close enough to kiss her forehead. Instead of brushing his lips against her soft skin, he breathed in the scent, savoring the ozone buzz of her magic, and the sweetness of her own perfume.

She should have smelled like blood and fear, but she didn't. Instead, the warm fragrance of desire pulsed around her like a living thing.

Like every man alive, he knew lust when he smelled it, and the buttery scent of her warm desire wrapped around his cock, caressing him as surely as if she'd used her hand. Or her mouth.

"I need . . . space." Her voice was a whisper now.

"Shh. I know." He carried her to his huge bed and set her there, gently cradling her head in a pillow. He knew about space. His centaur form was none too small. "You have space here—and privacy." And she was the only woman he'd ever known whose need for space would have matched his own.

Even as he set her on the most comfortable mattress invented in millennia of humanity, he hoped she really could heal herself—because he'd have a hard time explaining her horn to a vet or a doctor. There was no way in hell he'd sit back and do nothing while she died.

"Don't leave me," she said, touching his shirt, smearing it with her blood. "Not until I'm whole again."

"I'll be right here, by your side."

Within seconds all traces of her humanity were gone. No bare, golden skin of her forearms and neck. Silvery white hair slithered across her body as her legs turned into gaskins and stifles, as her arms morphed into horse forelegs. Her wrists gave way to dainty fetlocks, complete with small tufts of silvery hair.

Until she'd witnessed his own change, he'd never thought of his shift into centaur form as stunning, only something animalistic, something to be . . . not ignored, but trivialized. Akantha had had to overcome her own prejudices and the prejudices of her people before she could claim him as hers in the Mother Rite. And while his animal self had never disgusted her, she'd never celebrated it, either.

But this woman, she wouldn't be repulsed. Not by hooves or manes or tails. She wouldn't need to fight any prejudice against anything equine.

In that moment, her horn sprang from her forehead, bringing him back to the present with a gasp. Opalescent and long, it spiraled to a needle-sharp tip. It didn't look like an instrument of healing, although she'd told him it was. Lying against the sheets of his bed, it looked like a weapon—a dangerous and mighty weapon.

He sat back on one of the leather sofas in the room and straightened his injured leg. He stuck his finger through the hole in his pants made by the bullet, and clenching his teeth, he ripped the tough synthetic fabric of the track pants and exposed the wound. His own regenerative powers worked quicker when the wound had space and exposure to air.

He should have done this earlier, would have done it earlier if he hadn't been so distracted.

Deep in his thigh, his flesh pulsed like something from a horror movie. He was healing faster than he ever had in his life. Was it because of Ann?

He leaned back as the pain engulfed not just his thigh, but his calf and gut too. His brain throbbed behind his eyes. The healing process hurt like Earthshaker's balls. The magic seemed to tear him up before it put him back together.

Closing his eyes, he exhaled and sat back, wishing the processes of putting his body back together didn't hurt quite so much.

Her soft nicker pulled him out of his funk. She still lay on the mattress, but she wasn't prostrate. Her legs were tucked neatly beneath her, and her luxurious mane floated down her neck. Her eyes, dark as the night sky now, met his, and her velvet nostrils flared.

"Hey," he said. "Are you feeling better?"

In reply, she extended her legs from beneath her white barrel and rolled off the bed.

Which was probably a good thing since he didn't know if the mattress warranty covered holes from horse hooves or unicorn horns.

"That's great." He stood—and swooned. His leg wasn't mended yet. Sometimes the healing was like this. He didn't feel the injury, could completely ignore it, until his immortality kicked in. Then he paid the price. The longer he'd ignored physical damage, the more painful the healing process hurt.

She snorted now, and he read equine annoyance. He felt like shit, and she could see it. She thought he was being stupid. She was probably right.

"I'm fine," he said.

Again, she snorted.

"Maybe not one hundred percent." Looking down, he could see deep purple flesh pulsating against the bullet, trying to push it out. His magic would succeed—eventually. "But I'm fine."

She moved toward him, but he waved her away. "I can help things along," he said. "Hang on."

Gritting his teeth, he sat back down on the sofa. Even the act of sitting hurt. Taking a deep breath through clenched teeth, he pried the bullet out with his fingers, grabbing the slug with his fingernails.

The vortex of pain was not for young men, he thought as the ceiling swirled above him. He should have just been patient and let the Earthmother's gift do its thing. He shouldn't have been so damned heroic. Macho. The stiff-upper-lip thing had gone out of style more than one hundred years ago.

Covered in a sheen of cold sweat, he lay back on the sofa and focused on breathing.

She walked toward him, her hooves clattering against the hardwood. Deliberately, she brought her horn closer to his thigh, the razor-sharp tip a mere handspan from his groin.

"Be careful with that."

She snorted, her eyes narrowed with what he took to be exasperation.

"No, seriously. The last woman who held a weapon to me like that . . . well, let's just say things didn't end well for either of us."

She ignored his jest, and the same emerald swirls he'd seen enveloping her while she healed now looped from her horn. The thick vapor dripped like honey, slow, inexorable. Watching her now, he knew he had no reason to be nervous.

Still, when her horn touched his flesh, he gasped—not with pain but with surprise. He recognized this magic with certainty now. *The Earthmother.* Without a doubt, it was her enchanted touch. It was her warmth and sensuality.

As Ann's healing mist sank into his flesh and rushed through his blood, he felt like he'd just downed a single-malt highball. Satisfaction burned through him, leaving him . . . alive and happy and loose.

The Earthmother's touch had felt like that—exactly like that.

And then he realized something: the Earthmother must have left this gift to the unicorns. This healing magic could only have come from her. He couldn't mistake the flavor of the Earthmother's workings. Akantha would have loved this, and for a heartbeat he ached for her, longed to talk to her just one more time.

Another emerald swirl lazily wrapped itself around his thigh, distracting him. Endorphins crackled, sending out their delicious sense of well-being.

Dreamily, he looked at his leg. Through the hole in the borrowed pants he examined the wound—or the place where the wound had been. The bloody, pulpy mass had closed up completely. No ichor. No scar. Not a trace of it remained. He saw only skin, unscarred skin.

"Thank you," he said, looking up. But no unicorn stood before him now. A woman did. And he couldn't believe he'd ever thought her austere.

The desire burning in her eyes made him hotter than anything the Earthmother had ever envisioned.

At her most vulnerable, he had saved her. Knowing her darkest secret, seeing her at her worst, he had saved her. She was no longer an alien to be studied. With him, she wasn't an outsider.

Lust coursed through her veins and belly, around her breasts and over her wrists. She hoped he couldn't smell the desire pouring off her skin.

And if he did, she hoped he wouldn't judge her for it.

Controlling her need to change, healing herself, and healing him took so much energy. In her weakness, her mastery over her lust was hanging by a thread. Thank God he wasn't a predator or Daniel. Thank God he was exactly who he was—unlike any other person she'd met outside her family, he was worthy of her trust.

She took a deep breath and released it. He knew what she was and trusted her. He had trusted her with his deepest secret, and he'd asked for nothing.

"Come here," he said, but it wasn't a command. He held out his hands in invitation. He would have allowed her to refuse him.

She closed the distance between them, and her heart raced. His hands and mouth and cock would soothe her, slake the fire in her veins. She could give in to her need with someone who knew her, knew exactly what she was. That was a luxury she'd never experienced.

His eyes locked on hers as he touched her shoulder. The gray swirls within the green mesmerized her. She could lose herself in them. Her lips yearned to taste the sweetness of his eyelids. Her fingertips longed to follow the rugged line of his jaw, to drink in the solid muscles of his arms and shoulders.

He invaded her space, got too close with his hand on her shoulder, but she didn't move away. The heat of his palm burned through her T-shirt. She could let herself go, let herself enjoy the carnal pleasures of her kind. He would kiss her now.

But he didn't.

She remembered the sensation, the slide of his lips beneath hers in the parking garage. She had kissed him then to save him from Meena, but her passion hadn't been feigned. He'd shifted in front of her, trusting her with a secret he'd shared with no one in four thousand years. That did something to her.

She moved in toward him, inviting without pushing.

Instead of delighting her lips with his though, he gently turned her so he could inspect the wound on her shoulder. Her T-shirt, ruined from the bullet and stiff with blood, got in his way. Her jeans were soaked with blood.

"May I look?" he asked, tracing the collar of her shirt along the base of her neck. His touch sent a light shiver over her skin.

"If you wish."

As he moved the tattered shirt aside, cool air kissed her flesh, fanning the lust as it uncoiled in her belly. The chill traveled down her shirt and cooled the small of her back.

"You're completely whole again." His fingers traced the curve of her shoulder, sending a delicious shiver through her breasts.

"You're not surprised," she said. She took a breath and touched his thigh, felt the thick strength of it. But she kept her fingers gentle, not insistent. "Your leg is better."

"Yes." For a moment she saw indecision in his gaze. Would he take this further? Would he assuage her need? Could she finally share a moment of passion with a man who knew—and accepted—everything she was?

"Yes," he said again, and her heart leaped.

Except he moved away. "I think it's my turn to lend you some clothes. That shirt is ruined."

She fought to keep the disappointment from her voice. "It is."

"The bathroom is here, if you'd like a shower."

She followed him, desire making her knees feel like they belonged to someone else. Or maybe that was chagrin. He was pawning her off. Maybe their trust didn't extend to the bedroom.

He flipped on the lights of the huge room and walked over to the oversized shower. He turned a knob and water poured out of a nozzle.

"I'm guessing you like it hot," he said with a wicked grin.

She let her eyes travel down the length of him. "Yes."

"You're never going to be able to get all that blood off your back by yourself. Would you like some help?"

A better man wouldn't take advantage of her, he realized as he left her alone for a minute. She had enemies nipping at her heels. *They* had enemies, he corrected himself. Together, they would smite them.

But right now, he was going to fuck her like tomorrow's sun would never rise.

He was a jerk.

He opened the door.

"Chiron?" The way her voice slid over the syllables of his name went right to his cock.

"I'm here." He could back out now, be the civilized gentleman for which history celebrated him. But he didn't leave. He stepped into the room, inhaled her luscious scent. "If you want me."

"I really would enjoy your . . . help."

And that did it. He shed his clothing, his cock erect.

Through the thick steam he saw her. And if he'd found some mythical creature in some goddess-blessed glade, he couldn't have been more awed than he was right now.

Water sluiced over her, running off her shoulders and over her ass. Her hair, freed of that chignon, hung past her shoulders. Water gave the deep blond color an otherworldly sheen.

"Ann." He could think of no other words. What words could convey his appreciation of her beauty?

She turned and smiled at him, not embarrassed and not brash. Water streamed over her breasts, pouring off the tips of her erect nipples.

Myron or Polyclitus could have sculpted her in marble or bronze and done justice to her beauty. But Phidias couldn't have. He'd never have caught the sensuality in her expression. In his hands, a sculpture of her would've looked like a whore or a child.

"You're right," she said, her voice thick. "I can't reach my back." She handed him the sponge and poured some body wash onto it. Even the woody scent of cedar couldn't mask the perfume of her desire.

With an efficient movement she shifted her hair off her back, letting it drape over her breast. Hot drops of water splattered him, and his cock throbbed so hard it ached.

The curve of her ass begged to be savored, especially when she put her hands on the wall and stood with her legs spread, bracing herself.

"Please," she said, nodding to the sponge in his hand. "Scrub hard."

Her sex glistened, and not only from the sluicing water. He was not taking advantage of her. He would not hurt her. She wanted this.

And by Earthshaker's Balls, he did too.

With the first swipe of the sponge the last vestiges of blood left her back, but he didn't stop. Her shoulders, her neck, the small of her back, and her ass: he washed them all, covering every inch of her skin, admiring the golden sheen of it.

He also enjoyed the way she hummed in pleasure as he touched her.

"My thighs?" she asked, looking over her shoulder at him with a gleam in her eye. She was almost laughing. "Would you mind getting them too, especially the backs?"

He knew she laughed because he couldn't resist, because he was clay in her hands. Still, he rubbed the sponge over her thighs. Never had more perfect thighs been made, either by nature or in art. But maybe he hadn't watched enough porn.

No, he realized as his fingers lathered the soap from her knees to her hips, no porn star could have better thighs than this woman.

As he reached down, his cock pressed against her ass, slid over her sex. And she didn't move away. Instead she stepped back and impaled herself on him.

For a heartbeat, the pleasure was so intense he couldn't move, not even to breathe. But then she balanced high on her toes, and the length of his cock slid through her slick heat. Before the tip of his cock could slide out of her, she rocked back, and this time, he groaned, bending his knees a little to bury himself completely into her.

She took one of his hands from her hips and put it on her soapy breast. As his fingers slid over her nipple, around the perfectly formed globe, she rocked back.

"I'm going to . . ." she started to say, but he stopped her, pulling out and turning her around.

"Not yet." He saw her lips begin to move, no doubt to complain, so he kissed her. He touched her top lip with his tongue, then eased across her bottom lip. She gasped and shivered but didn't move away.

"Don't stop." Her voice was thick with desire.

Water poured over his shoulders, across his stomach. He pressed his lips fully against hers, let the smooth warmth of the shower steam slide between them.

She returned his kiss, and her lips didn't disappoint. They were hot and skillful, and . . . tender. He hadn't expected that.

He withdrew for a moment, just long enough to look at her face. Her eyelids were half closed with desire. He took her lips again, harder and more possessively this time, and she moaned, pressing her slick breasts against his chest. His erection slid over her, and she pressed against it, the scent of her lust threaded through the steam.

He touched her mouth with his tongue, teasing and questing. Her hands slid over his chest and rested on his hips like she owned him. Skilled fingers twined through his wet pubic hair then wrapped around his cock, stroking and caressing.

But no way would he let her make him come too soon.

Nipping her neck, he took her wrists in his hand and held her arms above her head. Hot water ran over her breasts and the flat of her stomach. She was completely at his mercy.

He brought his face to her breast, keeping her hands trapped above her. He captured a tight nipple between his teeth and softly bit. He circled with flicks, then slowed, swirling his tongue over the bud. She arched her back in pleasure.

His cock pressed against her thigh, and she shifted her weight so that her wet heat met his. When she slid him inside her, he wondered who was at whose mercy. He'd swear he was at hers.

Dropping her hands, he met her thrusts with a hunger of his own.

"Yes," she moaned, pushing herself toward him. He grabbed her hips and pulled her to him. He thrust his hips upward in an invitation that she accepted. Pressed against the tiled wall, she wrapped one leg around his hip so that he had no choice but to thrust deeper.

Gasping, he couldn't look away from her face. Her eyelids were sleepy with lust, but her jaw was tight in her effort to control herself. He forced himself to keep his strokes short, sliding over her clit with each push.

"I need you to . . . !" she cried as she thrust herself up.

And he was right there with her. He thrust down one more fulfilling drive and let the orgasm sizzle across his nerves in a delicious explosion.

16

"Don't tell me you cook, too." The smell of simmering olive oil and something lemony wafted through the kitchen.

He looked up from the stove and gave her that wicked grin, the one that left her quivering. "Too?"

He was fishing? Cute. "Seems like if you've been alive as long as you said you were, a man like you would've accumulated enough compliments." She wrapped the silk robe he'd left for her more tightly around herself as she walked all the way into the kitchen.

"Not from you." He had a pair of jeans that fit his ass perfectly, and the way his thin cotton T-shirt clung to the muscles of his back made her mouth water more than dinner did. She was glad the aphrodisiac effect of her shape-shifting had died back, or she'd be jumping him right now.

"I'll try to work on that," she teased. She knew the difference between love and lust, and just because they'd been thrust together—*some thrusting*, the snide part of her brain said— against a mutual enemy, that didn't mean she was in love.

The possibility was there though. In this world filled with

violent, needy humans, she and Chiron together found a way to belong. They didn't need to lie or hide from each other—and that was the basis for a solid relationship. Ann suspected this could grow into love.

Catching herself, she snorted at the thought, but at least sleeping with this guy hadn't made her feel slimy and used, which was more than she could say for Erik Sutherland. Oh hell, it was more than she could say for Daniel Hallock.

"Can I start by flattering you about dinner? It smells great."

"You hungry?" Chiron took two plates from the cabinet.

"Yes. Very." He placed sautéed chicken breasts on the plates and set one in front of her. Tiny green capers and artichoke hearts teased her. "This looks fantastic. How long have I been asleep?"

"It's about five."

"Five!" She laughed. "Guess we missed the tour of the Brode Institute. What about your boss? Wasn't he expecting us?"

"He agreed that I escort you home as soon as you're up to it."

Wrapping the robe's thin belt tighter around her waist, she didn't say anything.

"We can call airlines after dinner, okay?"

"I don't think so."

"What?" Chiron took out two wineglasses. The cut-glass edges glittered in the evening light as it poured through the oversized window. "We need to keep you safe."

She knew where she was safe—by his side. Ann took a deep breath and marshaled her thoughts. "Erik Sutherland steals a DNA sample from you, and an hour later his girlfriend shoots you and my mother is taken captive." She paused. "Humans have a bounty on me, and they're making a pheromone that lures unicorns and centaurs to their death."

"Or at least captivity."

"I won't be safe in North Carolina," she said. "Not until we stop them."

He looked at her a moment, his coppery lashes gorgeous against his angular cheek, and she wished she could just lean over the table and kiss him. Chiron touched her arm as if seconding that thought. "Agreed. Which is why I quit my job on the force."

"What?"

"I knew you'd want to hunt down the predators with me, and there was no way anyone on the SDPD would understand that."

"When did you resign?"

"While you slept. I need to focus on this case, and I can't do that with my hands tied. I also washed your clothes—"

"The vial! It was in my back pocket."

"It's in your backpack."

She breathed. She could trust him. "Let's leave all scary conversation until after dinner, shall we?"

He clinked her glass.

"So." She looked around the spacious room, admiring the ocean view from the huge window. "What does an ancient centaur fancy for a topic of dinner conversation?"

He gave her that grin, the one that made her mouth water. "Why don't you tell me how good the chicken is?"

"More compliments?" The chicken *was* delicious. Tender and tangy with little bursts of citrusy explosions. "This might be a topic where a picture is better than a thousand words." She pointed to her nearly empty plate.

"And hors d'oeuvres?"

She laughed. There'd been no hors d'oeuvres, not the kind people serve on tables. "Delicious," she said, meaning it. "The ultimate hors d'oeuvre whets the appetite, and yours did that."

"So that only whetted your appetite?" His gray-green eyes met hers across the table. "I think we can do better than that. I think I can come up with something much more . . ." He gave her that look. "Satisfying."

"I'm glad to hear it." She raised her eyebrows and gave him a challenging expression. Exhilaration raced through her, both from the promise of his bed and from the freedom to talk about it. "You have something in mind for dessert?"

"The possibilities are endless."

"You look like a man who might enjoy . . ." She ran the tip of her tongue over her bottom lip—and was gratified to see his eyes follow the movement. "A tart. A cherry tart."

He laughed, but he shook his head.

She gave him a flirtatious glance from between her lashes. "No tarts for you?"

"You're not exactly wrong," he said, toying with the stem of his wineglass. "Few men will refuse a hot cherry tart set temptingly on his plate."

"Or a slice of cherry pie," she added, looking at him from under her lashes.

"Or a hot piece of pie."

"I hear an invisible 'but' at the end of that sentence." No one-night stands for Chiron the centaur? That surprised her. Weren't centaurs supposed to be raunchy and rowdy?

"Sometimes he might want a dessert that sticks a little more to his ribs."

Was that an invitation to a more serious relationship?

She realized the idea didn't scare her. When had she ever felt more accepted, more trusted? Together they could stop the predators.

She stood and walked over to him, letting her heavy desire sink to her hips and heat her belly. Standing behind him, she reached down and caressed his torso through the thin T-shirt. "You want something to stick to these ribs?"

Wordlessly, he set his fork down.

She skimmed her palms over his chest, feeling the heat rising through the thin cotton, before she went back to his sides. The ropy cords of his muscles invited her lips and tongue, but she kept her fingers at his sides, traveling higher under his arms. "These ribs?" she asked, letting the sultry heaviness of her mood permeate her voice.

"Yes."

"Oh." She dragged out the syllable, tracing his sides down to his hips and then back up. Then she tickled him hard, digging her fingertips into his tender sides. He jumped, and then he yelped.

"You—" He leaped from his chair, and she giggled but took two cautious steps back. "You vixen."

"I think you need to update your vocabulary, centaur. No one's used the word 'vixen' since King George."

"You tickle me? And then you mock?"

I wouldn't mock a man as old as you. I was taught to respect my elders."

He moved toward her, his shoulders menacing but his eyes laughing. If he took another step closer, he'd catch her. To her left stood the kitchen table, but to her right, nothing was in her way.

She sprinted left, in the unexpected direction, and she was fast.

He was faster. He caught her in a heartbeat and wrapped his arms around her waist.

"Now what were you saying about ribs?" he asked, running his fingers over her sides. He didn't press hard, but the promise of the torment made her catch her breath.

"Ribs?" she asked, pressing her ass into his cock. Anything to avoid clever fingers on a tickling mission. "I thought we were talking about dessert. Hot tarts?" She pressed her ass against him harder.

"Homemade apple pie."

"Nothing that wholesome." But before she could come up

with a smartass reply, his teeth were gently tracing the line of her neck. His hands were firmly on her hips like she belonged to him.

Maybe she didn't need to escape his embrace. She lolled her head back on his shoulders, and he nibbled her ear, sending goose bumps down to her knees.

"That tickles." She held up an arm. "Look what you've done to me."

"That's not all I'm going to do." His hands, slow and inexorable, left her hips, following the curve of her waist. As she leaned against him, the edge of his thumbs caressed the sides of her breasts so lightly she might have imagined it.

Except she hadn't. Because warm fingers traced the length of her neck and gently convinced the silk of her robe to slide open. The texture of the warm fabric gliding over her breasts hardened her nipples and released the lust that'd been slowly curling through her belly.

He skated one hand down to her stomach, spreading his palm over the flat expanse of it. The knuckles of his other hand caressed the edge of her areola.

Her nipples hardened to little knots. She had never been more aware of the short distance between a man's fingers and her clit. She wanted him badly. She felt as hot as if she'd just shifted between forms or scented a predator, but her desire for him didn't stem from that. This was natural.

She tilted her head away from his face so that his lips and teeth and tongue would be tempted to travel lower.

"Do you want me?" he asked.

This was like asking if she liked his dinner. Actions were speaking louder than words. She shifted her weight and tilted her hips, inviting his fingers to discover the answer to their own question.

And his did. His fingers looped through her pubic hair, and then the tip of his thumb dipped lower. He slid over the wet length of her, and she realized her own hands felt empty. Her fingers found his thigh, and then his zipper.

"Do you want me?" he asked again.

"Yes." The way his fingers skimmed over her clit made it hard for her to breathe. "How can you—" She gasped as he slid inside. "How can you doubt it?"

"I don't doubt your desire." He pulled her more tightly against him, making it hard for her to unzip his jeans. "Still I wonder . . ." His fingertips pebbled her nipple as he caressed her breast.

"Wonder what?" She thrust against the fingers inside her, knowing the orgasm was coming, and it was coming hard.

"Is this natural, or is this lust the byproduct of your shapeshifting?"

"I haven't shifted in hours." The length of his cock pressed hard against her ass, so she wrapped her fingers around him, ignoring the jeans as she tightened her fingers. "This is natural."

The words must have affected him because he moaned as his fingers plumbed her. The pleasure of the orgasm ripping through her made her buck her hips against his hand. The shiver of delight lasted forever, and all she could do was quiver in his arms and feel grateful for the support.

When the storm died back, he placed tiny kisses behind her ear and across the top of her shoulders. Each one felt like a gift, like something delightful to be savored, like a truffle or a morsel of caviar. "You honor me."

"Is that what you call it?" she teased.

"I am serious. I feel honored that you desire me so."

She looked at him, realizing he sounded archaic for the first time since she'd met him. "Desiring you isn't difficult, Chiron. You're gorgeous." She swallowed, daring to say the words aloud. "And you trust me."

He held up his hand. "Let me correct myself. I feel honored that you desire me, in spite of my animal nature."

"Animal nature?" She laughed. He was the only person she'd met who didn't want to study her or trap her, or hell, even put her on the front of the *National Enquirer* with the aliens from Roswell. "At least you keep your face when you change forms," she said. "I'd be the last one to criticize an animal nature."

"Still, you honor me."

She didn't know how to reply when someone said, "You honor me." Was "you're welcome" the right response?

"You have earned that honor," she said. "Since the predators ruined my life fifteen years ago, I've haven't trusted anyone—no one's deserved it." She leaned against his shoulder. "I'm beginning to think things have changed." She took his hand in hers, marveling at its beauty and strength. "We can stop the predators together."

He scooped her up as if she weighed nothing and carried her into a room too cozy to belong in a mansion. "To stop them, we need to understand them, figure out what they want and why."

He set her on a huge deep navy couch. It sunk beneath her, cocooning her. She pretended that curling up on a rich man's—centaur's—couch was a very normal thing to do.

He went to a side table made of dark cherry, poured two glasses of cognac, and handed one to her. "We need to put our heads together."

"Yes," she said.

"How about if I ask some questions?"

"As you wish, detective."

"Meena used a pheromone on me?"

"Yes, and on me, but it wasn't so strong."

He flashed her that wicked grin, the one that grabbed her heart and twisted—the one that coiled through her belly despite the fact that the delicious postorgasm haze hadn't completely dissipated. "You broke through her hold pretty easily," he said.

"Easily?" She pretended to be affronted. "I gave that kiss everything I've got."

"Which kiss? The one you bestowed on her—or on me? Both were hot."

She sunk back into the feather cushion behind her, amused with his delight. "I have news for you, centaur." She pretended to be annoyed. "No one uses 'bestowed' anymore."

"Not even in conjunction with 'hot'?" He shrugged. "What a shame. When I think of the kisses I could bestow on your hot . . ." He leaned toward her thighs.

She threw a pillow at him.

"Think of what I could bestow while I tied your hands."

"Stop!" she said, laughing. "We need to figure this out. How can I think when you're doing this to me?"

That grin, the one that lit his eyes. "I have to turn in my handcuffs. You'll probably be safe then."

She smiled as she took a sip of the velvety cognac. The idea of cuffing him to a bedpost and giving herself free rein over his gorgeous body wasn't without its attractions. "I don't know." She eyed the muscles on his arms. "You look kind of dangerous."

"I thought we were supposed to be serious now."

"We are." She struggled to erase all signs of play from her face. "Now tell me, why did you quit the force? Couldn't they have helped us?"

"Help us?" His brow was furrowed in doubt. "Humanity doesn't help our kind, and I'm sure I'm—we're—going to uncover things we don't want to explain. They'll hunt us down."

She knew the truth: humans were vicious. "After the predators killed a bunch of us," she said, "our neighbors hunted us down. They'd been our close friends for years."

"And Akantha and all the centaurs of the past and the—"

"Aliens at Roswell."

"Were those real?"

She laughed, but she sounded sad, even to herself. All the hiding and lying exhausted her. What she wouldn't give to just live her life as herself. Change when she wanted. Live as she wanted.

That world didn't exist though. At least she had him. At least she had him for now. In their small cocoon, she could be true to her heart.

"Tell me about Akantha. What happened to her, exactly?"

"I don't know. Someone killed her, and Sutherland was the last person with her. We spoke," he tapped his head to indicate the mindlink, "and she was scared and hurt, on the same beach where Daniel proposed to you. She couldn't articulate what was happening to her or who was doing it. And then . . ." he paused and swallowed. "Nothing."

"Which suggests she's dead."

"It does."

"But who can kill an immortal centaur?"

"She wasn't a centaur," Chiron said. "She was human before the Earthmother blessed us with immortality."

"Still. She was immortal. Who can kill an immortal?"

"That's the question, isn't it? That, and why."

"Was she happy?" she asked. "I mean, before she disappeared."

Chiron didn't answer at first, perhaps asking himself the question for the first time. Finally, he said, "Who can truly tell if another is happy?"

"That's such a male answer. You can tell."

Again Chiron paused. "I think perhaps living for four thousand years can make a heart jaded."

"In what way?"

"She was always seeking new thrills. New ways to risk her life—which was simply never at risk."

"You mean like skydiving? Bull riding?"

He laughed. "She came from a culture of bull riders. She'd have found no thrill there."

Ann sighed. "You know what I mean."

He nodded. "Yes." He toyed with his glass a minute.

"Look, if you feel you're betraying her, I understand, but we have to know what's going on."

He met her gaze, and she saw guilt. "For the last two or three hundred years Akantha was looking for a new thrill. She slept with rock stars, politicians, and kings. She starred in porn flicks and tried every new drug that came her way. She drove race cars and rode fast horses." He looked at her then, and she saw only sorrow. "But she always came back to me. Sometimes I joined her. We had fun, a lot of fun. Once, we ran against each other in the Grand National, her on a bay mount and me on a dun." He laughed. "She won—but not easily."

"You sound . . . disappointed."

"Not in her. Never in her. I should have stayed by her side. I could have saved her."

"Chiron." She touched his arm. "I don't think she wanted you to. You can't protect someone who doesn't want protection."

"I could have saved her."

"I've seen you take a bullet in your thigh, your *profunda femoris,* to be exact. That artery wasn't nicked—it'd been severed. If she could do what you just did . . ." She shrugged. "She didn't need protection."

"I don't see how this helps us." From the stubborn set of his jaw, she could tell he was finished with the topic.

She wasn't finished though, and she was tired of playing by everyone else's rules, bowing to everyone else's sense of propriety.

"The way she was acting makes me think the predators hadn't blindsided her." Ann forced Chiron to hear her words, staring

at his face and refusing to cut him any slack. "They had something she wanted. What was it?"

Chiron froze. She could almost see his mind racing.

"What did Akantha want more than anything else? Was it a
new drug?" she asked. "A night with the predator, maybe?
Maybe they made a pheromone just for her like they made one
for you."

He shook his head, his hair almost black in the dim evening
light. "She would have fucked him without the pheromone,"
Chiron said. "She always liked sex."

"Then what? What happened to her?"

"What if they told her they'd bring immortality to all of humanity?"

Ann blinked. "I thought she was bored with immortality.
Would she want to foist it on everyone else?"

"She thought it would bring an end to a lot of humanity's issues. If no one could die, wars would end. With no death and
disease, people would have more joy. They'd have time to consider the long-term effects of their actions, and they'd take better care of the world."

If Chiron were right . . . She paused as pieces fell into place.
"They're after immortality," she said, trying the words out for
size. "The predators are after immortality."

"Yes. Consider the evidence." He put his empty cognac glass
onto the table between them. "First, Akantha. Sutherland, who's
associated with the Brode Institute—self-proclaimed mecca of
longevity and genetics studies—seduced and stole her."

"Okay."

"Point two. He seemed to be doing the same thing to you."

"And he sabotaged my job, tried to get me to run to my
mother, I think."

"That might be important." He held up a third finger. "Point
three. He stole my DNA and I'm immortal."

"But you?" Chiron's gaze met hers. "You're not immortal. Why do they want you?"

Before Ann could answer, she heard faint notes of the William Tell Overture. "My phone." She stood. "Where is it?"

"Bedroom." He pointed out the hall and toward the left.

"Only one person has the number for it," she said as she sprinted.

"Who? Daniel Hallock?" He followed her.

"No. Carl Stoller. From Harvard." She bolted into the room and dove toward her bag. "We were supposed to go to the party tonight, but he called me a slut and told me I'd never get the job, so I doubt he wants to dance."

"Brode's part of Harvard. Maybe Stoller's another piece of this puzzle."

She pulled out the phone, wanting to object. The old professor couldn't be part of this. "Hello, Dr. Stoller," she said.

"Ann," he said, his voice warm. "How many times must I insist that you call me Carl? We've shared fingers of scotch, after all."

"My apologies, Carl." She gave him a gracious laugh, shunting all bitterness to the background. "What can I do for you?"

"Well, I'm glad you're safe."

"Why wouldn't I be?" Had someone seen them in the garage? Surely there were video cameras all over the place.

"I'm sorry to be the one to tell you, but the woman who starred with you in your infamous video this morning has been killed."

"Killed?" Meena was dead?

"Yes. Strangled. In the parking garage, apparently. The police are questioning everyone right now. They're watching security tapes and all that."

"Oh." The woman had died like a prey, but she'd been a

predator. "I'm . . ." What was she besides confused? "I'm sorry."

"Yes. So am I." He paused. "But I called for a different reason. You remember that the formal dance is tonight."

"Yes."

"Would you be so kind as to add some magic to this old man's night and accompany me?"

The last thing Ann wanted was to do was go to a dance with a man who'd called her a harlot.

He must have sensed her reticence. "Please, forgive me, Ann. I was rude over drinks this morning—and premature."

"Premature?"

"The man you were up against for the job gave a terrible talk. He isn't suited to teach high school, much less Harvard students."

"Are you . . ." Her mind raced, trying to make sense of this. Could she really provide a safe haven for her family fair and square? "Are you making me a job offer? An honest job offer?"

"I believe it's possible," the old man said. "Please, accompany me to the dance and allow an old man to beg forgiveness. We can talk about the position, negotiate the details. Will you come with me?"

She glanced at Chiron, hoping he'd heard this conversation. He made a face like he thought Stoller had lost his mind—then he gave her a quick nod. "Go," he whispered.

"I'd be delighted to go with you, Dr. Stoller."

Ann held up a palm with a question in her eye for Chiron.

He pointed to his wrist and then held up an index finger.

"I can be there in an hour," she told the Harvard professor.

"You know it's a trap, don't you?" He'd led her back to his bedroom where he'd brought her suitcase and backpack.

"Saves us having to figure out what the next step is, I suppose. Although I have to say . . ."

"What?"

"I wish I really could land that job, or one like it. It was for my family. With Harvard's name on my field site, we would have had acres and acres of privacy. We could run wild if we wanted."

"I heard your talk. It was great. You'll land a better job."

"Only if the Playboy Mansion starts its own university," she said. "I just need a minute." She took her dress and went into the bathroom. She piled her hair up, put on enough makeup to feel glamorous, and went to find her dress boots.

"Wow!"

He said it at the same time she did, and they laughed. No man in a tux ever looked as good as this one. His shoulders were broad and his waist was tapered, which is what one expected of a man in a tux. He had something more though. Had a jacket ever made a man's jaw look so strong or made his eyes gleam so beautifully? She knew exactly how strong the arms beneath all that black cloth felt, and looking at him now made her long to be near him, her skin on his.

"Now I wish I were your date for a completely different reason," he said, taking her in his arms and caressing her bared shoulder with his lips. "Did I ever tell you I have a weakness for women in clingy dresses?"

She laughed. "I might've guessed it from the first time we met. You couldn't take your eyes off my tits," she teased.

He gave her a look of mock incredulity. "I could so. I knew right away that your eyes were the color of the Aegean."

She wrapped her arms around him then. She didn't wait politely. She didn't have to. She brought her lips to his, knowing he wanted her just as she was.

And he met her there. Curling his fingers around the back of her neck, he caressed her cheek with his thumb as she touched her lips to his.

Skin gliding over skin, she memorized his feel, but that wasn't enough. Slowly, she opened her mouth, twining her tongue around his. For a heartbeat she couldn't tell where her flesh ended and his began.

He slid strong hands down over the curve of her waist, and she pressed into him, savoring his strength and the safety of his arms. If the night went badly, she'd have this memory. She'd know that at least once, someone knew who she was and loved her.

He pulled away from her at the same moment that she stepped back, and she gave a little laugh. "We're in synch tonight."

"Let's get you packed."

"Packed?"

"What do you need with you?"

"I assume you mean besides lipstick?" She went to her backpack and dumped it out. "I need the vial I stole from Meena's back pocket and the vial I stole from Sutherland." She found the vials and put them in her handbag. "If I open the vial from Meena, you'll go mad with lust."

"I'm already mad with lust."

"Cute." She looked at the contents on the bed as she put the vial in the purse.

"Is there anything else you need?"

She spied a white plastic card. "I have a key to Daniel Hallock's room. If he hasn't checked out, that might come in handy."

"Why?"

"I don't know. Maybe we'll need to hide?"

"I hope not." He picked it up and handed it to her. "But it's small."

"Thanks."

Then he reached in his breast pocket and pulled out the tiniest gun she'd ever seen. "It looks like a toy," he said, handing it to her, "but it's very real."

She took it, appreciating the weight of it in her hand. "Look." She put it in her clutch. "It fits perfectly."

* * *

Carrying her backpack, Chiron led her to the garage, admiring the way her black dress hugged her hips and breasts.

"What?" she asked when she saw the cars. "You only drive Crown Vics?"

"I like to keep a low profile."

"They're all white."

"No one knows I have three cars this way."

She looked at him like he was crazy. "And you've lived four thousand years like this? No wonder the predators are after you. They probably just want to talk to you about mixing it up a little."

"You're very funny." He opened the door to the closest car. Like a model, she sat first and then slid her legs in. She looked great.

"No, seriously. Your suits aren't all the same color, are they? You're not like some weird Batman fan or something? Didn't Bruce Wayne have rows of identical clothes?"

"No." He put her backpack in the backseat and shook his head.

"No, what? You don't like Batman? Bruce Wayne didn't have military underwear?"

"No, I'm not like Batman. I find it easier to let my boss—my ex-boss—think the SDPD loaner is always pristine. I can take it to the shop for repair without him noticing." He gestured around the room. "No Batpole. No Batphone."

"See? If you lived in Gotham, you could get those things. And get real chummy with Commissioner Gordon, too. Batgirl was always looking for a good boyfriend."

"But you live in North Carolina."

His comment shut her up.

"I'm sorry," she said as he slid the car into reverse. "Words fall out of my mouth when I'm nervous."

"I'll help you, you know. We can fight this together." He

touched his lapel. "I'll go to the party too. Complete in Batman tuxedo."

"I know."

He looked over his shoulder to pull out, but the red light on the security panel blinked on, snagging his attention.

"What is it?" she asked, probably because the car wasn't moving.

"I think I've changed my mind."

"About helping me?" She looked appalled—and that touched him, made something in him vow to live up to that expectation.

"No," he said. "I'm staying by your side until this is over." He pulled the car back in and pointed to a door at the back of the garage. "I've changed my mind about the Crown Vic. Let's take something else. Grab your bag, will you?"

"Okay." She said the word slowly as she retrieved it. "But I really didn't mind the car. I was just teasing you." She closed the door.

"Over here." He pointed at a door at the back of the garage. A second light was blinking on the security panel now. He pressed a keypad on an oversized locker next to the door, opened it, and pulled out a hard black case. "Head down those stairs," he said, pointing at the door as he closed the locker.

He followed her. Her hair glowed golden in the stairwell as she went down, and then she entered the second garage.

"Wow!" She dragged out the word. "You have this, and you drive a Crown Vic? Are you mad?"

He laughed. "I don't always want to look inconspicuous." He pressed the buttons to close the garage door upstairs and open this one. A second button made the Shelby's engine roar to life.

"Wow," she said again, touching the silver hood like it was a work of art. "A gorgeous man wearing a tux and driving this . . . I have no idea what kind of car this is, but I can guarantee it's conspicuous."

He opened the passenger side door for her and handed her her backpack. Then he put the heavy black case from the locker into the trunk. "It's also fast."

"And we need speed because?"

"Because someone is trying to break into my home right now."

17

The engine rumbled like a tiger's purr as they sat in the garage. "Why aren't we leaving?" she asked.

"Let's sit here a minute. See who it is."

"I don't really want to see an army of men with guns." She swallowed, her right foot pressing an imaginary gas pedal in her itch to get the hell out of there. "Or a news crew. Or a predator."

He touched her arm. "I can handle those, I promise. Besides, whoever it is has tripped every wire between the fence and this building. He's not a professional."

"But what if—" A flicker in the mirror caught her glance and shut her up. A man stumbled into the garage just then, his blond hair greasy in the light. "Someone's here!"

Chiron pulled out his weapon, but Ann stopped him with a touch to his wrist. "Wait," she whispered. Something about him seemed familiar. He walked like he'd been drinking, staggering from the wall to the locker.

Chiron recognized him first. "That's Daniel Hallock."

"No." The man was hunched over himself, and he was

crooked. His chiseled features had melted in on themselves. "It can't be," she hissed.

Chiron opened his car door, gesturing for her to stay in the car. "Dr. Hallock," he said in the same voice that might soothe a scared child. "Can I help you?"

"You!" Daniel swung toward Chiron, and Ann gasped when she saw his face. A purple lesion, greasy and hairy, crossed his face like some alien slug. Large portions of his hair were gone, and what was left hung in lank, greasy hunks. "Where is she?"

"You look like you need help," Chiron said in a calming voice. "Maybe we should get you to the hospital?"

"Fucking doctors can't help me," he said. "Only she can."

"Who?"

"The fucking unicorn." He stepped toward Chiron, but his leg crumpled beneath him, and he fell to the floor.

"What happened to you?" Chiron moved closer and helped him stand. "Is this radiation poisoning?"

"Those fuckers made me their guinea pig." She could see that the vile lesion crossed his eyelid, making the thin skin pulse. His irises had a white cast to it. "Those stupid, stupid fuckers. I told them I'd break out. I told them I'd tell everyone, the press, the other scientists, everyone, and they just laughed at me. But I *did* escape."

The predators allowed him to escape, Ann realized. Daniel just hadn't behaved according to their plan.

"Which fuckers?" Chiron asked.

Daniel's leg gave out again, and he caught himself on the car. "The lying cheaters from Harvard."

In the safety of the car Ann gasped. Stoller's invitation truly was a trap.

"No one from Harvard did this to you," Chiron said. Ann knew Chiron was purposefully patronizing her ex, probably to see what he knew. "Let me call an ambulance."

"You don't know fuck-all." He spat at Chiron's feet. "It was that old professor, mad as a hatter." He gave an insane giggle. "He's crazier than I am!"

Stoller? Stoller did this to him? The blood in her veins felt like it was on fire. It was one thing to suspect Stoller was part of a trap, but had he orchestrated the ruin of her career? Even now, was he plotting her death—or worse, her imprisonment in the name of science?

"Who really did this?" Chiron asked.

"Stoller and that asshole from the Brode Institute. They jabbed me with some shit, told me it'd do the same thing to me as it did to my wife." He leaned against the car's hood like he couldn't stand. What the *hell* was wrong with him? "But it didn't work. They want the unicorn, but I want her more. Only she can fix this. Where is she?"

"She's not—"

Then Daniel spied her with his good eye. "Bitch!" he said. "This is your fault! Heal me!" He slammed his fists on the hood. "Heal me!"

"I—"

But Ann didn't get a chance to answer because Chiron hauled off and punched him. He crumpled to the floor in a heap.

"That's the most disgusting thing I've seen since leprosy," he said.

Ann opened her door and looked at her ex-fiancé. Something wet dripped down her face, and she realized she was crying. What had they done to him?

"He can't hurt you, Ann."

She looked at the puddle of humanity on the floor. "I'm not afraid of Daniel," she said, her voice thick. She was afraid of the lengths people would go to keep alive. She pushed the tears from her eyes, trying not to vomit. "I've seen these lesions before."

Chiron looked at her as he put his pistol back in its holster. "Where?"

"Carl Stoller had a purple mark like that on his hand after my talk this morning." She touched the neatness of her bun. "And I swear it wasn't there yesterday."

"Hmm. Help me drag him to the back room here." He took his ankles as she took his shoulders. She sent tiny tendrils toward him, seeking the cause of his injury.

"What're we going to do with him?" she asked.

"We'll lock him in here for now. I'll call the SDPD when we're done with the folks at the Brode Institute."

Ann shook her head. "That's not a good idea."

"Why not?" Chiron hit the door. "No one can get in or out once this is locked."

"It's not that." She brushed her hair from her eyes. "He's not going to live through the night if I don't help him."

"After everything he's done to you, you're going to help him?"

She nodded. She wasn't a judge or jury. She was just a person watching another suffer as his cells fell apart.

"This changes everything, you know. You can't go to the formal with Stoller." The muscles in Chiron's face were tight. "Not knowing what Stoller's willing to do to people."

She was going, and she wasn't going to argue about it. Instead, she tried to change the subject. "Daniel's chromosomes were filled with more genetic mutations than I've seen." The lust from her change left her weak with desire, and as the car thrummed all around her, it was all she could do to resist taking Chiron's thigh in her hand, his cock in her mouth. He could drive while she tasted him. Win, win.

"I don't care about his chromosomes. I care about you."

Chiron's anger helped her push that lust away though. The

speedometer showed they were going close to ninety miles per hour. The walls of the low-slung car seemed to press in on her. "Just a reminder, Speed Racer, I'm not immortal."

He didn't slow down.

"Don't be pissed off with me. There's no other way."

"I'm not going to let you risk yourself like this."

"Chiron." She tried to keep the exasperation out of her voice. "I won't be risking myself. You'll be there. How much safer could I be?"

His expression softened a little. "A lot safer. Stay at my house until I take these guys out," he said. "Whatever they did to Akantha, they'll do to you."

She understood then, what this meant to him. "I am not Akantha."

"Don't be unreasonable." Irritation muffled his voice. "That's not what I meant and you know it."

"You want a chance to save me because you failed—you think you failed—Akantha. Well, I'm not your living therapy session."

"Ann."

"Look. This is not a dangerous idea. We'll go to the hotel. I'll allow Stoller to accompany me to the formal. You can lurk in the shadows until he and his minions do whatever the hell they're going to do. you arrest them."

"I'm not a cop."

She gave him an exasperated look. "You arrest them, and they leave us alone for their natural lives—and if Stoller is in the same condition as Daniel, that won't be long."

He shook his head, his expression grim, but at least they were only going seventy now. "And what happens to you if something happens to me?"

"It's a chance I've got to take."

"I don't like it."

"This is not a stupid risk."

"Why not?"

"You'll be with me the entire time."

"And if something holds me up someplace?" He'd asked this twice now, and she realized it scared him, the idea he couldn't be there when she needed him.

"You're immortal," she reminded him.

"I wouldn't have been able to walk away from Meena if my life depended on it."

"Meena's dead. She can't seduce you away from me."

"And where did we get that information?"

"Stol—" Then Ann realized he was right. Reaching into her backpack in the back seat, she found her phone."

"What are you doing?"

"Asking the front desk." She dialed, and when the operator answered, she asked, "Hi, I'm a guest at your hotel, staying for the genetics convention. I heard someone was killed in your parking garage today. Is that true?" The woman on the phone said it wasn't—but she hesitated. Ann wasn't going to accept anything half-baked. "Listen," Ann said, "if I park down there and someone attacks me because I didn't know the truth, I'll hold you—and the hotel—responsible."

"No one was killed, ma'am," the woman at the front desk said, "but I'd park someplace else. There's street parking just off Orange."

"Thank you."

"And ma'am?"

"Yes?"

"I wouldn't go outside alone for the next few days, but you didn't hear that from me."

She closed the phone and looked at Chiron. "Okay," she said with a small shrug. "Meena's dead."

Chiron grunted, not appeased. "We don't have to do it this

way." The intermittent light from the streetlamps made his face hard to read, but his voice was grim.

"What are you suggesting?"

"We go to the Brode Institute and blow it up."

"And what if that's where my mother is?"

"We'll find her and then blow it up."

"And you just happen to know how to blow up a gigantic building?"

He nodded, a curt movement of his chin. "I put a case in the trunk. It's full of explosives."

She looked at the man next to her, all hot in his tux and driving his fast car with explosives in the trunk. She wasn't in the car with Speed Racer—she was with James Bond.

"What do you think?" he asked.

"I think you've learned some scary things in four thousand years of living."

"Seriously."

She shook her head. "If Stoller tries to kidnap me, you can arrest him. If you blow up his stuff, he'll make someplace new to play. And he doesn't play nice."

He was silent for a minute. "I don't like it."

"I know." She touched his leg, her fingertips drinking in the shape of his thigh. "But I can't live my life protected from every threat, Chiron, and I can't keep running."

"If I blow up the lab, you won't have to run."

"I ran fifteen years ago and I've been running since—and if we don't stop them now, it'll only get worse."

"How could it get worse?"

A fear that hadn't been there before swirled through her gut. The predators weren't playing around, they weren't asking nicely. If she failed—no, if she and Chiron failed together—one or both of them would spend the rest of their days locked in the lab's basement, guinea pigs. Worse. They'd become the rabbits who had chemicals put in their eyes to see if they went blind. They'd become the rhesus monkeys who had their spines severed to see if the new nerve-regeneration treatment worked.

Ann looked at Chiron and let him see her fear. She touched his thigh, hoping for understanding. "I just can't run anymore."

"Look," Chiron said as he slid the car into the parking garage. "We'll go straight up to his room, and I'll stay out of sight. I'll follow him wherever he takes you."

She nodded, too nervous to say much.

"You okay?" he asked.

She swallowed, but something had just occurred to her.

"What is it?" he asked.

"They could've kidnapped me the night I spent with Erik Sutherland. They could've kidnapped me when I was alone with Dr. Stoller."

"They didn't." He glanced at her. "You know why?"

That was the problem her mind had been mulling in the last few minutes. Both Stoller and the predator had mentioned her mother. Stoller had actually suggested she call her mom, for moral support, he'd said. "They left me alone because they wanted me to lead them to my mother."

"Your mother?"

"She's the only one of us who ever turned back the biological clock for someone—and got caught."

He looked at her, probably thinking of Daniel Hallock and his rant. "And now they know you made someone younger," he said.

"They're not going to wait for me to lead them anywhere. They're going to try to capture me tonight. So I can make them younger."

Anger tightened his jaw. "Let's just blow the lab up."

She shook her head. "I can't. No half measures. We have to absolutely stop the predators. I can't live wondering how and where they'll strike."

"I'd protect you. Stay with me."

She gave him a small smile, touched by his loyalty. "And my entire family?" She ran her hand over his muscled thigh. "I don't think even your house could accommodate all of us for the rest of our lives."

He didn't say anything, so she put her hand on the door handle. "You ready to go?"

"Wait a minute." He touched her arm. "Your entire family can stay with me any time they like for however long they want to."

"That doesn't solve the problem."

"I know." He gave that curt nod. "So in case something happens to me, the black case in the trunk is filled with explosives. There's also a pistol in it. You know how to shoot?"

"You're repeating yourself about the case, and I've already told you I can shoot. I have your mini-pistol in my purse."

"I wish I found any of that reassuring."

She laughed softly, reassured. "Thank you," she said. "For helping me do this."

He took the keys from the ignition. "I'm not going to lock the car. Just press the trunk button if you need the case."

Ann looked at him. He was so damned strong he was mighty—and that was in his human form. With him at her side, what could possibly happen? "Everything will be fine," she said. "We'll be—"

Anemone!

"What is it?" Alarm filled his face as he looked at her.

"It's okay. My mom." She held up her hand a second and tried to respond to the mindlink.

I'm here, Mom.

We have a problem.

Beside the predators breathing down their backs at every turn? *What's that?*

I was wrong about the vials. There aren't two of them—there're three.

Three?

Someone named Daniel Hallock has the third. It's in his hotel room, in a small, paper-wrapped box. It attracts females of our kind, like the kind you stole from Erik Sutherland. The one you took from the woman is something different. I don't know exactly what it does.

Ann suspected she did. It attracted centaurs. Male centaurs.

You need to find it, her mom said.

We're going to arrest the predators and destroy their lab.

All of that will be for nothing if you don't destroy every vial ever made.

Are you at the lab?

Yes, I'm—

The terrible scream of agony that came from her mother tore Ann's self-control to shreds. Her own shriek filled the car and reverberated off the windows.

"Ann!" Chiron's warm hand grounded her, severed her contact with her mother. "Ann!"

"I'm . . ." She touched her head, and it ached. "I'm okay."

"And your mom?"

"They caught her. They're doing something horrible to her. Her cries! You should have heard them!"

"Shh," he said. He wrapped his arms around her, banging an elbow on the dashboard. "Shh. I'm here with you. Now tell me what she said."

"Daniel Hallock has a third vial." She savored the strength surrounding her, relishing the fact that someone would help her, that someone knew her and would help her. "It's in his hotel room in a brown package. We have to find it."

18

The door key to Daniel Hallock's room still worked. Given the shape the man had been in before Chiron punched him, Chiron wasn't surprised that checking out wasn't high on the list of his priorities.

"Did your mom say where the vial was?" The room was still a mess with twenty or so shopping bags thrown onto the floor next to the bed. Chiron wanted to find the vial and get out of there—but his heart ached with what he had to do first.

"She said it was in a box wrapped in paper." Ann moved some of the bags on the floor, her face calmer now. "She said it was a square box."

He scanned the floor, knowing she might not forgive this betrayal—but he didn't have a choice. He couldn't let the predators do to this woman what they'd done to Akantha.

Then he spied a likely suspect. "This it?" He picked up the small brown box, which had been lying on the floor by the door. Hallock's name was written on the top, but there were no stamps.

"Maybe." She gestured to the mess of shopping bags. "Good eye finding it in this mess."

"His wife said that's how she caught him. Someone hand delivered a package to him, and he acted weird about it."

"Cheating bastard." He handed her the box, and she slid her finger under the packaging and pulled off the tape. White packing peanuts spilled out of the box and onto the bed. She dug in her fingers and gave a small sound of satisfaction. "Someone sent him a vial. This is it."

"Smell it," he said, hating himself. "Is it really the perfume?"

She fingered it without sniffing. "Why? Why would someone send it to him? I'd have followed him wherever he wanted."

"Backup?" He tried to keep impatience from his voice. "In case he couldn't lure you here."

She considered the tiny thing in the palm of her hand, and then nodded hesitantly. "Maybe. Only a unicorn would have responded to it. The human women in the town where I grew up were immune to the predators."

Chiron was interested despite his need to hurry her. "Then why did he try to shoot you instead of using the pheromone?" he asked.

"I don't know."

"Is that really the perfume?" he asked. He sniffed for himself, detecting only bergamot and vetiver. "It smells nice, but not particularly beguiling."

Ann tentatively brought the vial in the package to her nose and sniffed. Immediately, her eyes grew drowsy with lust. He hardened his heart.

"It's the real thing." She quickly put it back in the box and closed the lid. It didn't really help much, he could see. Her pupils were dilated, and her face was flushed. He knew the scent rushed through her blood, making it impossible for her to think.

The vibrant exhilaration of being alive filled her. The tension in her stomach softened and her core yielded to the unfurling desire as it pulsed through her. Her neck longed for Chiron's lips, his mouth. Her lips longed to taste his.

He took one look at her, perhaps reading her half-closed eyes correctly. "I've become your predator, haven't I?"

"Mmmm." She touched the tip of her lip with her tongue, and her eyes were still half closed. She touched his thigh, moved her hand higher to his cock. When it hardened immediately, she chuckled.

He kissed her. He'd never met Judas Iscariot, but Chiron felt every inch of his pain with this kiss. Her lips tasted like honey in his mouth, and he wanted her more than ever—and he wasn't alone in his desire. She pressed her hips against his cock and curled her arms around his back as he moved his hands to her neck.

"Mmmm," she said again, and he did his best to ignore what her body was doing to his. As she ran her lips over his, he caressed her neck—at least that's what he wanted her to think. But while he caressed her, he pressed her brachial plexus origin on both sides of her neck, right above the collarbone. He knew where her carotid artery and several nerves ran—and he knew that pressure on the artery and nerves would make even Dr. Ann Fallon unconscious.

She passed out in his arms.

Chiron took out his badge, held it to the peephole, and knocked. He heard a shuffling sound behind the door and then it swung open. Hairy gray eyebrows rose as if in surprise. "Mr. Atlanta, do come in. I've heard so much about you."

Chiron put his badge away and walked into the room, hiding his alarm. If everyone went along with the farce that Chiron was a simple detective and Stoller was a simple professor, Chiron would not be on Stoller's radar. "And what is it that you've heard about me, Dr. Stoller?"

"Why, that you're one of the immortals, of course."

Chiron blinked. The purple lesion Ann had mentioned covered his entire right hand and vanished up his tuxedo sleeve. "If I'm an immortal, sir, what are you? A gremlin? An alien from Alpha Centauri?"

"Very clever." The older man made a welcoming gesture into the suite. "I've no doubt that living as long as you have has provided you every opportunity to learn how to deflect even the most persistent questions."

Chiron paused, weighing the odds that a bluff would work. Not high. "*If* someone had managed to obtain immortality, sir, I think you could understand how important it would be to keep that ability away from the focus of the public."

The man shook his head, the wattles on his neck shaking. "On the contrary, if someone had managed to achieve immortality, Mr. Atlanta, he should realize how much the public would hunger to achieve the same feat. Just think, humans take thirty years to develop their minds, their brains, and what do they get for this investment? Thirty years of service. Just as they hit their strides, cognitive abilities decline." His rheumy gaze met Chiron's. "You could save us from this."

Chiron understood. The man standing before him was looking his own mortality in the eye, and he didn't like what he saw.

Like Chiron gave a rat's ass. He took out his handcuffs. "What if I could assure you that there is no way for the public to achieve such a feat?" He met the mad scientist's gaze. "I can't save humanity, and you need to come to the office with me and answer some questions." He'd hand him over to his boss, even if he wasn't officially on the force anymore.

"You're wrong."

"I'm not wrong. You can come with me peacefully." He held up the cuffs. "Or I can use these."

"That's not what I meant." Stoller laughed as if Chiron had told a delightful joke. "You're wrong about re-creating what made you special. If immortality happened once—no, twice—it could happen again, Mr. Atlanta. We can make it happen."

Chiron remembered the day the Earthmother had blessed him and Akantha with her gift. He remembered the crackling ozone and the ethereal blue tendrils snaking through the air around her like otherworldly fingers. He remembered owls and fireflies decorating the forest around her—and he doubted she could be coerced into any action. And more than that, the Earthmother was dead, replaced by goddesses who'd been replaced by goddesses.

"That is very unlikely." Chiron gestured toward the door. The old man's physical presence wasn't remotely intimidating, but the room held a vibe Chiron didn't like, something that unnerved him. He was very glad he hadn't let Ann walk into this trap. "Some things only happen once. We're leaving now."

Stoller didn't move. "But how do you know? What seemed like magic centuries ago can be explained with the cold logic of science, which has advanced quite dramatically in just the last one hundred years." Dr. Stoller cocked his head and asked, "Surely, you're familiar with Clarke's Law?"

Chiron nodded, slowly walking toward the madman. He'd use the handcuffs. "Any sufficiently advanced technology is virtually indistinguishable from magic. I'm familiar with it." Chiron couldn't shake the feeling that something big was about to happen, but looking around the room and seeing only the old man, that feeling made no sense. "But I'm also familiar with the fact that Clarke was a science fiction author, not a scientist or a mathematician. It's hard to give too much credit to a law penned by a genre author."

"And the common folk accuse scientists of being elitists." Stoller chuckled at his own joke, then he waved Chiron's objection away with the flick of his shaky fingers. "You will tell me how you obtained immortality, and we will replicate it—even if you believe you obtained your immortality through magic."

"No, you're coming with me to meet the sergeant." Chiron shook his head, bemused. "And if I were immortal, don't you think I'd have better things to do than sit in your lab and let you back-engineer me?"

"Oh, you'll join my work at the Brode Institute. Just think! You'll be benefiting all of humanity!"

"And Akantha?" he asked. He was close enough now to feel the man's body heat. "Did she volunteer her services?"

"Ah, Akantha." Dr. Stoller did the flicking thing with his purple fingers again. "You should be asking about Dr. Fallon, no? I understand you two have become good friends."

A rush of adrenaline zinged through Chiron's veins, and he grabbed the old man, snapping the steel bracelets over his wrists. What if this mad man was right? What if the scientists could harness the power of the unicorns and the immortals? "What have you done with them?"

"Oh, Detective Atlanta, you worry too much. Let me get my coat and I'll come with you. No need for handcuffs."

Chiron nodded. "We'll leave the cuffs on, but you can get your coat."

"If you insist."

Together, he and Stoller walked over to the door that separated the suite from a second bedroom—and a whoosh of lust hit Chiron, carried on a floral scent he couldn't describe if he wanted to.

Meena walked out of the room, and Chiron knew exactly what a male praying mantis felt like just before a female ate him—alive with sexual pleasure. He dropped his hold on Stoller's handcuff.

"Kai," she purred as she approached him. "I'm so sorry we were interrupted last time." She twined her arms around his neck and pulled him toward her.

"I thought you were dead," he said, sliding his lips against hers. Her mouth tasted like ambrosia; her skin felt like perfection. Her breasts pressed against his chest, and he couldn't stop himself. He pressed his cock against her hip.

"As you see," she said in her Italian accent, "I am quite alive." She gave a throaty chuckle. "I'm sure you'll come with me now. You'll find yourself," her fingers caressed the length of his cock, "very nicely rewarded."

And Chiron knew then that he would follow her to the ends of the earth if she asked it.

When Ann woke up, she blinked. Where was she? The air held Chiron's scent, but it was faint. He wasn't here now, and where was here?

She sat up and realized she was in a hotel room. If the clock were right, it was just after nine, so the party was just starting. How had she gotten here?

She slid her legs off the bed, still in her black dress and boots. Where was Chiron?

And then she remembered.

That bastard!

He didn't trust her, didn't think she could actually help take out the predators. Did he really think he could do it himself? Fool! If the predators had made up any more fragrance like the kind Meena had worn, he was doomed—if they found him.

She scanned the room. It was empty, but she spied the room service cart they'd ordered this morning, still covered with uneaten French toast and an omelet. Eww. Where had Chiron gone?

For a heartbeat, she felt really lonely. For her entire life, she'd had to pretend to be human, play by human rules, except when she was with her mother and cousins and siblings. Then she'd lost that. When she and Chiron found each other, discovered each other's nature, she'd felt complete for the first time in her adult life.

And he'd just left her here, abandoned her. Anger burned hot through her veins. How could he? She should just let him tackle the predators alone and see how far he got. He might be immortal, mighty, and wise, but he had no idea what they were up against—and she did.

Which is why she couldn't abandon him.

She looked around for her small purse. He'd left it on the bed next to her. She opened it and found everything as she'd left it: oxblood-red lipstick, keycard to the predator's bedroom, two vials of wretchedness, and the impossibly small gun. Then she spied something new: the third vial from Daniel's room.

Ann stood, ready to kick predator ass and save Chiron to boot—but how?

Where would Chiron have gone first? With the case of explosives to the lab?

No. He knew Stoller was waiting for her. He would have gone there.

Ann took the gun from her purse and unlatched the safety as she opened the door to the hall, but when she got to Dr. Stoller's room, she didn't have to knock to know Chiron wasn't there. His scent left the faintest trail in the hallway—and so did Meena's. Apparently rumors of her death had been greatly fucking exaggerated.

Ann followed the scent as much as she was able to, but when it ended at the elevator, she knew she was out of luck. She wasn't a bloodhound, and she wasn't trying to find someone wearing pheromones targeted to her personal biology.

Shit. Now what? Where would Stoller have taken an entranced, immortal, shape-shifting centaur? Not to the party, that's for sure. To the lab.

She pressed the down button for the elevator, and when it opened, she walked into it.

Chiron's scent was thicker here, trapped by the four walls. She inhaled his warm cedar scent, the scent of his strength—and the scent of his desire. Ann had no doubt then—Meena had enthralled Chiron.

She could get the explosives from his car and get a cab to the Institute. She started to press "P" but chose the button for the seventh floor instead—the predator's floor.

Because what if Stoller had taken him to the predator's room? At least she had a key.

She sniffed the air in the hall. No Chiron. The air was thick with the predator's dark scent, but no Chiron. Still, she'd look—and she'd hold her gun while she did it. If she happened to find Sutherland . . . well, accidents happened.

When Ann inserted the key into the steel slot, the whirr and click sounded deathly loud in the silent hallway, but she pushed the door open anyway.

The room felt too still. The dark perfume laden with pheromone hung in the air, from his clothing and bedding—it was too weak to belong to the man himself.

Despite the weakness of the scent, lust swirled through her blood, filling her with erotic languor. She couldn't help but remember the weight of the predator's hands over her neck, the feel of his cock buried inside her.

She shoved the traitorous thought to the back of her mind. Maybe she and Chiron didn't know each other well enough to detect real love in their relationship—but the potential existed, and she wanted the chance to discover what they had.

She sniffed again, trying to puzzle out the weird stillness of the room. Chiron might not be here, but someone was. She smelled the pungent scent of fear and . . . duct tape? What was going on here? "Hello?" she said. "Is anyone here?"

"Hmghmhg," she heard.

What? Then she knew. Someone was tied up in the room, probably with duct tape. Someone—but not Chiron.

She sensed a trap, and considered turning and running. She couldn't, though. First, if someone needed help, she was the last person to walk away. And second, between her gun and her magic, what could anyone do to her?

She stepped into the small entryway. What had happened here?

"Hello?" she called into the room. "Are you okay?"

"Hmghmhg," she heard again, only this time the cry was more desperate—and she caught the slightest flash of movement from behind the door. Who?

Knowing she should run the other way, she slammed the door open with her free hand, and when it was at its widest, she lunged inside, toward the voice. She spun around and aimed her gun just as the door closed.

She wasn't fast enough though.

Like an uncoiling tiger, the predator sprang from the bathroom, his teeth white in the moonlight. He roared as he leaped at her, and she could see death in his eye.

Ann didn't have time to shoot or think—she changed, amazed at the strength of her power here. Ripping ligaments and tendons with her speed, she whipped into her equine form, the ozone scent of her magic filling the room.

His body slammed into her while she shifted, knocking her half-unicorn form to the carpeted floor. Perhaps surprised to find horseflesh where there should be none and a lack of human flesh where he had every reason to expect it, the predator fell to the floor too, sprawling atop her. His scent curled through her, but she shoved away the lust as she tried to push him off. Her hands, braced against his chest, turned to hooves, and her full equine form coalesced. Unicorn magic healed all the tissue she'd torn while changing so quickly—at an astounding speed.

She looked down at him, expecting to see shocked surprise,

but his dark face was too inscrutable. His black eyes looked at her with as much emotion as she'd seen in a panther's face. She couldn't blame it on the light—her animal vision had no excuse.

She lowered her head defensively, letting the sword-sharp tip glint in the white moonlight pouring in the window. She gathered her haunches beneath her, ready to slay him.

The predator jumped to his feet and jabbed his left fist at her nose. Maybe Muhammad Ali could have swung faster—most horses would have watched that muscle-bound fist rocket toward their face helpless to stop it. But Ann was a unicorn. She didn't have time to duck. She didn't have time to kick or bite. Instead, she angled her face so that his fist slammed into her thick equine jaw, reinforced by nature to hold massive, grinding teeth.

Bones cracked—and they weren't her bones.

"Fuck," he muttered, but he swung with his right. From the play of his chest and the rippling of muscle in his arm, she guessed he put all his power into the second punch.

Ann couldn't let that happen. Even as the punch flew toward her, she tucked her nose to her chest and moved toward the door. His fist hit the wall with a resounding thud. Drywall dust filtered into the air between them, and the wainscoting popped off the wall and fell to the floor.

"Fuck," he said again, and Ann doubted he cursed his redecorating skills. She didn't wait to defend herself again, didn't wait for another fist to fly. In the cramped entryway, she wheeled around and lashed out with her back legs.

Her back hooves hit his hip and shoulder. He grunted but didn't move, so she spun around again and reared as high as she could without hitting her horn on the ceiling. Then she leaped at him, connecting her front hooves with his chest.

He fell this time, but he didn't try to protect himself. His powerful hands wrapped around her forelegs and tried to drag her down.

She ripped more energy from the hotel floor and pulled from his grasp, sweat coating her body now. She reared up a second time and smashed down on him, feeling a rib crack beneath her. He didn't try to grab her again, so she barreled over him, making sure to smash his skull with her back hooves. And then—

And then he was down flat. He wasn't moving.

She stood for a minute, trembling. She'd done the impossible. She'd inhaled the full scent of a predator and not fallen under its thrall. She'd done more than that. She'd vanquished a predator, attacked him despite the fact that her body craved him.

Her trembling had stopped.

She huffed a long breath through her nose and looked at her prey. The coppery tang of his blood filled the room, and she immediately saw why. Blood poured from his nose and from a long gash across his forehead. The way he breathed made her wonder if she'd punctured one of his lungs with a smashed rib. His collarbone looked smashed too, but there was no way in hell she'd heal this man. Hell, he had two lungs. He could use the other. Even 911 might be too good for him.

Okay, no. She'd have to call 911. Death wasn't something she needed to deal in, not even for this. At least not until you questioned him, the snide part of her mind said.

She stepped back from him, sure he wouldn't move while she was most vulnerable, and she shifted back into woman form. She took her time now, allowing her ligaments and tendons to reshape themselves at a natural pace. As the opalescent green light of her magic receded, Ann felt hocks give way to knees and hooves give way to feet. Her eyes regained their ability to see multiple colors.

"Ummgh." The garbled cry came from the corner. Her gaze fell on Brad Scrimshaw. He was duct taped to the oversized hotel chair, his eyes open and locked on Ann's.

Shit. He'd seen her change form. *Shit and damn.* What the hell was she going to do? She couldn't knock him out.

She walked over to him and ripped the tape off his mouth with a merciless tug. One thing was certain: if he were the predator's friend, he wouldn't be swaddled in silver duct tape.

"Jesus," he said, rubbing his mouth. "You sure know how to make a man cry."

"Brad, what the hell is going on?"

19

―――――――――

"I knew you were a unicorn," Brad said. The skin around his mouth was red from the tape. "I saw blood samples from one of your kin when I was working for Zim, and I knew it. But I never thought I'd get to see you change! That was so damned cool!"

"Glad to amuse you. Now what the hell is going on?"

"That bastard was about to bring me to the lab."

"Why?"

"To run the same experiments on me as they did on Stoller and the vet."

"Experiments?"

"They're trying to harness your biomolecular magic to cure aging and disease—and if you've seen Stoller lately, you'll know how well that's working."

"Jesus Christ." She pulled the tape from around his ankles and wrists. "You think they went to the lab?"

"Yeah." Brad gestured toward the predator and snorted. "He was about to drag me to the car when you busted the place up." He looked around. "Looks like Velvet Revolver's been staying here." Brad looked at Ann. "What are we going to do?" he asked.

He was dressed in a suit, complete with dress shoes. He'd obviously been going to the formal dinner tonight. "Go to the formal," she said. "You won't even be late for the dinner if you hurry."

"Dinner!" He scoffed and ran his fingers through his hair. "You're kidding me. They were going to use me like a guinea pig! Just like that vet—and did you see what happened to that poor bastard?"

"Brad, go."

But he crossed his arms over his chest. "Freaks interested in the fountain of youth just captured me, I've seen a woman change into a unicorn and back before my very eyes, and—" He stopped. "Where's your guy? The cop?"

"They got him."

He snorted. "And you want me to go to dinner."

"Brad, this is serious."

"I know. That's why I'm going with you to the lab."

"What?" She laughed. "I don't think so."

"I do. You want me with you."

"Go to dinner." She picked up the gun from the floor and put it in her purse. "You'll just get in the way, Brad."

"I know where the lab is, and I've been inside it. In fact, I was on the tour just this afternoon."

The tour she missed—but then another thought occurred to her. Why was he duct taped to the chair? "They caught you there, didn't they. Snooping?"

"Yes." He looked sheepish. "After I heard Sutherland talking about the vet, and after I saw your biomolecular info—I had to snoop."

"You'll get yourself killed one of these days."

"But I know how to get to the lab, and I bet you don't have a clue."

He was right—and even if she left him, she knew he'd follow. Better to know what he was up to. Ann looked at his wingtips and dress pants. Not optimal, but not as bad as say, flip-flops.

"Do you ride?" she asked, although she knew the answer. Of course he did. Anyone who studied equid microsatellites did it because they loved horses.

"Oh, man!" Brad threw his hands in the air. "I get to ride a unicorn! Does life get any better than this?"

"A Shelby?" Brad said when she led them back to the parking garage. "The man drives a Shelby?" He touched the gleaming metal of it in appreciation. "No wonder you picked him over me."

"Brad, you're what? Twenty-one? You're a baby."

"Yeah, but he's like a gazillion years old. He's an old man!" He peered inside the car. "He drives a fast car, but he's still really old." The he stood and grinned at her. "I'm only six years younger than you. With the lights off, you wouldn't even notice. And with the lights on—"

"Shut up, Brad." Ann popped the trunk, glad Chiron had had the foresight to leave it unlocked. She pulled out the plastic case Chiron had carried so easily. It weighed a ton. "Can you carry this?"

"Sure," Brad said before he tried. Ann almost laughed when she saw him try to hide a grimace at the case's weight. "What's in it? Gold bullion?"

"Explosives."

"Explosives? Have you lost your mind?"

"They've got Kai and my mom. We're going to rescue them, then destroy that lab."

"Oh, man!" He shook his head. "Could this night get better?"

"Now we need to get to the beach."

"The beach?"

"I'm not going to change near the cameras. I hope you know how to get to the lab from the shoreline."

"Can't we take the highway?" He touched the car again, awe in his voice. "And the Shelby?"

"No car. I don't have keys, and they'll see us coming." She walked toward the far end of the beach. The earth's power was so strong here this close to the pounding surf. It practically begged for her to change form. "And a unicorn on the highway might raise some eyebrows."

"Uh, true." Brad struggled with the case in the sand.

"Can you get us to the lab from the beach?"

"Umm," he paused and she knew he was getting ready to lie. "Sure. We want to go . . . north."

Since south would bring them to Mexico, it was probably a safe bet, but then where?

"You don't have a clue, do you."

"Not so much."

She laughed and shook her head. "I hope you're better with the directions inside the place."

"I did go on the tour, and a tour of my own."

"Excuse me a moment, please." Then she let the surf's power wash through her. The change from human to unicorn was effortless. Tendons and bones eased into the secondary form. Hair and skin grew and stretched. Her horn appeared so smoothly in her forehead it was like some goddess on high painted it there.

"Oh, my God!" he said as she finished. "That is the coolest damned thing I've ever seen!"

She walked over to him, lining her shoulder up with his hip. *Get on!* she said with her body. One nice thing about hanging out with Brad Scrimshaw was he actually dampened the lust from her shift. Did anyone else in her family know that? Or was the dampening effect the result of her newly honed control in the face of the predator?

Brad struggled to pull the explosives case to her back, but then he leaped on like he'd been riding bareback his whole life. At least he hadn't exaggerated that. When she felt he was balanced and had a good hold of the case, she turned north and eased into a trot. He sat easily—no bouncing or bumping her tender sides with his legs—so she broke into an easy gallop.

As she ran, waves washed over her hooves and power flooded through her veins. Miles slid away under her speed, but she would have felt better about this had she known where they were going. It wasn't like she could stop and ask directions. Brad might be able to, but what person would take him seriously? He wore a suit stained with sweat from her shoulders and back, and he smelled like a horse.

But then she had the answer—she just didn't know if it would work.

For the next handful of strides, she pulled the energy from the earth. She lured it from her hooves and through her veins, and she stored it in her horn.

And then she tried it.

Chiron, she called using the same mindlink she used with her mother. Maybe a conversation between her and Chiron wouldn't be possible—she'd never used this form of communication with anyone but her family. Still, her powers resembled Chiron's in so many ways. It seemed worth a shot, especially with all of the power coursing through her as she ran.

Besides, what did she have to lose?

Chiron! Energy coursed through her, and she wasn't even panting. *Chiron!*

Ann. He dragged out the syllable of her name like it was something to be savored.

Chiron! You can hear me! Are you okay? Where are you?

Oh, Ann. The barrage of questions didn't seem to bother him. *You taste so good.*

What?

Your lips taste like ambrosia. Your nipples like—

Chiron! She understood then. He was talking to Meena. *You're with the predator.* And the sense of jealousy that zinged through her caught her by surprise. She didn't like the idea of Meena's hands and lips on him, not one little bit.

Chiron, where are you? Ann galloped north, appreciating the way Brad barely intruded on her balance, especially with all of the weapons on her back. *Try to focus. Tell me where you are.*

In between your perfect thighs. In your delicious shirt. Your breasts . . .

At least he thought Meena was her. It could be worse. But more importantly, his voice was getting louder in her head. They were getting closer.

"Ann? I mean, Dr. Fallon?"

She snorted. It wasn't as if she could speak to him.

"I have no idea where we are. I can't lie about it. I might have been able to get us there in a car—I paid attention to the exit numbers and all that, but from the beach?" She felt the muscles of his ass move as he shrugged. "I'm useless."

She nickered, trying to tell him that it was okay.

Chiron? She didn't care what he answered now, only that he answered, only that he was alive and she could find him. *Chiron?*

Don't tease me. Let me touch you. Let me . . .

She knew what the predator was doing now. Meena had enough control to prolong the pleasure, to keep him enthralled long enough to manipulate him into a car, and then into a building.

But she also knew that he was east of her, and he was closer.

Chiron, tell me. She filled her voice with sultry longing. *Tell me what you want me to do to you. Tell me every last detail.*

Black stockings, he said. *And high heels. And a very short dress.*

Yes?

And your lips on mine.

Oh, yes.

And the knowledge that you want me as badly as I want you.
I want you, Chiron. The first time I saw your eyes from
across the room, I wanted you.

But your heart, he said. *When I saw your true heart, your*
courage and bravery, that's when I knew I wanted to stay by
your side as long as you'll have me.

And with those words, Ann knew she'd be able to find him
wherever the predators had taken him. How could someone
lose their heart?

When she came to the salt marsh she broke her canter and
walked. The only thing that separated her from her centaur was
the swamp. Lowering her head, she put a cautious foot into the
black water, and Brad grabbed her mane with his free hand.

"We almost there?" he asked.

She nickered her assent, spying the lab before Brad did. The
lights from its parking lot, dim with distance, intruded into the
dark night. Even from this side of the swamp, she could see that
the Brode Institute was a huge, low-slung monstrosity, hugging
the contours of the hills.

What the hell was she going to do here? She didn't know
shit about security systems or breaking and entering. She only
knew Chiron and her mother were captives in that building,
and the predators were probably using them as bait.

She waded through the swampy plants, avoiding fallen logs,
but she wouldn't run like a scared rabbit. She stopped just outside the swamp and took a deep breath. No bergamot. Not yet.

"You found it!" Brad slid from her back. "Jesus, does that
mean that when you're a unicorn, you can home in on things
like pigeons?"

She snorted and shook her head in annoyance. They were
less than a mile from the shoreline, and the thick power she
channeled to use her magic still pulsed through her feet like a
living thing.

She didn't have time to think about it. Instead she let that power slide through her like liquid satin, and she changed from unicorn to woman in the blink of an eye.

"Man, that is so cool," Brad said. "Too bad about your clothes, though."

She looked down and saw she was wearing exactly what she should be: her slinky dress with her pocketbook hanging over her shoulder. "What do you mean?"

"I was kind of hoping to see you naked." He shrugged and didn't even look slightly embarrassed. "In all those werewolf movies, they shred their clothes."

She shook her head. "Someday I might understand why I like you."

He laughed like he didn't care. "So your power must work more like a *Star Trek* transporter."

"I have no idea."

"You must wonder. You're a damned good scientist."

The funny thing was, she never had. "What I really wonder is how the hell I'm going to break into that building and rescue my mother and Chiron."

"What about your horn?"

She blinked at the non sequitur. "What do you mean?"

"Can't you use it to break in?"

"Brad, you're making my head spin. You've suggested about eighteen novel things that unicorns should be able to do in the last three minutes. First, I'm not a homing pigeon. Secondly, I'm not a transporter. Thirdly, I'm not a locksmith."

He crossed his arms and looked at her. "With no disrespect, Dr. Fallon, I think you have no idea what you can do. What if you use the so-called magic of your horn on a lock? What'll happen then?"

She glared at him. "I'll heal it?" She let sarcasm drip from her tone. "I'll poke a big hole in it?"

"You don't know, do you? You don't have the slightest clue."

"I—" But she had no answer, because she didn't. "I think I can only manipulate things at a cellular level."

He swatted at a fat mosquito that had just landed on his arm. "Maybe now's the time to find out."

She stared at him, trying—and failing—not to feel stupid. "I've been a pompous ass," she said.

"A pompous unicorn." He laughed. "Which is still damned cool—and hey," he said, turning toward the building, "maybe zapping the lock will help us understand your powers—without locking you in some Frankenstein dungeon."

"Which door should we attack?"

"That one," he said, pointing to the southern side of the building. "There was an entire wing on that side that I couldn't get into—and I'd even swiped someone's ID card."

"Good." She started to walk toward it.

"And I'm also thinking that it might not hurt to see if you can short out their security cameras."

"Another thing I've never tried."

"Well, if you're channeling energy through your horn somehow, a discharge from it might fry the cameras. They're pretty sensitive."

Mr. Spock would be proud of this guy.

Through his haze of lust, Chiron followed Ann's gorgeous ass into the building, hardly looking up, even when she swiped the door open. Where'd she get the key card? As she walked down the hall, her high heels clicking on the floor, her ass tempted him beyond reason. He wanted nothing more than to thrust his cock into her, savor the silky glide of her skin beneath his.

Did I ever tell you how fuckable your ass looks when you've got those heels on, Dr. Fallon?

Chiron, I'm almost there. Talk to me.

He'd make love to her until she screamed for mercy, until

every drop of semen his body could produce was spent inside her. *I want you to claw my back until my flesh is nothing but a tattered mess. I'll still want more. I want more. I want more now.*

She stopped by a second locked door and paused to open it.

I'm coming, Chiron.

She was coming, and he wanted to join her. He couldn't help himself then. He pressed against her, grabbing one of her breasts in his hand. He wasn't gentle. Even as he nipped her glorious breast through her shirt, he knew she'd like it.

"Detective." Her foreign voice shocked him. Ann had an accent? "Just wait a moment. We have a bed waiting, a very special bed. Just for you."

Ann? You speak like an Italian. And then he laughed, getting the game. *Si, signorina. Non posso vivere senza voi.*

Oh, baby, I love it when you talk so dirty to me.

Dirty? He'd just told her he adored her. He groaned at the thought. He'd talk so dirty to her, show her how the masters did it.

I'll rip the clothes from your back, Ann. I'll throw you on that bed and we'll revel in the glory of making the ultimate love.

The door swung opened and he followed. Her ass was calling his name. He couldn't resist it. He grabbed her ass and squeezed. Ann chuckled. "I've always loved enthusiasm in my men."

In her men? He didn't want to be one of her men. He wanted to be her man. Her only man. And he wanted that now.

She opened another door. "Here we are."

Chiron spied a small bed under a rectangular fluorescent light, and he shoved her to it, growling with need.

Ann. She curved her body to fit his, pressing her breasts into his chest, grinding herself into his thigh. He grabbed the neckline of her shirt, and she laughed.

"Not so fast, big boy." She flipped herself so she was on top of him. She pressed her thighs against his cock, her heat penetrating her skirt and panties, and his jeans.

Running her lips over his neck, she grabbed one of his wrists. The bed had ties on its side, and she trapped one of his hands there.

Undeterred, he grabbed the back of her neck and pulled her face to his. *I have to taste you, suck your lips. Ann, oh, Ann!*

She bit him hard, drawing blood, and trapped his other hand in the second tie.

"You like it dirty, don't you?" she asked.

"Oh, yes."

Wait for me, Chiron! I'm almost there with you!

He'd bring her closer, so close she'd meet him there.

She brought her face to his chest and nibbled. The heat of her mouth through his T-shirt made his cock ache for her, and when she brought her face to his groin, he prepared himself for the blowjob of a lifetime.

"Don't stop." Her face had reached his fly. He would have unzipped his tux, but she'd tied his hands. Oh, she did like it dirty. The woman was full of surprises. *Don't stop.*

"I won't, big boy. Don't you worry."

She dragged her face lower, and before he realized what she'd done, both of his feet were tied to the bed, which wasn't so much a bed as a gurney.

Ann, where are we?

She took a step back, and he groaned in frustration. "Come here," he said, his voice thick with a slow-growing anger and a roiling desire.

Ann had vanished, though. Meena took a step away from him and toyed with the buttons near her neckline.

"Get away from me, bitch!" He struggled with the restraints, but he couldn't free himself.

Then Meena vanished, and Ann was back. She undid the

first button, letting the tiny pearl slide through the hole. He could see the tops of her tiny breasts.

"Undo the next one." He craned to see her better. *Your breasts are so beautiful.*

"You want to see?" she asked. Coyness laced her voice. "Want to taste and touch?"

"A tease." *That's what you are. A tease.*

She undid the second button. The black lace of her bra peeked through now. "More?" she asked.

"Yes!" *Yes!*

"Then tell me about your immortality." She ran a long-nailed finger over the black lace. "Tell me how you achieved this feat." She approached him, bent so that her luscious breasts danced just out of reach of his mouth. Her scent floated around her like a cloud.

And he knew he'd give her whatever she desired.

Ann shifted back to unicorn form, still amazed at the ease of the transformation. Lust simmered in her veins, but she ignored it more easily than had ever been possible.

Chiron, where are you?

I'm coming with you. His voice sounded almost manic with need, and she tried to hurry.

When she dipped her horn toward the lock mechanism, she hardly had to pull any energy from the earth below her—it flowed like sap in the spring. Within heartbeats, coils of energy looped from her and fell onto the mechanism.

I'm coming, she said. *Hold on!*

"See?" Brad said as the door clicked. "I knew it'd work!"

Ann sent him a baleful glance as she dripped more of her energy onto it. How could he tell if it worked? But then the mechanism whirred—and a klaxon shrieked through the night.

"Well, I guess they know we're here." Brad swung the door open, and they went in like they'd been invited.

Eyeing the wide hallways, Ann followed him in her horse form. Her horn would slay, and her hooved legs would run much faster than anything she could do in her human form.

Chiron, are your safe?

I always have condoms.

Brad threw a look over his shoulder, obviously struggling with his heavy suitcase of explosives. "Good idea, staying a unicorn," he shouted over the klaxon. "You're great at picking locks!"

She snorted. She'd have to get used to the idea that her horn was good for more than impaling things and healing them. Although impaling Meena was high on her to-do list.

Suddenly, she heard doors open at the far end of the corridor. The metallic click carried to her unicorn ears even over the electronic wailing. They needed to run.

She trotted past Brad, grabbing his shirt with her teeth. He picked up the hint and vaulted onto her back, grunting with the effort of hauling the weapons. She broke into a gallop then, heading toward a set of large swinging doors twenty yards ahead.

Your breasts are so lovely.

When she tried to stop, her hooves slid on the linoleum. She managed to turn so that her shoulder rather than her face slammed into the door.

"That was cool!"

The taste of your skin makes me crazy, he said. *And between your thighs, honey. The sweetest honey from ancient Crete.*

She didn't reply to either man. Footsteps pounded in the distance. She dipped her horn and let the energy drip onto the lock mechanism. She pushed it open the heartbeat she heard the catch tumble, and she started to gallop forward.

"Wait!" Brad sat back, forcing her to slow. "Can you relock the thing? It might slow them down."

When you grind against me, love . . .

She turned, her magic forming its coiling loops even before she dipped her head. As the energy dripped onto the lock, she heard the metallic click. Brad had been right, again.

She needed to find Chiron and her mother, then they could bomb the place to hell, with or without the wretched Meena.

"Okay," Brad yelled as they galloped forward. "I have no idea where the prisoners are. I only suspect they're in here."

Ann could do better than that. *Chiron!* She yelled his name, hoping to break through whatever mind-haunting reverie had caught him. *Talk to me.*

I'll talk to you. I know you like it when I talk dirty, baby.

His voice was so close! And a little to the left. She took the next turn, her hooves sliding from beneath her as the slippery floor refused to support her.

"You realize only a really good horseman could stay on a ride like this," Brad shouted over the alarm.

Funny boy. No, man.

Chiron?

Mmmm. Your breasts. I'm not lying. The Earthmother bestowed the gift. She blessed me. She blessed Akantha. She took form and walked the island and gave us her blessing in order that we could defeat Earthshaker.

Shit! Chiron was telling someone—Meena, no doubt—his story. He shouldn't talk to anyone, not about this.

She knew where Chiron was, though. She slid, neatly this time, to a stop outside a single stainless door. A quick peek in the window horrified her. Chiron was tied to a gurney while Meena stood over him, her blouse unbuttoned.

"It's them!" Brad's voice was a whisper.

But Ann was already shifting into human form, dropping Brad onto the floor in a heap.

"Sorry!" she whispered.

"It's okay. My God, did you see that woman? She's gorgeous. What an ass! Angelina Jolie, move over."

In that moment, Ann knew exactly how she would defeat this predator.

Tugging his suit jacket, Ann pulled Brad away from the door. "Brad? If I had a cologne to put on you that would make you absolutely irresistible to that woman, and you had to spend the night . . ." She searched for a polite phrase.

"Fucking her brains out?"

"Exactly. Would you want the cologne?"

He laughed. "I'd feel cheap and used." He laughed. "And I'd love every minute of it!"

Ann reached into her purse and pulled out one of the silver vials. The one from Meena's pocket had a pink lid. Ann opened the blue one and dabbed a little on his wrists.

"Get ready," Ann warned. "When we open that door and she smells you, she's going to be all over you." At least Ann hoped so.

"And when I want to stop?"

"I'm not sure." She shrugged. "Get her in the shower. Use lots of soap. You'll need it."

And then, even as her extra-sensitive ears registered the sound of fumbling at the far door, Ann burst into the room.

"Who—" Meena started. She was holding a syringe, and Chiron's arm had a tourniquet around it. She was getting ready to take his blood.

"Hey, baby," Brad said to her, swaggering in her direction. "I'm going to fuck your brains out. You can call me Daddy."

Meena turned toward him, her lids drowsy with desire. "Sounds like fun," she purred, her accent lending an exotic flavor to her words.

"I knew you'd say that. Now come here. Daddy wants some sugar."

"She's mine!" Chiron said, but Ann didn't try to change his mind. Instead, she hit the wheel locks on the bed to free them and swung the gurney toward the door.

"Thanks!" Brad said. He flung the case of explosives into the gurney, banging Chiron's shins. Meena had already twined her arms around his neck, and his big grin made Brad look like the happiest man alive. "And when I say, don't blow me up, I'm talking to you, Ann." He let Meena give him a lingering kiss. "Not you, babe. You can blow me all you want."

"Have fun, Brad."

"Oh, I will."

The klaxon suddenly stopped, throwing the room into a heartbeat of silence, but it didn't last long. Ann shoved the bed through the door with a loud clang, and she and Chiron were alone in the hallway. Pushing the bed with all of her might, she ran opposite the way she'd come.

Next on her list was her mother. If the trick worked with Chiron, it ought to work with her own mother—although Ann tried not to think of the way their last conversation ended. *Mom?* Ann called. *Where are you? Mom!*

No one answered. Shit. What was she going to do?

Mom! she tried again. *Mom!*

"Ann. Ann, I'm so sorry." Chiron's words were a little slurred, and his eyelids were still heavy with lust, but his erection had died back mostly.

"It's the predator. No one can withstand them."

"For more than that. For the nerve pinch. But I can't let you get hurt."

"You're in a gurney and I'm pushing you. Who got hurt?"

"I can't let you—"

"You have to trust me. I know these predators. I know how to escape them."

He paused, and she hoped he was taking the message to heart. He could not desert her—not even for her own good.

"How do you do it?" he asked. "How did you walk away from Sutherland?"

"Lots of practice." She heard footsteps. Their pursuers had

made it through the second door, and they needed to run—a task made harder by her need to push him down the hall. "You back to yourself yet?"

"Yes."

She paused and ripped his restrains, freeing his hands. *Mom!* she called as she freed his ankles. *Mom!*

"Let's get out of here," Chiron said, leaping from the gurney.

"I've got to find my mother." She started to run.

"Mindlink?"

"She won't answer." She was grateful when Chiron didn't suggest the obvious—that her mother was dead. But then, he'd been chasing a dead woman for so long, how could she expect anything short of understanding?

"We'll find her the old-fashioned way then." He flung open the next door. The room was dark, but Ann's inhuman vision let her see its emptiness. "Nothing."

Chiron turned and opened the next door. Nothing. And then the next.

"I can hear security, Chiron. There're two or three of them, and they're marching up the adjacent hall."

"Maybe that means we're close." He flung open the door to the next room. Nothing.

Ann started to open the opposite door when something hissed past her head. The room smelled different than the others; it smelled like—"Damn!"

"What is it?"

But she didn't have time to answer. A yellow tranquilizer dart landed in the flesh of her upper arm.

20

"Change, Ann!" Chiron's voice was hushed, but his tone was insistent. He pulled her into the room. "Change!"

Obeying without thought, she shifted from human to unicorn, eradicating the poison from her body.

"Oh, Ann!" Chiron called loudly, winking at her. "Don't pass out!" She knew his words echoed down the hallway. He was laying it on for them. "Stay with me!"

Suddenly, her eyes caught on something in the darkness. "Shit, Chiron, look at that," she whispered.

He didn't look. He didn't have time. He was bolting the door, shifting into centaur form at the same time. Then he bent over his suitcase, and opened it. He took out a pistol and locked the ammo into it. Apparently, this was the place to make a stand.

She walked toward the back of the room. Something smelled familiar—and wrong—and she spied two beds in the back. Machines hissed at their sides and poured milky blue light into the room. Even though she didn't need light to see, she hit the switch.

Two women lay on the beds, both apparently unconscious.

Neither had reacted to the light. Comas? Then she spied her mother. Taped to her upper lip, a tube ran into her nose. An IV stood near her head. "Mom!" she called. *Mom!*

Her mother didn't answer. Fighting a growing panic, Ann looked at the label in the IV sack, wondering if she'd even recognize whatever drug they were putting into her. Lactated Ringers Solution. Ann breathed in relief. That was for rehydration. Nothing terrible.

Then a small pump on the other side of the bed kicked in, its soft whirring almost gentle. She recognized the machine immediately—an apheresis machine, the kind that plasma donation centers used to take blood from willing donors.

There was nothing willing about her mother.

"Chiron!" she called in a hushed whisper. She glanced at the second patient. A wild mane of red hair floated over the pillow in otherworldly beauty. Jealousy knotted her stomach. Ann suspected she knew who this second woman was. "I found my mother!" She paused. "And someone else too."

"Stay there! They're coming."

"You need to—"

She didn't get a chance to answer because the door burst open, kicked to pieces by two men with rifles. Rifles? What kind of people used armed men to guard a lab? Brode Institute was a lot of things, but it wasn't a National Laboratory housing federal secrets.

"Ah, Dr. Fallon, I thought I might find you here." Dr. Stoller looked worse than even last night as he stepped through the debris into the room. The purplish lesion on his skin had spread from his hands to his neck. One crept up his face. Oozing drops of oil beaded on the bruise-colored flesh.

Chiron stepped toward him, and she could see he'd overpower the mad professor as easy as anything, despite the men holding rifles to his side. Stoller wasn't well—and never had a man seemed more powerful than Chiron.

"I've had enough of you, Dr. Stoller," Chiron said.

"Wait." Ann held up her hand, and he stopped. "Don't hurt him. Yet." She nodded at Stoller. "Get rid of them." She pointed at the security guards. "Then we'll talk."

With a shaky movement, Dr. Stoller turned toward the armed men. "Please, wait in the hall for me."

"Chiron, look behind me," she said. "In the beds. It's important."

He did. "Akantha!" His hooves clopped on the hard floor as he moved to her side.

"My God, man, what have you done to her?" Chiron's cry told Ann everything she needed to know. The flame-haired woman was his lost love—and he still loved her.

"We need answers," Stoller said. "And we need them now."

"We're not lab rats!" She wanted to shake the old professor's shoulder, but he'd probably break into pieces. "Dr. Stoller, you disgrace Harvard's name—and the name of science," Ann said. "You can't treat people this way."

"I haven't." He shook his head, his eyes rueful.

"Of course you have. Look at them." She waved her hand. "My mother was a healthy, vibrant woman, and look what you've done!"

"There's where you're wrong."

"She *was* healthy! I just spoke to her—"

"You misunderstand." Stoller shook his pale head. "She was healthy, just not a human."

"What?"

"I'm afraid that your karyotype is quite distinctive compared to that of *Homo sapiens.*"

"Are you saying I'm not a person?" Her tone couldn't quite carry the depth of her disbelief.

"One could make that argument." Stoller raised his hairy eyebrows. Even as she watched, the lesion seemed to spread toward the bridge of his nose.

"Are you kidding me?"

"Look at him." He pointed to Chiron, the very image of glorious masculinity and power. "He has hooves and a tail."

Words escaped Ann for a moment, and she wanted nothing more than to obliterate the fool standing before her, the fool who'd ruined her life and the lives of anyone she'd ever loved.

"His soul is more humane and more noble than yours." She gestured toward him. "He has more power than you ever had."

"Ah, but you misunderstand again, Dr. Fallon. Chimpanzees are so closely related to us, and yet we conduct gruesome experiments on them daily. You have hooves and ask for more rights? That makes no sense. No human would agree with you."

"I—"

"I'm going to kill him." Chiron moved away from Akantha's side with a blurring speed. He grabbed the old man's neck, and started to squeeze.

"Chiron, stop."

He paused, and Ann could see the effort it cost him.

"And this is the creature supposedly known for his wisdom." Stoller's mocking voice dared Chiron to finish the job.

"You'd prove him right if you killed him," Ann said. "You'd prove your inhumanity."

He nodded, sorrow clear in his green eyes. Then he threw Stoller aside like he weighed no more than a rag doll. "I know."

"We might need him alive anyway," she added. "Who knows what they've done to them." She nodded toward the unconscious women.

Ann turned toward Stoller. With a sigh, she helped him to his feet. "How are you keeping her comatose?"

"How isn't as important as why." The old man's voice shook now. "Her genes hold the secret to immortality for humans—and so do yours."

Ann looked at Carl's stooped form and the oozing lesions on his face. "How's that working for you?"

He shrugged, and that merry twinkle came back to his eye. "Not so well, as you can see. I tried to rush things along." He made a futile gesture with his crooked hands. "Perhaps I should've waited a bit longer. We're testing the new serum on others."

"She would have healed you." Ann gestured to her mother. "Why did you—"

"Will you heal me?"

"I—"

"Actually, that wasn't a request. It was an order. You will do more than heal me. I know you can turn back the clock—just like your mother did all those years ago. I know you can make people young again—just like you did for Mrs. Hallock. And you will do that for me. Now."

"You presumptive bastard." Chiron nearly leaped toward him again. "You drain an immortal human—and Akantha *is* human—of all that makes her herself, and then you demand help?"

"I—"

Ann didn't need to hear the argument. She was already shifting into unicorn form. The power radiating from the floor of the building poured into her so fast that she almost passed out. She didn't actually shift, she realized. She slid from one form to another like silk slides off a shoulder.

The lust was there, beckoning her. She tried to shove it away, but it refused. Deep in her core she longed for satisfaction. She longed for his hands and mouth, and his cock, but no matter how hard she tried, it refused to step back.

Then she realized why she couldn't push the lust away.

What she felt for Chiron was more than lust—and she couldn't shove it away. Except now he stood by the bedside of his beloved, his wife—and Ann's soul wanted to weep.

Holding back tears, she funneled the throbbing energy into her horn. She walked over to the prone woman at Chiron's side, and she dipped her horn. She would save her, if she could. What better gift could she give him?

"Ann." The word seemed ripped from Chiron's throat. "Oh, Ann. What are you doing?"

He knew, though. From his tone, Ann heard he knew.

"Remarkable!" Carl Stoller's eyes were hard on her. "Your mother refused to change in front of me." That gave Ann a start—even yesterday she herself would have refused. "She refused to help."

In this heartbeat, Ann would change in front of the world. She was tired of hiding who she was. Chiron had done that for her, shown her that she could be herself and still be accepted . . . and maybe more than accepted.

"That ozone!" Stoller said. "I'd never have guessed there'd be the feel of ozone. Look!" He held up a wrinkled arm. "My hairs are standing on end."

"If you make a move," Chiron said, "I will kill you."

"And centaurs!" He shook his grizzled head. "Akantha gave no indication of that. Who knew there were centaurs in this world?"

"Thanks to people like you, you slimy bastard, I'm the only one."

"People like me?" Stoller seemed affronted. "I'd never kill something as unique as you."

"Yet you refuse to acknowledge my humanity. That was the Lapiths' first step toward genocide—they refused to acknowledge our humanity, and that gave them the right to slaughter us, to drive us to extinction."

Ann turned away from them, both of them. She knew normally she'd need to inspect the woman for injuries, but as she stood next to Chiron's beloved, the air felt strange, charged. Her magic was stronger here than it'd ever been in her life.

She dipped her horn and let the power she'd channeled flow through the woman's chest and into her cells.

And then—If Ann had been in human form, she would have gasped. There was no injury in this woman, at least, not of the sort that Ann could help. The woman in the bed had more power than Ann could even imagine. In fact, the woman might actually be the reason Ann's powers had been so strong since she arrived in San Diego.

The woman in the bed was growing and changing. She was . . . becoming.

Knowing Akantha would never need her help, Ann turned toward her mother.

"Heal me!" the old man cried. He ripped himself from Chiron's side and flung himself at her feet. "Make me young again!" Ann ignored him.

Her mother's blood was filled with a toxin Ann didn't recognize, immobilizing her tissue without damaging her. Her unicorn heart couldn't fight it because it wasn't an actual injury.

Ann could flush it, though, and she did. Ann imbued her mother's blood with her healing energy, and within heartbeats, her mother's blood cells had regenerated. The poison was gone, and her mother's eyelids fluttered.

Mom, she said. *How do you feel?*

Oh, my Anemone. Her mom reached out her hand and touched Ann's equine jaw. *I can't believe how good it is to see you—but you shouldn't have risked it. If they hurt you, I'll never forgive myself.*

I have help. No one will hurt us.

Only then did Ann turn toward Dr. Stoller, her ears forward.

"Ann," Chiron said. "He's the last man on the planet who deserves your help. Don't do it."

The fact that he didn't think she'd shish kabob him made her grin to herself, but she was her own master. She let her healing tendrils loop around Carl's sickened form.

Aging had ravaged his cells, but the twisted concoction he'd made from Akantha's blood caused the lesions, which were abundant along the walls of his liver and pancreas. Without her help, death would come for him within the hour.

She staved it off for him.

But she wouldn't turn back the clock.

Chiron looked at Akantha's pale face, perfection. The rise and fall of her chest was shallow—but it existed. She lived. For two years, he'd thought her dead—and here she was, returned to him by Dr. Ann Fallon.

His heart twisted at the thought.

"Beloved," he said for her ears only. Her red hair spilled over her pillow as if arranged by magical hands. What had they done to her? He bent to kiss her—and she opened her eyes.

"Chiron," she said, and she closed her eyes as if weary beyond living.

"Beloved—"

"Security!" Stoller's voice, stronger than Chiron had ever heard it, bounced through the room. The two armed men who'd been in the hall rushed into the room, and Chiron left Akantha's side for Ann's.

"Kill her." Stoller pointed to Ann's mother. "We'll keep the younger one." He gave a dark grin. "She appears to be much more obliging than her mother—and they are equally powerful."

Still in unicorn shape, Ann gave a sharp equine scream, but Chiron didn't have time for words. He gathered his hindquarters and leaped across the room. The slippery floor couldn't provide enough friction to keep his feet beneath him. He slid into the men, bowling them over. One of them shot the ceiling, and white dusty fibers filled the air.

"Immobilize the unicorn," Stoller called to the men, but Chiron didn't give them the chance. He grabbed the closest man's head, and he shoved it toward the second man's head with focused strength. Bone hit bone with a loud crack.

Another sharp equine scream caught his attention. Green wisps were already looping around Ann's horn, and she moved back toward her mother.

The cracking of skulls had masked a lucky shot. A bullet had landed in her mother's chest.

Stoller—with an alacrity and strength given to him by Ann herself—jumped toward his downed security. He grabbed a rifle from one of them and aimed it at Ann's mother.

This wouldn't do. Chiron jerked his equine legs beneath him, and knocked the weapon out of the man's hand with the punch.

"I've had about enough of you." Chiron extricated his legs from the tangle of unconscious security guards, and moved toward the old man. She might have healed the bastard, but she hadn't made him younger.

Stoller must have seen his death in Chiron's expression. "You can't kill me." Stoller pointed toward the corner of the room, where the black eye of a camera impassively reflected Chiron's face. "That's live video feed. The whole world knows."

Chiron shook his head. "No one believes photography and videos anymore. Digital manipulation has made photographs a thing of the past."

"That may be true, but I have genetic material. When scientists see the karyotypes and the sequencing oddities, they'll have no choice. They'll believe you and your girlfriends exist."

"You know," Chiron said, "I really have had enough." With that, he hauled back and punched the man in the face. Ann could heal him if she wanted, but he wanted nothing more to do with the man. Chiron then walked over to the camera and pulled back his fist to punch that too—but a warm nuzzle between his shoulders stopped him. He looked at Ann, and her dark equine eyes met his.

"What?" he asked, and she gently nudged him out of the way.

With a graceful hop, she reared onto two legs. She bent her neck nearly to her chest so that her horn touched the camera. Then she let the green loops of mist fall on the device.

The camera crackled and the wires running from its rear panel to the wall sizzled green. The green traveled along the wires like sparks along a fuse.

"I didn't know you could do that." He touched her shoulder, ran his fingers through her silky mane. "No more digital images."

She shifted back to human form in a heartbeat, and the scent of desire wafted around her. "We have to destroy this place," she said. "They have genetic material, and we can't run from it."

"You brought the gear." He nodded at his case of explosives and weaponry. "We'll destroy it."

"We have to get everyone out." She looked at the heap of unconscious—and unworthy—humanity lying at his feet. Stoller and his men didn't look evil right now, but looks could be deceiving. "Including them."

"Fair enough."

"I can walk, Anemone." Ann's mother sat, her movements gingerly. "Strap them in this bed. We'll push them out."

"Good idea." Chiron picked up the men and dumped them on top of each other while Ann and her mother fumbled with ankles, wrists and straps. "Who else is in the building?"

"Brad's here with Meena."

"I knew that." He flushed with the memory.

Chiron?

He stopped in his tracks. He really was hearing Ann's sweet voice in his head. *Ann?*

We can keep in contact this way. I'm going to get everyone out. Don't blow anything up until I've emptied all the rooms.

Ann? Chiron understood that he was hearing Ann's mother as she spoke to her daughter. The unicorn and centaur gifts were remarkably compatible, and now that he'd seen Akantha, he thought he knew why.

There are many rooms, Anemone, Ann's mother said. *I'll take Akantha and the men. You search. Chiron can do whatever he's going to do with those explosives. We'll meet out front?*

Do you think Akantha can walk? Ann wasn't at all sure.

Either that, or she'll fly, her mother replied.

As Chiron started toward the north end of the building. Ann slipped into her unicorn form. Doors might be more difficult, but her sight and sense of smell were better.

Ann pushed open the door to the room where she'd left Brad and Meena, but even as she did, she knew they were gone. Their scent—Brad's lust mingled with Meena's—trailed down the hall.

Mom? she asked. *Do you know of any prisoners here?*

No, but that doesn't mean there aren't any. Ann heard something uncertain in her mom's tone, something that was unrelated to other prisoners.

What is it, Mom?

There's something very odd about the woman with me. Ann could hear the testing tone in her mother's voice.

Akantha? Ann pushed a door open. She smelled no one. Saw no one.

Yes.

What is it? Ann asked this, although she thought she knew. Even as she trotted to the next door and shoved it open with her chest, she thought she knew.

She's really not herself, is she?

I would think not. Ann saw two more doors in this hall. Quickly she opened them, looked, and sniffed. *But I didn't know her before . . . this.*

As Ann pushed opened the final door of the hall, she wondered if her mother had noticed the strength of this spot, the ease with which they could access their power. Did her mother know the source? Did her mom understand that the source ran at her side?

No one was in the room, and Ann trotted to the next hall.

Ann! The voice didn't belong to her mother.

Chiron?

You need to run. There's a whole team of security guards here, and they're loading stuff into a truck. Another team just went down the hall, and they're armed to the teeth.

We can't blow anyone up, Chiron—

I can't blow you up.

Ann started to form the words to object, but a ground-shaking explosion rang through the building.

Chiron!

Run!

She sensed frustration and anger in his tone, and it wasn't at her. *I didn't set those explosives,* he said. *They went off by themselves.*

Run! she called to anyone who'd listen, to anyone who was sensitive to a mindlink.

A second explosion rocked the earth beneath them.

Get out of here now, Ann! These men are insane. They're blowing up the building as we speak.

She doubted it was the men. In fact, she'd bet the source was the woman by her mother's side. *Isn't that a good thing the place is exploding?*

If the men weren't taking all sorts of things out of here in armored cars, it'd be a good thing. Get out! I can't let them take the trucks!

Running as fast as she could, she smelled burning plastic, burning wood, burning linoleum—but not burning flesh. If she was wrong about Akantha—wrong about her true identity— Ann would probably die here.

Ann burst through the front door, gasping in the fresh night air. A group of people was huddled in front of the building—security guards, an older man in a lab coat, a woman wearing a janitor's uniform. Where was her mom?

"That was the weirdest thing," the janitor said. "I heard a voice in my head telling me to run, and I ran. And I'm glad I did, because the next thing I know, the place is in flames."

"Amazing," Ann agreed.

"It was my guardian angel."

"Yes, it was," a masculine voice said with a chuckle.

Ann was relieved to see Brad there. He'd fashioned a pair of cuffs from the gurney, and he used them to control Meena, sort of. She was still trying to slide her hips over Brad's, and he didn't seem to be fighting her too hard.

"What are you doing?" Ann asked with a laugh. She scanned the crowd for her mom.

"What can I say?" Brad flashed Ann a grin. "Chicks dig me."

"I'm glad it's been a good day for someone."

He laughed. "When your guy actually used the grenades, I knew no night was ever going to get better than this one." He started ticking off his fingers. "First, a unicorn shifting shape right in front of me, then that car, then that ride, then . . ."

Ann turned away from him, not needing to hear the litany. She spied her mother standing next to Akantha, brushing her red hair out of her face. Her mom patted Akantha's hand in a soothing gesture, and Ann could tell she was speaking calming words to the immortal. When her mom spied Ann, she jumped to her side and embraced her.

"My Anemone," she said, burying her face in Ann's hair. "Oh, I've missed you. I never thought I'd see you again. Or touch you or smell you."

"Mom." Ann had imagined that when she finally saw her mother, it would be against the backdrop of her herd of wild horses and the majestic Sierra Nevadas—not against the Brode

Institute, twenty-foot flames shooting from its interior. "I love you."

I can't destroy the armored cars. Chiron's voice carried a deep fear. *I'm—*

What? Chiron, what?

Something caught her gaze. Next to her mother, Akantha was holding her hand at an odd angle, flicking her fingers.

Jesus Christ, the armored cars, Chiron said. *The drivers just—I don't know. They fell out of the seats, and now the trucks are hovering ten feet above the ground!*

Akantha brought her hands to her sides in a fast motion.

Now they've crashed!

Oh, my God, Ann thought to herself. Akantha's red hair floated around her face like it was charged with electricity. She'd been right about the ancient woman.

The woman with the red hair turned toward Ann. "He came back for me." Wonder filled the woman's voice. She wasn't gloating.

"Yes." Ann touched the woman's—the being's—arm. "For two years he's been looking for you."

A radiant smile filled the woman's face. The woman had lovely cheekbones and startling green eyes. Ann hadn't seen a more beautiful woman in her life. "He's found me—and you would have given me back to him."

"He—" But Ann faltered. "He loves you. Of course I returned you to him."

Another beatific smile crossed the woman's face, and then she turned away.

That was the craziest thing I've ever seen, Chiron's voice intruded in her thoughts. *But we're safe. No one can prove anything about us. No more genetic material.*

That's a good thing, Ann said. *Because I hear fire trucks and helicopters.*

"When we run this time," Ann's mother whispered in her ear, "we'll run together. You can bring Chiron with you."

Something in her heart broke at those words, because Chiron's beloved was standing here, waiting for him.

The sirens were getting louder. Ann saw the humans turning toward the road, hope and confusion in their expressions.

"We should run now, love," her mother said.

"We can't leave Akantha." The woman's expression was off, almost zombielike, but Ann knew she'd trashed the armored cars—the armored cars no one on this side of the building could see.

"Look!" her mother said. "There's your Chiron."

He was striding from behind the building in human form, the very picture of rugged masculinity and power. He had soot smudged across his face, but it didn't detract from his beauty.

Ann could see the flashing red lights of the fire trucks now, and the helicopter above them bore the letters KNSD. A huge light from the helicopter panned over the building and then the crowd.

"Ann." Chiron stood right next to her, but didn't take her hand or wrap her in his arms. "Let's go. I'll carry Akantha. You and your mother can run. We'll get out of here. I have a place in Mexico. No one will find us."

Cop cars and a news van were pulling into the parking lot. They had only minutes.

"You going to run?" Brad asked. "Your secret's safe with me." He winked.

But she wasn't going to run. Not anymore. Not from predators, not from humans, not from her own fears of loneliness and persecution.

She turned toward Chiron and said, "Do you know any civil rights lawyers?"

"What?"

"And constitutional lawyers."

"Ann," Chiron said, his voice tight. "What are you talking about?"

The news van had parked, and the reporter and cameraman were getting out.

"Did you ever see *Alien Nation*?"

"*Alien Nation*?" He looked at her like she was nuts, and then his brow cleared. He understood. Of course he understood—because even though they'd just met, they knew each other better than anyone else.

"You're going to make a stand?" He shook his head. "After all you've seen, after all the slaughter, you're going to make a stand?"

"I can't run anymore."

"You can't trust civility." He glanced at Akantha. With her vacant expression, she seemed human, but Chiron would learn the truth soon enough. "Civilization's a veneer, a very thin veneer."

Ann nodded. He was right. Humans had slaughtered centaurs, and humans had enslaved unicorns for their magic—but it didn't change her heart, the heart he had opened for her. She couldn't go back to hiding and running. She couldn't go back to the fear.

Next to them, Akantha began to hum. Ann had no idea what this meant, if her notes corresponded with some unseen force of nature unleashing itself someplace.

"You need to take Akantha. Take her away from this." Ann ran her hand through her hair, missing the neatness of her bun. "She doesn't need to be here for this, Chiron, really." And humanity might not be ready for what Akantha could reveal.

Chiron looked between the two women, torn.

"Go." Ann knew she'd cry later, but she felt nothing but determination now. "Go!"

"I know lawyers. I have a friend who argues Supreme Court cases regularly. I'll call her."

Ann's mom wrapped her hand around Ann's, a question in her eyes. "Go with him, Mom. Come out of hiding when it's safe."

"No way," her mom said. "I argued for this among our kind a hundred times. I'm staying."

"Who said I'm going?" Chiron asked, but she knew. His need to protect Akantha would outweigh any other need—even the need to protect her.

Or maybe he'd learned something about protecting her.

Maybe he'd learned the lesson too well. Did she really want to be alone for the rest of her life?

What choice did she have? Ann took a deep breath, realizing she could live with this. She was strong enough for this fight—thanks to him, thanks to his acceptance and . . . his affection.

"I'll be okay, Chiron." For a moment she watched him look at the reporters. The cameraman was walking toward them now, the spotlight coming their way. If Chiron stayed just a few more heartbeats, his choices would be fewer.

"It's okay. I'll be fine." She leaned in toward him, inhaling his delicious scent. With her eyes closed she could almost see the cedar trees his fragrance invoked, see the horses thundering over the plains. Then she touched her lips to his, as lightly as a hummingbird touches a blossom. "Go," she said, moving away.

Akantha's humming broke into a forlorn lament now, and all of her hair stood on end.

Chiron touched Ann's face. "Thank you." Then he swept Akantha into his arms and ran.

Ann was wrong about her tears—they came now, hard and fierce.

But when the camera's spotlight fell on her and her mother, she let her human form slip away. Her tears evaporated, because animals can't shed tears.

21

The path through Baltimore's Druid Hill Park was steep, and Ann lengthened her equine stride to eat the miles. A nice sweat covered her body from her poll to her fetlocks, and she liked how people had quit staring at her, at least here. Having a unicorn gallop through their woods had become commonplace.

She slowed to a trot and then a walk, appreciating that at least this part of her life was complete. The parking lot was just ahead, and she shifted to human form, relegating the accompanying lust to the back of her mind with an ease that left her a little sad. Ever since Chiron had vanished, she could change forms and heal people with almost no change to her libido.

As she turned on the car, the reporter's voice filled the car, and Ann turned up the volume. The Supreme Court reporter was describing the soon-to-be-argued case regarding full civil rights and definitions of intelligence in nonhuman species. Since several members of the newly discovered species *Homo unicornensis* actually had doctoral degrees—Dr. Ann Fallon had her doctorate from Stanford, the reporter informed the audience—the case was expected to be straightforward.

Ann turned it off. As she drove past the throngs of people lining the streets near her home, she knew her life was anything but straightforward.

A dark-skinned woman with huge sad eyes watched Ann drive by and held up a sign. "I have AIDS." The woman next to her wore a huge pink ribbon on her breast. A man held a small boy's hand, beseeching her with his eyes. The child stared into the sky with an off-kilter smile, and Ann knew he was blind.

She pulled over. As her shoes hit the ground, they changed to hooves, and loops of green mist spiraled from her horn. Such ease would have astounded her before, but Akantha's magic had done something strange to the world. Now, she pulled energy from the earth and poured her energy into all the supplicants at once.

Despite the fact that her cousins had set up an around-the-clock center in Nashville to heal anyone without question, people still sought her and her family here. She healed them without question, but she never made anyone younger. She'd keep that skill secret, at least for now.

"Thank you!" someone cried. "Bless you." Voices fell over each other. Only the fact that she didn't have hands stopped them from showering her with gifts. Someone had installed a box in front of her apartment, and people stuffed that with tokens of gratitude. She gave the checks and cash she found there directly to a foundation to fight homelessness.

On four legs, she clattered up her stone steps and changed into human form to open the door. She paused a minute in the lobby to collect her mail, hating the sick hope that coursed through her heart every time she sorted through the mail, every time the phone rang. Would Chiron ever talk to her again? He could at least do her the service of telling her good-bye.

A masculine-sounding clearing of a throat made her jump. "Forgive me," he said. "Are you Dr. Fallon?"

She spun around, green swirls curling around her ankles. "Yes."

"Can I talk to you for a minute?"

She took in his suit and military build. "FBI?" she asked.

He blinked and then let an impassive expression take hold. "Yes." He reached for his ID. "How'd you know?"

"The CIA and NSA have already talked to me, and I'll tell them the same thing I'm telling you. No."

"But—"

"Listen, the military already asked my mother if she'd work with them to develop a unicorn-based weapon. No. I don't want to be an instant healer on your battlefield, I don't want to provide instant communication, and I don't want to—"

The man held up his hands in a mock plea for mercy. "I'm here about Dr. Carl Stoller."

She shut up. "I'm sorry." Dr. Stoller's body hadn't been found in the Brode Institute explosion, and Ann figured the Earthmother must have had something to do with that. She doubted Akantha's weird song had been a sign of joie de vivre. "I can be an ass. Do you want to come in?"

"No, thank you."

"Okay." Ann assumed he didn't want to be seen. "What is it then?"

"We found Stoller in Cambridge."

"He's at home?"

The man shook his head. "No, he was wandering around like a homeless man. He doesn't remember who he is, where he came from, anything. But *where* he's wandering is interesting."

"What do you mean?"

"Apparently Harvard had a number of very low-profile research facilities, which just happened to have exploded on the same night as the Brode Institute."

"FBI," Ann said, looking at him more carefully. He'd taken

off his glasses, but his eyes didn't give much away. "You're here because you suspect domestic terrorism."

A slight tightening of his lips told her he suspected something else. "I'm here because a number of people think the unicorns did it, blew the place up, that is."

The unicorns? Dear God. "We're healers by nature. None of us did it." She knew who did, though. The Earthmother. Akantha.

"A number of people believe that too. I'm just here to warn you, tell you you have enemies. Be careful."

"They can join the health insurance companies," she said. "They hate us, too. Thank you, Mr . . ."

"You're welcome." He slipped through the door to the basement.

Ann sighed as she climbed the steps to her apartment, but she wasn't exactly surprised to be talking to spies. Yesterday, her mother had talked to the Vatican, who wanted to make her a living saint for all the miracles she'd procured.

As Ann opened the door to her apartment, the scent of gingerbread wafted over her. It should have made her mouth water, but she was hungry for something else—someone else.

"Come join me," her mother said from the kitchen table. She pushed a pot of tea in front of Ann as she sat.

"Thanks." Ann's words were polite, but she ached inside.

"So?" Her mom pushed cookies in front of her. "You ready for your big day?"

Ann took a pink-frosted cookie, but the only sweet thing she wanted had run off with the Earthmother incarnate. She doubted she'd see him again. What man would leave a goddess? What goddess would let a man like Chiron go? "Yeah," Ann said. "I think I am."

"Don't take this wrong, Anemone, but I'm glad to see you going into medicine."

"I know, Mom." She tried not to feel annoyed.

Johns Hopkins had made her the only interesting proposal. They'd offered her a position as a graduate student in both biochemistry and genomics, all expenses paid plus free room and board. The goal of her dissertation was to unravel the mystery of her ability to change shape. They suggested that she save the exploration of her healing ability for a postdoctoral position— and they'd hired Brad Scrimshaw, at her suggestion.

"I was so proud of you for your doctorate in animal behavior," her mom said. "But I always felt like you were shunning your true nature. Something in you has changed, and I like it." She touched Ann's arm. "I'm proud of you."

Something in her had changed—her heart. Chiron had seen the truth of her soul and accepted it, embraced it. And that had given her courage—no, that wasn't right. It had shown her that she couldn't live a life without truth. She deserved to be valued for who she was—not what she could provide.

If only Chiron had valued her enough to choose her.

"At Johns Hopkins," her mom said, ignoring the fact that Ann was brooding, "you get to be your own guinea pig and your own mad scientist." She chuckled warmly as she ate a cookie.

"I'll understand myself better, understand my biology," Ann said. "That's the important part."

"What is it that you want to know?"

The question had so many layers of potential answers that Ann couldn't speak. Looking at the line of people waiting for the healing power of unicorns out her window, she could see the wisdom of Stoller's plan. If unicorns could distribute their abilities in a pill, she and her kind would be free to live normal lives. Maybe figuring out how the healing worked wasn't a bad idea—as long as it didn't subjugate an entire race in the process.

She had faith in her ability to puzzle it out under the tutelage of the scientists at Johns Hopkins—but that wasn't the kind of understanding she really sought.

"He'll come back to you, Anemone." Her mom touched her arm, and Ann fought back tears. These days should taste like victory, but the successes tasted as dry as the cookie in her mouth.

"Why should he, Mom? I hardly know him. I spent one weekend with him."

"You just wait and see." Her mother took a sip of tea. "Sometimes I'm right."

"He's over me, Mom."

"Love isn't that simple, and men are proud creatures. He probably thinks you hate him."

"Hate him?"

Her mother looked at her, pale eyebrows raised. "He did leave you alone to face the reporters and the world." She picked another smidge of icing off her cookie. "Not everyone would think that was behavior worthy of a gentleman."

Ann looked at her, dumbfounded. "I don't hold that against him."

"But he might hold it against himself."

When Chiron first received the document, he was pleased. It would make a fine olive branch. He spent long hours inspecting it, the ornate scrollwork along the edges, the State of Nevada's seal at the top. The document was beautiful.

But could he send it to her? Should he send it? Unable to decide, he had slid it into an envelope and put it in his desk.

He had thought he'd forget about it. It was a stupid gesture. Ann Fallon, through her own personal strength and courage, had found her own freedom. The freedom he offered her with this document was a copout. He saw that.

Still, he couldn't get the deed out of his mind. The gold scrollwork haunted his dreams. No, the fall of her hair over her shoulders haunted his dreams. The idea of giving her the document, beautiful for both its scrollwork and what it represented, haunted his dreams.

In some dreams, she gave him that glorious smile and thanked him.

In the nightmares, she shredded it in his face and called him a coward.

As if the deed itself could solve his dilemma, he walked over to his desk and pulled out the envelope. The document was as intricate and graceful as he remembered. By hiding the thing away, he was just putting off the inevitable. He had to know the truth.

"Shit."

He picked up his pen and wrote her address on the envelope. Then he headed out the door to the post office. He'd make the phone call when he got home.

Ann was right. Living like this—living a lie—was no way to live. Four thousand years of cowardice was enough.

"Ann!" her mother gasped from the kitchen. "You've got to hear this!"

"What?"

Her mother rushed to the stereo and flipped on the power. The cool voice of the reporter filled the room.

. . . repeat, this is breaking news. There has been a stunning new revelation today. Just as humanity has begun to adjust to the fact that it is not the only intelligent species inhabiting this planet, a second new species brings itself to our attention: the centaurs . . . or, at least, a centaur. On the day when opening arguments begin at the Supreme Court to establish the civil rights and liberties of Homo unicornensis, *the creature scientists are calling* Homo centauri *has appeared at Johns Hopkins School of Medicine, where he has agreed to undergo scientific examination—but only by a team that includes at least one unicorn.*

Unlike the unicorns, this creature cannot heal others—but he can shift between human shape and that of a centaur. And, perhaps most surprisingly, he claims to be immortal. He claims to have been born on what is now the island of Crete in the year 1992 B.C.

Here to discuss the cultural implications of this are . . .

"What's he doing?" Ann asked. Her heart was beating so hard in her chest she couldn't hear her own thoughts.

"I told you," her mother said. "It's love. Maybe he's fighting for you."

"I—" Ann started to say, but the doorbell interrupted her.

"Yes?" Her mom opened the door.

"There's a package here for Ms. Ann." The FedEx man's voice was always polite. It helped that her mother had cured his wife's breast cancer.

"Thank you." She gave the package to Ann, and somehow, she knew it was from Chiron.

Apparently her mother felt it too. "I told you," her mother said. "He's fighting for you."

Ann pulled the tab. A sheet of paper slid from the envelope, its gold embossing catching the room's light and glowing. "It's a deed—and it's in my name."

"To what?"

"I think . . ." Ann read the property's coordinates and description and understood what land she now owned. "I think it's my research site."

"To the place you were going to get Harvard to buy so we could all hide away?"

"Yes." For years Ann had had her sights on this place as the ultimate location for hiding. She fingered the heavy document, savoring its beauty. Chiron wasn't giving her a hiding place with this deed—he was offering her something different.

"What's the note say?"

He'd stuck a sticky on the back of the deed. " 'Enjoy the solitude,' it says."

"So, he's not going to be there," her mother said. "That's a shame. I'd have liked to meet him."

"Accepting this gift puts demands on us." Ann had to point it out. She'd thought that being beholden to Harvard would be acceptable, but only because she'd have been working for them.

"I think the land belongs to you whether you accept it or not. That's what a deed means, Anemone."

With a sick feeling in her stomach, Ann realized her mother was right. And more than that, just imagining the open mountains, the grassy valleys, and the scent of horses made Ann so homesick she almost cried.

"We should go visit." Her mom ate another cookie. "Get away from these crowds, out of this apartment."

The same longing coursed through Ann. And it wasn't like Chiron would be there. She wouldn't have to see the rejection in his eyes.

The sprawling fields sparkled in the early afternoon sun, green glinting off wet grass. The gray mountain crags called to her. Some were still peaked in snow.

Ann changed shape, her feet craving the freedom of speed. Or maybe it was her heart craving that freedom. Her mother followed suit, her pleasure at seeing the wide-open spaces evident in her prancing hooves. Like Ann, she held her tail high, and they waved them like flags as they trotted in tight circles.

The air is so clean here! Her mom stood, all muscles frozen as she sniffed.

It was true. The jagged mountaintops kept smog at bay, and the sky sparkled a blue so clear it reminded Ann of sapphires.

I want to run, her mother said.

Ann stopped and held her equine nose in the air. The herd of horses who'd been her study group—more like pets—stood in the near distance, and Ann whinnied, calling to them.

The lead mare saw her first. With a scream of delight, the bay galloped toward her, her black mane and tail flying, her neck arched.

Ann whickered as the mare approached, and they blew their breath into each other's nostrils in greeting. Ann wondered how she'd managed to stay away for so long. She'd been so busy fighting for her civil rights, she'd forgotten how much her soul needed soothing.

The bay mare squealed and kicked out a foreleg, begging Ann to run the same way a dog begs its master to play.

Do you mind? she asked her mother.

Go! Run like the wind, Anemone. I won't bother you.

She needed no further encouragement. She tossed her head at the bay mare, who took off toward the herd. Ann followed on her heels.

Caught up in the joy of the moment, the entire herd stampeded the valley. Babies leaped and bucked in a show of strength, and Ann's heart did the same. Yearlings challenged each other to sprints. Hooves pounded over the hard-packed dirt, and the sweet scent of horse sweat filled the air. Ann ran hard, intoxicated by the bliss of freedom.

One by one, the horses dropped out of the race. They weren't built like thoroughbreds. Forty-five-miles-per-hour gallops weren't in their make-up. Neither was a twenty-mile sprint.

But once the joy of running filled Ann's veins, she didn't want to stop. The white-hot sun pounded on her back, and the sound of her thrumming hooves filled her ears. She left all her cares in the dust. She knew if she changed shape right here, she'd have a huge grin on her face.

After miles—too many miles to count—sweat lathered her flanks and shoulders. Still, she knew this land, knew a lake of snow runoff lay not too far to the west. She slowed to a trot.

As she turned, a scent—delicious and familiar—assaulted her nose, and she spun toward it.

Him.

She shifted back to human form. The bright mountain light

burned through the sky. "You," she said. Her heart pounded in joy and fear. He was so gorgeous. Even if he'd come to tell her good-bye, he was gorgeous, and her eyes savored him. "You've been following me."

"It wasn't easy." His flanks and chest were lathered, but he stayed in centaur form. "You're fast."

Her eyes drank in the glint of his coppery hair and the planes of his muscles, but hurt made her voice sharp. "You lured me out here, making me think you wouldn't be here."

He shrugged. "I was afraid you wouldn't talk to me."

"You could have called."

"You deserve a bigger gesture." He waved his hands at the mountains.

"I appreciate the sentiment." She noticed then that he'd lost weight. His face was leaner, his cheeks a little hollowed. "But if actions speak louder than words, I think we've said everything that needed to be said."

"You think it was easy for me to leave you to face the reporters? I had to do it. You know I did. I was afraid that Akantha would make the building vanish or float to the moon."

She'd been afraid of the same thing, and in fact, the goddess seemed to have trashed everything to do with the Brode Institute. Erik and Meena Sutherland had lost their minds, just like Carl Stoller.

"Months have passed, Chiron." She swallowed. "I can't make you love me, and I won't be the other woman." She hesitated, now understanding he'd come to say good-bye. She hated the secret part of her heart that wildly hoped he'd pick her over the goddess. "Still," she said. "Thank you for the deed—and for meeting me here."

"Ann," he stepped toward her, but she moved back.

"Don't touch me. I don't think I can stand it."

"Ann." He held up his hand. He wouldn't touch her. "It wasn't what it looked like."

"You never lied to me or made me promises you didn't plan to keep." She shrugged. "You thought she was dead."

"She *was* dead."

"I healed her, Chiron. She wasn't dead."

"That wasn't Akantha. The Earthmother is not the same person, and the person I loved is gone."

"What?"

"Akantha was tired of living and the Earthmother was tired of oblivion."

"What are you telling me?"

"They switched."

"So, the Earthmother is walking the planet?" She shook her head. It sounded like some weird comic book plot—but it explained why her power seemed so much greater than it had in the past.

"She's walking the earth with all the magic of a goddess at her disposal."

A choked laugh escaped her. She didn't even know why. "I can just see Johns Hopkins trying to apply the scientific method to the powers of a goddess." She sounded slightly hysterical, even to herself.

"Ann, Akantha is dead. Truly dead." He held up his arms in a futile gesture. "She'd been wanting death for so long, the Earthmother answered her prayers. Each is where they belong."

"And your heart?

He stepped toward her and embraced her in his arms. "It's where it belongs."

She tipped her head, and his lips grazed hers. As she held him, he shifted back to human form.

"Ann, I have to tell you something."

A hard pit formed in her stomach. Rejection was coming. "What?"

"I realized something while we battled Stoller in the laboratory, something I should have realized much earlier."

"And what's that?"

"You make me whole. You're a true partner running at my side, not a creature I'm racing to protect—and I beg your forgiveness for knocking you out, and for being so blind. I was wrong."

"Can I hear that last line again?"

"I was wrong?"

"That's the one."

"We're stronger together than either of us are alone." He touched her cheek. "And the world is a much better place when I'm near you."

She didn't say anything for a minute. She buried her face in his chest and savored the scent of him and the mountain air. "You know," she said finally, fitting her hips against his erect cock, "unicorns don't live forever. This might be a bad idea."

He shrugged, nuzzling his face in her hair. "You could. The Earthmother is wandering the planet, and your own powers have yet to be tapped. What if your mother turns back your clock for you?"

"But—"

"It's not the point," he interrupted. "I don't care if you live forever or not. My only job is to convince you to enjoy every minute of your life." He brought his mouth down to hers for a kiss that left her aching with need, a kiss that left his cock throbbing against her thigh. "Maybe that enjoyment will convince you to spend the next four centuries with me."

"You planning to use your glorious sexual prowess to convince me?"

He gave her that wicked grin, the sun gleaming in his eyes. "Oh, yeah."

She traced the line of his chest muscles with a light fingertip, trailing that finger down to the lean line of his hips. "I can live with that."

The Chanku story continues in
WOLF TALES VIII!

On sale now!

1

The narrow chin strap was uncomfortable, but it held her night vision spotting scope in place and made it easier to focus on the pair of wolves crossing the meadow behind the house. Even with the scope, it was difficult to keep them in sight for long. They moved like magic through the dark Montana night, and once they disappeared into the heavy overgrowth bordering the forest, she knew they'd be gone for hours.

Stillness descended as the last wolf slipped through the brush. Still, she watched, her vivid imagination taking her where eyes couldn't follow, taking her into a world of dreams, until exhaustion won out and the dark line of the forest lost its attraction.

Packing up her gear took only a few minutes. Climbing down the fragile rope ladder and raising it once again took a few more, but there would be other nights to watch. Other nights to contemplate the next steps . . . as many as were needed, now that their den was no longer a secret.

Father would be pleased to know she'd come this far. To know that her journey was almost over. She owed him this much, didn't she?

* * *

Head down, tail hanging, the dark wolf that was the wizard Anton Cheval trotted slowly through the towering trees with two things on his mind—the tantalizing scent of his mate and his own terrible failings. Keisha stayed just ahead, blatantly ignoring him. Without even trying, she still managed to entice him with her sleek wolven body and the musky perfume of her arousal. Her sensual appearance and seductive scent flaunted the invitation he'd felt in warm lips and soft breasts only moments before their shift.

He'd not embraced her then. He'd felt unworthy . . . almost unclean. Would he be able to here, in the depths of the forest? Here, where the feral side of his nature might finally overcome the issues confusing his woefully inadequate, deeply flawed human side?

For a man who'd taken great pride in his unflattering reputation as a presumptive, arrogant bastard, he'd certainly had the self-importance knocked out of him. Nearly dying could do that to a guy. Giving up and embracing death when those he loved still fought on, when even his infant daughter showed more backbone than he had . . . dear Goddess, that was even worse.

Would he ever find his way past the pain—the utter humiliation—of his own failings? He'd promised to keep his family and packmates safe, but he'd failed—intruders had breached the very walls of his home.

More than once.

There was no excuse for the fact that Keisha and her cousin Tia, pregnant with her first child, had been forced to defend not only their home and their own lives, but Anton's infant daughter.

They'd done an admirable job. A much better job than he or any of the other males had. As the so-called alpha of this pack of Chanku shapeshifters, he was a dismal failure.

Even now he felt that all was not well. Despite all their precautions, their nightly searches and increased surveillance, his senses jangled with the subtle awareness of some unseen danger hovering just out of sight.

Was it really a threat, or merely the fact his personal world seemed to be spiraling out of control?

The first frost of autumn blanketed the ground and dried grasses crackled beneath their paws. Other than the sound of their passing, the night was silent . . . unless he considered the unwavering clamor of self-flagellation. Creatures stayed warm in their dens. The soft hoot of owls and whisperings of other denizens of the night remained curiously muted, as if the cold imprisoned their voices.

The chill wind didn't reach beneath his thick fur or cool the heat of his desire. No, he figured he'd manage to do that entirely on his own. Even Keisha's magic hadn't been enough to rouse him earlier. Now, her cool, amber-eyed gaze as she glanced over her shoulder drew him, even as his inner demons held him at bay. Still, he moved closer to her, drawn by love and respect more than sexual desire.

That alone reminded him all was not well. A creature normally ruled by his libido, Anton felt nothing. Nothing beyond a sense of terrible desperation.

Keisha slipped beneath a tangle of brambles and led him to a small glade protected from the chill night wind. There she waited, her feral pose as regal as a queen's, head held high, ears forward, feet planted firmly in the frosty grass. She was everything he desired in a mate. Everything he'd ever dreamed of, hoped for.

Everything he no longer deserved.

Anton trotted up to her. Ears lying back against his skull, he dipped his head and touched his nose to hers in an uncharacteristically submissive gesture. His long tongue wrapped around her muzzle. She tilted her head and acknowledged his touch, but her thoughts remained closed to him.

What more could he expect? He'd locked her out for days, an even more cowardly act than the one that had brought him to this point. He still wasn't certain if he was ready to open to the woman he loved. Not certain if he was brave enough to share the doubts and questions dominating his thoughts. For a man who embraced honor, integrity, and personal courage, the realization had come to him slowly—he was no longer worthy of her. No longer worthy of the esteem of his fellow Chanku.

Failure was a painful meal to swallow.

His packmates looked to him for guidance, for safety, for leadership. He'd failed them at every turn. Failed his pack, his lovers, his mate, and even his daughter. Failed to keep them safe, to protect them from those who would do them harm. In fact, he would have failed at life if not for the telepathic words of his child and the life-giving power of his packmates.

They'd shared their own life force to keep him from crossing through the veil when he'd hovered in that dark place between life and death. Seduced by the light and the peace it offered, he'd wanted so badly to follow. His people had given all they had to save his worthless soul when he'd been more than ready to leave this plane for the one that beckoned him.

It had taken the surprisingly powerful voice of baby Lily to force him to choose life with all its pain over the easy escape of death.

The truth unmanned him. The truth had nearly destroyed him. For all his abilities, all his empty words of wisdom and his arrogant orders to those who loved and respected him, Anton Cheval knew he had to face the truth.

He was a coward. Unworthy of the love and sacrifice of his fellow Chanku. Unworthy of their respect.

Unworthy of the woman who waited now, so patiently, for the physical love he couldn't bring himself to share.

Do you love me, Anton?

Keisha's question caught him by surprise. She doubted even that?

More than life. He met her forthright stare and once more felt unworthy.

Then love me. Here. Now. No barriers. No lies.

I've never lied to you. How could she even think that?

When you block me, when you refuse to open to me as my mate, you might as well be lying. Our bond is built on sharing, on complete and total honesty. You've been unforgivably selfish with your thoughts.

Her words were a coldly accurate assessment. They stung. Badly. Anton nodded in painful agreement. *Will you ever forgive me?*

Keisha's chest moved in and out with her slow, steady breathing. It terrified him, knowing she actually had to think about his request. Had he pushed her too far? Destroyed the finest thing that had ever happened to him? Without Keisha, there was nothing. Without her love, he would have been better to follow that seductive light through the veil.

Choosing death, not life . . . with all its pain.

Will you ever forgive yourself? There was no sympathy in Keisha's mental voice.

He hung his head.

Make love to me, Anton. Here. Now. Just the two of us, as open and free as we were when we first bonded. When you swore your undying love for me. When you pulled me out of my own hopeless pain. Do you remember how that was? Open your heart, your thoughts. Share what fears are holding you prisoner, the way you forced me to share mine. Prove to me that love is real, not just words without substance. Can you do that?

He trembled. Unbelievable! Anton Cheval, trembling before his mate, but he'd never been more frightened, not even when faced with his own mortality. To love Keisha here, now, with his barriers down and his thoughts open to her, was to show her the worthless creature she thought she loved.

She growled. *Give it up, Anton. You're wallowing in your perceived inadequacies. It's not all about you. What we have is bigger than you.* The sound rumbled up out of her chest and shocked him with the ferocity behind it. The anger. Her silent words stung.

The fur at her neck rose in an angry line along her spine and her lips peeled back to display sharp teeth. Anton's ears flattened against his skull. His hackles rose. Blood rushed in his veins. His lips curled back in a silent snarl.

She challenged him! Insulted him, belittled his fears. She stared him down with her legs stiff, her body posture aggressive and angry. He'd never seen her like this, not with her anger directed at him. How dare she challenge him!

Lust enveloped him. Fierce and ravenous, it rose in his veins, a feral hunger like nothing he'd felt in so very long.

Passion, anger, and arousal, all knotted together in a twisted tangle of want and need, of fear and confusion. He felt her questions battering at his mind, a demand that he grant her access to his deepest fears, his basest desires.

If he let her in, all was lost.

If he kept her out . . . all was lost.

His chest ached even as arousal blossomed, blinding him to everything but Keisha. His female, her body ripe with need, her scent a musky aphrodisiac enveloping his conscious mind, grabbing hold of his balls in a powerful, visceral grip.

He charged, snarling, teeth bared, saliva dripping from open jaws. Startled, she yipped and turned to run, but he was bigger, stronger. He caught the thick roll of skin at her neck between his teeth and clamped down. She twisted beneath him, and he searched for her thoughts.

Her mind was open, a blazing eruption of emotions, all the

fears she'd hidden from him, the desperate needs he'd ignored for too long. His fault. All his fault!

Keisha tore free of his grasp and faced him, legs spread wide for balance, head hanging low, breath charging in and out of her lungs. Her amber eyes nailed him and he felt her rage, the wolven equivalent of a powerful slap in the face.

No! The world does not revolve around you, Anton Cheval. The world is bigger than you. Our love is bigger than you! What is wrong with you? Where has the man I fell in love with gone?

Her angry words ripped a blindfold off his face and opened a window back into the world he'd fled. He saw himself through Keisha's eyes.

Saw himself through eyes of love.

Arousal surged. He reached for her. Gently, this time, his paw raked her back and she watched him warily. He mounted her as the blood rushed to his cock and when he slipped inside, it was with the amazing sense of truly coming home.

She was hot and slick, her passage ready for his entry. He felt her muscles clench as she braced herself to support his weight. His forelegs tightened around her shoulders and he filled her. His hips thrust hard and fast. The knot in his penis grew, sliding deep within her heat, swelling to fill her passage, binding the two of them together.

Arousal expanded, blinding him to anything and everything but the female he loved, the one who loved him. Power charged through his testicles, the sharp jolt of pleasure streaking from balls to cock as his orgasm swept over him, filled and overwhelmed him. Hot bursts of seed blasted into Keisha and she groaned, but he knew she hadn't found her own release.

Not yet.

Physically connected, his swollen cock locked tightly inside her passage, Anton searched her mind, opening his own thoughts to reach Keisha's. After so many weeks closed inside himself, he opened just enough to touch her spirit with his. He sensed it, then, her silent scream of pleasure, the climax she'd denied herself while she waited for this most intimate connection.

A connection even more powerful than two bodies locked together—the melding of two minds, the mating of reality and spirit.

Without warning, Anton tumbled gracelessly into her waiting consciousness. If he'd been human, he would have wept at the very moment the walls crumbled. The barriers he'd erected so many weeks ago dissolved and disappeared, leaving him naked and wanting.

No, my love. Never in my eyes. Never in the eyes of your pack.

He bowed his head until his muzzle rested against her shoulder. *They gave everything they had to save me when I'd already given up.*

If you'd truly given up, they wouldn't have been able to save you. Your life force, your force, *is stronger than that.*

I love you. You deserve better.

I love you, Anton Cheval. Now shut up and make love to me.

Did you just tell me to shut up? He bit back the unexpected laughter and they shifted as one.

The two of them lay together in the frosty grass with Keisha on her belly beneath him. His cock was still hard, planted deep inside her heat, but his mate pulled away from him and rolled to her back. "I want to see you when you make love with me. No more hiding."

Shamed once again, he hung his head as he knelt between her thighs. "I don't know what's happened to me. It's as if something is lost and I can't find it."

"It's your confidence." She reached for him. Her palm cupped the side of his face. He turned his head slightly and planted a kiss over her lifeline.

Keisha sighed. "You think too much, worry about too many

things. It's all inside you, that innate ability of yours to trust in yourself. Make love to me now. We'll worry about it later."

He smiled. The first time he'd felt like smiling in ages. "Bossy, aren't we?"

She raised her eyebrows but didn't say another word.

He rolled his pelvis forward and the hard length of his cock slipped back inside, finding a familiar home between her damp folds. She raised her knees and tilted her hips, giving him perfect access to her slick passage. He clasped her hands up over her head and watched himself, watched his thick shaft slowly disappear deep inside, his skin so fair to her dark, dark chocolate.

Keisha's vaginal muscles rippled along his length, pulling him deeper, tightening around him until he'd buried himself completely inside her welcoming channel, until his flat belly rested against the soft swell of hers.

Already wet and slippery from their first climax, their bodies slid together in a saturated tangle of damp pubic hair and straining muscles. The ripe, intoxicating fragrance of sex and clean sweat filled his nostrils, and the sound of their rapidly beating hearts, of breath rushing in and out of straining lungs, rose to his ears.

If he thought about this, if he lost himself in the sensory beauty of the act of sex, he didn't need to think about everything that was wrong. If he thought about loving Keisha, his world was once again right.

Your world has always been right, you idiot.

Shocked, he blinked and stared at her. She stared back at him with a ferocious look in her eyes.

"Did you just call me an idiot?"

Keisha's full lips curled up in a smile. "Yes, I did. Want to make something of it?" She tightened her vaginal muscles as if to emphasize her dare.

He groaned and slowly shook his head. "I have been an idiot, haven't I? I'm not really certain what went wrong."

She pulled one hand free of his grasp, reached up and stroked his cheek with her fingertips. "I'm not either, but almost dying can have a powerful impact on a person. I've been there, remember? I know what it's like. Then to absorb so much from so many people who love you, their fear for your safety, their determination to make you live . . . All of that lives inside of you now. I imagine it's a horrible responsibility, living your life for so many other people. Why don't you try, for a while, anyway, to live for Anton Cheval?"

He thrust forward, filling her completely. Slowly he withdrew. "And who is this guy? This Anton Cheval?"

Keisha's smile grew wider. "Why, he's the man I love. The father of the world's most beautiful little girl. He's the one who's taking me real close to a fantastic orgasm right at this very moment."

"He is, eh?" Anton drove forward, tilting his hips just enough to slide his cock directly over her clit. He felt her shiver and knew it had nothing to do with the icy ground.

"Oh, Goddess. Yes. He is!"

Again he filled her, and yet again. Keisha's back arched and her eyes closed. He slipped quietly into her thoughts and found nothing but love. No sense of condemnation, no anger at his foolish, self-centered behavior. She loved him, warts and all. He had no choice. None whatsoever.

No matter what, he would be worthy of the woman who called him mate.

This time, when they reached their peak, they found it together. With a fearsome cry, he arched his back and drove deep inside. Her body tightened and held him. Her nails dug into his shoulders, her ankles locked behind his thighs and she milked him with her warm sex, squeezed him tighter with each contraction of her climax, each beat of her heart.

For the first time since the night he'd almost died, Anton Cheval was finally fully, gloriously, alive.